WOLF TOWN

J.V. JAMES

Classic Old West Tales

for R.S. – Marge's real life hero

CONTENTS

1. Put Up Your Fists   1
2. The Man Was Short, but the Boots   6
   Were Tall
3. The Problem with Lead   14
4. "Arrest that man!"   20
5. Ol' Jimbo's Appetite   25
6. Knife's Edge   29
7. Outlaw's Warning   33
8. Baldfaced Lies   38
9. A Man Has to Be What He Is   46
10. "Anyone else care to dance?"   52
11. Blood on Our Hands   60
12. "I seen a pig fly once too..."   66
13. A Yellow Dog   71
14. Dull as an Ox   74
15. A Real Bad Feeling   80
16. The Problem with Horseshoes   84
17. A Real Bad Business   88
18. Fear, Not Remorse   93
19. Deputy Damn Double-Crosser   99
20. Friends in High Places   103
21. "Dead before he hit the dirt..."   107
22. Stick Yer Paws Up   113
23. A Long Slow Walk   119
24. Gabe Roach   125
25. A Girl Named Fred   130
26. Wrong End of the Stick   136
27. The Hideout   143
28. "A right fussy eater..."   149
29. The Problem with Daves   156

30. His Bark is Worse than his Bite 163

31. The Tracker 170

32. Attack on Wolf Town 175

33. Just About Dead in His Boots 182

34. Heart to Heart 189

35. Brown Derby Hat, Blue Bandana 197

36. Camp-Fire Plan 203

37. "If you find yourself knee-deep in dung..." 209

38. Last Time I Seen Bat Jenkins... 215

39. Hackles 219

40. The Devil's Own Man 223

41. Little Jack 228

42. The Shot 235

43. Roll With the Punches 239

44. World's Biggest Chucklehead 244

45. The Problem with Witnesses 247

46. Dirty-Work 255

47. Wish in One Hand 260

48. Squeal Like a Banker 265

49. "Who's small now?" 273

50. Jumping the Broom 278

51. Community Minded, Them Bankers 282

52. Clever as a Sheep 287

Also by J.V. James 292

Fyre – A Western 293

CHAPTER 1
PUT UP YOUR FISTS

Wyoming Territory, 1871

Stagecoach never was the most pleasant way to travel, but strong-worded argument between passengers helped the time to pass quicker at least.

Cleve Lawson considered himself a reasonable man, and not given to poking his beak in where it didn't belong — but he was right, dang it all, and he wasn't about to allow no maggoty sheep feller to convince him no different.

"Roach," he growled at the man seated across from him, "Yellin' louder don't make you less wrong."

"Dammit, Lawson," cried Matt Roach, "I thought *sheep* were the stupidest things on this earth! That's why I chose to farm them, convinced as I am that stupid's less trouble. But having met you, I regret not farming cattlemen instead!"

Cleve made two good fists from his hands and said, "Who you callin' stupid, Roach? You raise sheep, but you don't know the first thing about 'em. That sticky stuff comes from their toes, it ruins the pasture for cattle forever, they'd rather die than eat—"

"You're an obstinate fool, Lawson! How many times must I explain—"

"That's it," said Cleve Lawson. "When we stop at Little Horse Creek you'll put up your fists. You're old enough and ugly enough to know when talk ain't gonna settle things!"

That statement was true of both men in fact — maybe not quite *old* and *ugly,* for both were large men, six feet tall, strong of bone and heavy-muscled — but both were now the wrong side of thirty-five, and their days of youthful good looks were long gone. Whole lot of hard work and harsh Western sun had taken its toll, way it does — another broke nose or lost tooth wasn't gonna make much difference to either of 'em.

"You've made a real mistake now," said Matt Roach with a confident smile. "It will be my great pleasure to educate you on boxing, Cow Chip, the moment we step down from this conveyance." He sank back into his seat then, and they both wished the miles would go faster.

That was when the first shot rang out behind them.

Some shot too, it was. Those that looked out the left window caught a glimpse of the guard as he spun through the air and bit the dust hard. Never made a sound. Rolled once, never moved after that. Yessir, it was some shot, that first one.

"Guard's gone, hold tight in the coach," cried the hoarse-voiced driver, Dim Dave, as he kept his head down and his whip hand in motion. "And them that's got guns, right now might be time to get busy."

Matt and Cleve looked around quick at their three frightened fellow passengers.

Two shopkeepers and a useless over-wide banker — all three of 'em filling their britches, if wide eyes and shaking was something to go by. Banker gripped the handle of the small strongbox that sat between his feet.

Like that's gonna help, Cleve thought. *Maybe he's plannin' to throw it at 'em.* Cleve looked back at Matt then and said, "Looks like it's you and me, Sheep Boy."

"Out of my way, you old fool," growled Matt as he pushed past the banker, so he could access the left hand window, and commence to shoot his revolver from it.

The riders were still eighty yards off, and hard to see through the dust.

"I hope you know more about shootin' than you do about sheep," Cleve cried, as he thrust his Spencer repeater out the window and fired at the riders behind them.

"I know my weapon," Matt growled back before taking his first shot.

"Then you should know they ain't close enough for that toy of yours yet, and stop wastin' your damn ammunition!" Cleve fired his Spencer again, but Dim Dave had that stage moving fit to bust wheels, and with all of its bouncing, Cleve couldn't get a straight shot off to save his own life.

Matt Roach's luck wasn't no better, but his mouth still

worked fine. "You talk a good game, Cow Chip, yet the riders pursue us unharmed."

"Roach by name, Roach by nature," Cleve yelled. "You maggot farmers is all blood-related to your own wives, I heard."

The click of the hammer of Matt Roach's Colt was a sound that filled the whole coach then, and it seemed like everything stopped.

Cleve looked around, saw the Colt pointed at him, realized he'd gone too far. His own rifle was in his left hand, still outside the window. Useless to him in here.

Dim Dave cried out in pain and the coach slowed — but outside seemed no longer important. Bigger fish needed frying, right here, right now.

The barrel of Matt Roach's Colt was the biggest thing Cleve ever saw, way it looked to him then. Might as well been a cannon at that range.

"Listen," Cleve said. "I'm sorry. I should not have said what I did."

"Finally, you've said something correct," said Matt Roach. And his eyes blazed anger and death.

Only sound for a few moments was horse hooves and wheels, then even that stopped as Dim Dave pulled the brake on, and the coach came skidding to a halt.

Matt Roach seemed just about loco, and nobody moved. His top lip was turned up in a snarl; his hand was filled with his Colt, just a foot from Cleve Lawson's face; and his eyes were not getting *any* less wild or deadly.

Outside, one of the road agents called, "Drop all your guns out the window, or I'll spill the damn driver's brains all over the box seat — if I start, I'll get in the mood, and you'll all get the same."

"I really am sorry," said Cleve, looking into Matt's eyes. "It was wrong of me to say that, and I'm rightly ashamed." He remembered the road agent's order, and let his Spencer fall. Winced as he heard it land in the dirt.

Same road agent was still talking. "We *will* search you proper — and any man with a gun on him goes straight to Hell, that's a damn solemn promise. Guns out *now!*"

Matt still had the Colt pointed at Cleve. His eyes narrowed now, like a man making ready to shoot. Every man in that coach held his breath. "This discussion is *not* over," Matt said.

He turned, dropped the gun out the window. He breathed out real sharp, glared at Cleve again, and they waited for what would come next.

CHAPTER 2
THE MAN WAS SHORT, BUT THE BOOTS WERE TALL

W hat *did* come next was, that one big road agent kept up his yelling, and the other five did a whole lot of pointing and waving of guns at the passengers. Seemed like there was always at least three guns pointed at Cleve at any one time. Maybe everyone in that coach felt the same — they all did just what they were told.

What they *were* told, for the most part, was, "Climb on out, keep your hands in the air."

Cleve could do *that* real good. Seemed like they all could.

All but one of the road agents had climbed down off their horses, and they had tied them a good ways back from the action. Even that one feller who stayed mounted kept his horse back with the others. Seemed to Cleve like the cleverest thing — brands on the horses was clear as mud at this distance.

The loud-yelling feller's voice sounded strange through his mask. He was sorta tall, about right size for them big square-toed boots he wore. Kind of lean but built strong, most likely from years as a cowhand. Clean-shaved face covered by a blue bandana, paisley. Wore a brown derby hat.

Nothing really unusual about him — except that he was the mouthpiece, but *wasn't* the boss. Cleve picked up on that pretty quick.

In between every direction he gave, Blue Bandana glanced across at the man on the horse. That feller looked like no sort of horseman at all, even just sitting still. He was small, and wore *two* bandanas over his probably clean-shaved face — plain red one underneath, paisley green one over the top of it — and a tall white sombrero he kept adjusting with his left hand. Too big for him that hat was, and pulled down almost to his eyes. Stayed in the background not speaking, but no mistake, he was the boss.

The five passengers and the driver stood in line by the coach, awaiting directions. Never saw eleven hands so high in the air — shoulda been twelve, but Dim Dave the driver had took a bullet to his right shoulder, and it messed with the workings of his arm. Could only get that hand out to the side, needing to keep his elbow braced flat against the side of his belly.

Grimacing some he was too, which said plenty for how painful it was — Dim Dave being of that type not much given to complaining. Weren't much given to speaking at all, truth be known. It was how he had gotten his name, by being so quiet he *seemed* dim. But like many quiet fellers, he was plenty clever enough, and just felt no need to show it.

Blue Bandana walked right over to Cleve then and snarled, "What you lookin' at, Friend?"

That mean feller was pointing a big Army Colt, right in Cleve's face, from just a few inches away.

Must be the day for it, thought Cleve. But he couldn't say that. Had to come up with something, and quick. *Bad eyes'd make me no threat.*

He blinked some, squinted and said, "Sorry, Mister, my eyes ain't the best, that's the problem. It's why I went to Cheyenne, see a eye doctor there. He says I'm already half blind, and not much to be done."

That feller waved the gun about a little, one side to the other, and laughed. "You see this though, don't you?"

"I know it's a gun, but it's mostly a blur, is the truth. Please, Mister, I'm just tryin' to make sure I do whatever you need me to. I surely don't want any trouble."

"Alright," said Blue Bandana, satisfied by the answer. Then he viciously kicked Cleve's legs out from under him, pointed the Colt at him where he fell, and laughed it up big as he said, "Your lucky day, I reckon, Friend. I'll allow you to get up and empty your pockets, make us a nice contribution. And the rest'a you passengers too. Hand it all to my business partner here."

Cleve did as he was told, and so did everyone else. While they were putting their money in that one feller's hat — with *one* hand, while they kept the other raised up high — another of the thieves was searching inside the coach.

These road agents knew what they were doing — only one had spoken, they were all well disguised, each man seemed to know just what his job was. The feller on the horse never moved any closer neither — even the sharpest pair of eyes could not have made out a brand on any of the horses.

The banker had tried to hide the small strongbox under his coat, but that was never going to work. For a moment it seemed he might get his head blowed off for the deception, and even though Cleve did not like him, he felt sorry for the feller as he pleaded for his life.

But in the end that big road agent just laughed as he took the little strongbox. Then he took the banker's gold chain and pocket watch as well. Didn't rough him up though — that part seemed almost strange to Cleve later.

"But that watch and chain was my father's," the self-important man complained. "His name is engraved on the back. Romulus Hogg the Second — surely you can't mean to keep it."

"That's what you get for holding out," Blue Bandana said when he put the gold watch and chain inside his own pocket. But they woulda took it anyway, and everyone knew it.

Then Blue Bandana looked at the sombrero-wearing feller, the boss. Sombrero didn't notice at first, he was busy studying the faces of the passengers. Cleve saw that just fine, but remembered he was meant to have bad eyesight, and went back to blinking a little to keep up the ruse.

"I guess we're all done here," Blue Bandana said then, and he sounded almost disappointed. But when he looked back to his boss again, Sombrero crooked a finger, and Blue Bandana started to make his way over there.

Sombrero rode his horse forward to meet him halfway, and that's when Cleve Lawson noticed that mounted feller's boots. The man was short, but the boots were tall to make up for it. Not just the heel, but the whole sole was raised several inches, so much so they almost didn't fit in the stirrups. Most men would never even have noticed them boots — but Cleve had been a bootmaker before he came West, and them built up boots, to him, stuck out as good as red paint would have done to another man.

And though he had never seen the boots before now, Cleve just about lost control of himself when he saw 'em — for a man's name popped into his head, and almost came out his mouth just as quick. Thing was, though there were plenty of short men in these parts, and none wore such boots — only one man Cleve knew of would be vain enough to even consider it.

And while that small man was already rich, he was indeed one of that type whose greed knows no bounds.

Just hope it don't show on my face, Cleve thought. Went back to blinking, and tried to switch his thinking to *anything else* but them boots. Came up with thoughts of a prettier than usual soiled dove he'd once met. Wiped that from his mind quick though, worried that the smile it put on his face mighta looked even worse.

That pair of road agents turned their faces away, whispered a little to each other. Blue Bandana looked around twice, then he nodded up at his boss, turned and walked back to the passengers. Sombrero Tall-Boots stayed on his horse where he was, and Cleve made sure not to look in that direction at all.

Oh, Cleve *wanted* to look closer alright, look at the man's eyes and his build, decide it *was* who he thought, for sure and for certain. But he knew he might as well shoot himself through the head, as let Tall-Boots see he'd been recognized. Best place to look was the ground, so that's what Cleve did.

Blue Bandana walked along the line, close — too close — sniffing at each man in turn. You'd think what he'd have smelled most was fear, but he never mentioned it once. His sniffer worked fine though — that was clear, way he screwed up his nose after sniffing at Dim Dave, before saying, "You *really do* need a bath, Friend."

Blue Bandana just grunted after sniffing at the others along the line though. Cleve didn't even look up at him.

Then when the outlaw came to Matt Roach at the end of the line, he took a long deep sniff and said, "You smell like maggots," then put his nose right close to Matt's, almost touching. Got right up in his face then and added, "I know *sheep* when I smell it — and now I feel right *sick* from the stink o' you, Mister."

"I haven't been near a sheep in six months," said Matt. His voice was that of a man who was ready to explode, but he kept his hands in the air — had to, if he wanted to live.

Blue Bandana half turned, looked to Tall-Boots, who gave him a slight but deliberate nod. Then Blue Bandana turned back to Matt, smiled cruelly and said, "Well, what I smell is maggoty sheep. I believe you been beddin' down with sheep, same way real men bed down with women. You wanna call me a liar?"

Matt Roach's eyes blazed wild, then hardened again. A tremble went right through him too, but Cleve had seen such trembles before — and he knew, it wasn't from fear. But Matt played it smart, didn't utter a word, and kept his hands in the air.

Blue Bandana half turned away, looked down along the line at the others. "Anyone *else* here love sheep?"

Nobody moved, nobody spoke.

He chuckled a little, spat on Matt's right boot, stared into his eyes and waited. When Matt didn't react, Blue Bandana looked disappointed, then said, "You can all climb back in the coach now."

Cleve breathed a sigh of relief, asked Dim Dave if he'd be fit to drive.

"This ain't nothin' at all," said Dim Dave, his voice more hoarse than ever. "Had worse scratches from whores I was pleasurin' too well. Drove with an arm near hangin' off for a year once, afore it grew back all its strength. Thanks muchly for the offer, but you just climb on inside."

Cleve watched Dim Dave scramble up onto the box, no problem at all, while the two storekeepers climbed into the coach without any assistance. Then Cleve helped the trembling banker climb in. That banker was all gone to fat, and was weak in the legs from his fear. Took a goodly part of Cleve's strength just to push the man up.

He looked around then at Matt, who motioned for Cleve to climb in first, so he did. Then he reached out a hand toward Matt to help him up — Matt looked at him, nodded his thanks, reached out to take the hand Cleve had offered.

That was when Blue Bandana put his Army Colt to the back of Matt's head, and blew off the top of his skull.

CHAPTER 3

THE PROBLEM WITH LEAD

"**N**ooooo," cried Cleve Lawson, but that didn't do any good.

How could it?

Roundabout half of an inch. That's about the size of the hole that piece of lead made — going in.

Problem with lead is, it's soft. Everything it hits, it gets flatter and wider. And when a lead bullet goes through any part of a body, it hits more than one thing.

By the time it comes out the other side?

Let's just say — even though it hit only skull, and then brains, then more skull — the exit hole was some bigger, and not nearly so neat. Smashed out a damn piece of the man it did — took his life along with it. Dead before he hit the ground, poor Matt Roach.

That big bullet continued on forward, alongside the coach, past the horses. Sure scared them into action — and Dim Dave didn't waste no time either, getting out of that place.

For a feller with just one good arm, he sure got his whip going, and them horses ate up the ground, leaving the road agents behind with Matt Roach's body. Some of them outlaws were hooting and hollering then, and firing their guns.

Cleve held on grimly as the stagecoach lurched forward, clattering and bouncing while the horses flew along at top speed. He thought he was going to be sick, but he dared not put his head out the window, for fear of being hit by a bullet.

Dared not look back, for fear of being seen to see who it was who had robbed them.

They were a half mile gone from the spot before anyone spoke.

"Bad enough they killed the guard," Cleve said sadly. "But the guard knew the danger, and he died doing his job. But Matt Roach, another thing altogether. Unarmed, and doing exactly what they told him to."

It was the overfed banker, sitting across from Cleve, who spoke next. "They killed the sheep fellow then? You're certain of it?"

Cleve looked up, saw three anxious faces studying his own. He nodded. "Murdered the man where he stood. Blew out his brains."

"This sheep thing's out of control," said the smaller of the shopkeepers. He was sitting next to Cleve. "Why don't they just leave? Now innocent folk like ourselves are being dragged into it."

Before Cleve knew what he was doing, his left hand had shot out, grabbed the man by the shirtfront, and dragged him along the seat toward him. Cleve's wild eyes looked into the frightened shopkeeper's, just six inches away now, and saw the fear that raced through him.

But Cleve didn't move, didn't breathe, was lost in his own shock and fear, and something else too.

The coach plunged on along the trail, and a different voice, slow and soothing, came to Cleve's ear then. "Mister Lawson, isn't it? Please. Let him go now, this isn't helping."

Cleve moved his head, looked past the man he gripped, saw it was the *other* shopkeeper speaking to him. He was taller, somewhat older, gray-haired. Fastidious feller, polite. He and his wife were new arrivals, and they had a clothing store. *Friends with the barber,* Cleve now recalled. *Must be at least halfway decent, going by that.*

"Parris, ain't it?" said Cleve.

"Perris," said the man. Then, calm as if it was a church social, he added, "Call me Sam, please. Nice to make your acquaintance."

"Sam, then," said Cleve. He noticed he still had hold of the other feller, and took the opportunity to glare at him some more. *Sneaky skunk from the Dry Goods Store, that's who he is.* He looked back to Sam Perris again, and, with an effort, made his voice come out polite. "Cleve Lawson. Call me Cleve."

"Cleve," said Sam Perris calmly. "Perhaps you could release Mister Dobson now, hmmm?" He put a hand by his own mouth now, as if confiding some secret, and added, "I don't much like Dobson either, but choking him to death won't help, or bring back Matthew Roach."

True enough, Cleve thought, *though I don't believe I'm choking him that...*

Cleve looked at the loud-mouthed skunk Dobson again, and saw the man was indeed turning an interesting shade of blue.

He let go of the man's shirt and pushed him away — Dobson's hand quickly undid his top couple of shirt buttons, and he shrank away from Cleve, wheezing for all he was worth.

"That's better, isn't it?" said Sam Perris, moving across to the other seat next to the banker, so the terrified Dobson could get further away from Cleve. "We've all been through a bad thing today, Cleve. Sometimes men speak in haste when they've had a shock, and say things they don't really mean."

Cleve glanced at Dobson again, where he cowered in the corner. "Guess we all do that at times. But if the skunk don't want it filled up with fist, he'd best shut his cake-hole the rest of the trip."

"Terrible thing," said Sam Perris. "Anyone have any ideas about who they were?"

"The boss feller..."

The words had slipped from Cleve's mouth before he had time to think. He preferred to stay alive if he could though. So he let the words hang in the air a moment, then said something different.

"The man who did the killing wasn't the boss, I shouldn't reckon. He kept looking to that feller who stayed on the horse. Anyone else notice that?"

"I noticed it too," said Perris. "The bossman didn't sit a

horse comfortably either. Not much of a rider, in my estimation. And there was *something* about him. Even masked, and under that foolish big hat, he looked ... he looked sort of familiar."

Cleve tried to get Perris to stop. "Reckon it best not to speculate, just for the—"

"I wondered was all," Perris said. "I wondered if he might have been..." He shot a glance at Cleve, changed the track of what he was saying, tried to cover it up. "Well, I only wondered why he wore *two* bandanas over his face, instead of just one like the others."

"Wondering," said the banker in a pompous tone, "is the sort of thing gets a man killed. I shan't be wasting my time *wondering*."

"A man's been murdered," Cleve growled at the banker. "What if he was *your* kin? Your friend? Well?"

"But he wasn't," said the banker. "And he wasn't yours either. Best forgotten, that whole part of the affair. The real issue is, they stole my money, and my gold watch and chain as well!"

"Keep calm now, Cleve, please," said Sam Perris, placing a steadying hand against Cleve's chest before he could move to grab hold of the banker.

"Money!" Cleve growled at the banker. "A man is *dead,* and you're worried about a few damn coins."

"Seven-thousand dollars," huffed the banker, "is *hardly* a paltry sum. I'm an important man, and I was given a personal assurance both the money and myself would be safe on this trip."

"Well you weren't safe," said Cleve, "and you lost your

damn money. But at least you're alive, you staring fool. What of Roach's family? What of them?"

"Priorities, Sir," said the banker. "This is a matter of paramount importance!"

"Compared to a killing?"

The banker looked at Cleve as if he was loco, then jabbed at the air with a stubby finger and said, "There are killings and *killings,* Sir. And as the esteemed Mister Dobson so correctly pointed out — before you so thuggishly *brutalized* him — the dead man was, after all, just a lowly *sheep* farmer."

The punch Cleve threw landed flush on the banker's chin — the fool was still out cold on the floor when the stagecoach pulled into town, about four minutes later.

CHAPTER 4
"ARREST THAT MAN!"

T he old Sheriff had been told in advance that the banker would need an escort from the stagecoach to the bank. He was sitting on a chair on the boardwalk when he saw the stage roll in. Saw there was no guard right away, then saw blood on the driver. "Dammit, Dave, what's happened now? You alright?"

"I'm gettin' too dang old for all this shenanigans," Dim Dave said in that hoarse voice of his. "Road agents out by Bear Creek. Killed poor Sam'l with their first shot. Took all our guns, lined us up and took everything else we had too. Then they killed one of the passengers afore we left. Real bad business, way it went."

"Murdered him in cold blood," cried Cleve as he jumped out onto the ground. "Shot him in the back of the head. Man was unarmed and doing what they'd told him to."

Before the Sheriff could reply, the small shopkeeper,

Dobson, stepped out of the coach and said, "Never mind that, Sheriff Whipple, arrest that man!"

He was pointing at Cleve.

"You sniveling little—"

"He brutally beat me without reason, Sheriff, and he's half-killed Mister Hogg too." Dobson ran and hid behind the Sheriff, looking out at Cleve from behind him.

Sheriff looked at Dobson, skeptical-like, then turned back to face Cleve again. Said, "Any of that true, Mister Lawson?"

"Wish it was," said Cleve. "It's what they deserve."

"What happened?"

"I only held that snivelly hiding skunk there by his shirtfront, then gave the damn banker a light tap on one of his chins. He's sleepin' it off in the coach now. Thinks money's more important than men's lives, the damn filthy—"

"Alright, Lawson," said the Sheriff. "We'll discuss all that in my office. *After* I hear about this robbery. Dave, leave them horses for the liveryman to look after, and get yourself quick to the Doc. Come see me when he's patched you up, I'll be in my office."

Dim Dave grumbled some about it, but he did what the Sheriff told him to.

By this time Sam Perris was emerging from the stagecoach. In his anger he paid his feet no attention, and almost stepped in some horse dung when he alighted. Then he turned back around to face the banker still inside and said, "I'm just sorry I tried to help you, Hogg. But here's something to bank on — I won't make the same mistake twice."

"And *I*," came the pompous reply from inside, "might just think about calling in a few loans." Then louder, he barked, "Help me down, someone, right now."

The flabby outline of the banker appeared, his jowly face looking critically at the gathering crowd. Not a man came to assist him. Dobson had taken one step forward to do so, but immediately retreated back behind the Sheriff when Cleve looked at him, wide-eyed, and smiled like he was loco.

There came then a long moment of mirthful silence, during which the fat banker's face grew even redder in color.

"Seems you're on your own, Mister Hogg," said Sam Perris. "And for the record, you don't hold *anything* over me — I *own* my store outright, and everything in it as well."

The banker hung half out the door, still unsure of himself. The scene looked like a painting of some awkward beast that did not belong there.

It was Cleve Lawson who finally moved toward the stagecoach. He skirted around the horse dung before stopping nearby the open door. Immediately, Mister Romulus Livingstone Hogg the Third — it was how the banker preferred to be known — drew back his shoulders, untrusting, suspiciously sizing up Cleve.

Then sudden as snake-strike, Cleve raised his right arm into position for the banker to hold so as he could climb down.

Hogg jerked his head away just as sudden, and smacked the back of it against the doorframe.

"Oww," he cried, and the assembled gawkers broke into laughter. "You did that intentionally, Lawson. I demand you arrest this man forthwith, Whipple."

The Sheriff looked at him, took off his hat, scratched his head, put the hat back where it belonged. "For tryin' to help you down from a stagecoach?"

"For a vicious, relentless, bloody assault *inside* the stagecoach. I have witnesses."

"I witnessed it," said the groveling squeaky-voiced Dobson from his safe hiding place behind Sheriff Whipple. "Attacked us both, he did. The man is a menace to honest citizens."

"They both of them asked for it, Sheriff," said Sam Perris, calmly as ever. "Made light of the death of two men. I'm only sorry Lawson hit this fool banker before I thought of it. And it was barely a tap. As for Dobson there hiding behind you, nobody touched him at all." Then he turned his gaze on that sniveling coward and said, "No one's touched him *yet,* anyway."

"That's it," said Sheriff Whipple. "Enough of this foolishness. There's two men killed by road agents and another man shot, getting stitched by the doctor — and you two cowards are complaining about a little scuffle you brought on yourselves. Try acting like men or I'll arrest the both of you."

"On *what* charge, Sir?" cried the banker.

"On a charge of impersonating a pair of little girls,"

Whipple said, much to the amusement of the crowd. "Now, not one more word about it, y'hear?"

"But he—"

"Not another word, Hogg," said the Sheriff, stepping toward him, and the banker shut his mouth. "Now get down from that conveyance and waddle along to my office. I want the facts of the robbery, and that's *all* I want, nothing else."

Cleve took two steps back away from the stage, and motioned for Hogg to climb on down by himself.

The banker wasn't just overfed, he'd been lazy for years, and too much reliance on others does no good for a man. In his attempt to climb down from the coach, his foot slipped from the edge of the step; his clammy hand lacked the strength to hold his weight; and he fell down into the dirt in an awkward, tangled heap, to the raucous laughter of the crowd.

Best part came after that though, when he tried to get up — he put his left hand in the horse muck; the hand skated sideways in the slippery mess; his huge bulk shifted in that direction; and he fell face down in the horse dung, the way many had hoped he would all along.

Not exactly the image Romulus Livingstone Hogg had hoped to portray — a face of green muck with two small angry eyes and a flashing growl of teeth showing through it — but it sparked off the biggest cheer ever yet heard in the tough little town of La Grange.

Cleve Lawson was the only passenger who wasn't a town dweller, so the Sheriff interviewed him first, so as Cleve could pick up his horse from the livery and get home before dark.

He was no fool, Sheriff James Whipple. At sixty years young, he might not be so fast or so strong as he was in his youth — but those disadvantages were more than outweighed by the sort of experience and wisdom won by hard years.

That sort of wisdom was why Sheriff Whipple always interviewed witnesses one at a time — not together, the way most lawmen did it.

Didn't only do that though. The Sheriff also ordered the other witnesses to wait outside for their turn, under the watchful eye of his deputy. He gave the deputy strict orders they weren't to discuss what happened with each other until after they'd all been interviewed.

Problem with that was, Cleve had hoped to speak with

Sam Perris in private, perhaps compare what they'd each seen. Evidence of two witnesses would be stronger than the suspicions of one. But that conversation had to wait, at least for the moment.

Cleve followed Sheriff Whipple inside and sat at the desk facing him, as the deputy closed the door behind them for privacy.

"In my opinion," Cleve began, "Matt Roach was murdered because—"

"Facts first," said James Whipple, putting up a hand for Cleve to stop. "Your opinion's important to me, Cleve, don't get me wrong. But first, just tell me what happened. And don't leave anything out, no matter its smallness."

Cleve told the whole thing, best he could. Best he could for the moment anyways. Even included the bit where he and Matt Roach had argued beforehand about sheep on the range.

Sheriff raised his brows some at that bit, but he never said a word, just kept taking down notes on his writing tablet.

Cleve told him too, that the feller who did the shooting wasn't the boss — but that he *had* done so after seeking direction from the bossman. Told him too that the bossman was smaller, wore two bandanas, did not sit a horse well, and was almost certainly beardless.

Aside from asking a question to clarify things here and there, Whipple never spoke a word 'til Cleve was done.

Then he said, "Cleve, I know you for an honest man, and I wish we had more 'round here like you. But sometimes, honest don't stretch quite so far as it should —

there's something else you're not telling. Something important."

Truer words never was spoken. But while Cleve was not yet as wise as James Whipple, he planned on living long enough to become so. He knew that a pair of unusual boots wasn't enough to convict a man — especially when that man was a respected citizen who'd undoubtedly have a good alibi — and Cleve knew too, that the mention of the shoes would bring the wrath of their owner down upon him. And that such a wrath was likely as not to be deadly.

"If I've left something out, Sheriff," said Cleve, "it'd only be a thing that couldn't help. At least for the moment. Unless *you* think it'd help if I got murdered as well? That what you want?"

"Alright," said the Sheriff with a frustrated sigh. "You can go, I guess. Your dog's locked up in my house, most likely ate my pillow and blankets by now. Don't forget to pick him up on your way home."

"Wondered where he was at. When he wasn't here with you, I thought he must have ate somethin' he shouldn't and died."

"Iron stomach, ol' Jimbo," said Whipple. "I had to lock him up though, I've had four complaints from the townsfolk of half-eaten boots in the time you've been gone. Two from the wife of that snidely dry-goods feller, Dobson."

"Well, that half's good news at least," Cleve said with a laugh. "Funny thing, he only ever eats the uppers, he don't like the soles."

"That's what she said was left, so I knew it was Jimbo

for certain." For a normally steadfast up-keeper of the law, James Whipple sure seemed happy about the unruly behavior of that corrupt canine. But then the smile drained away from his face and he said, "Just remember, Cleve, two men are dead — and you know, well as I do, that they and their families deserve justice. You just come back and let me know when you ... *recall* ... the rest of those details."

CHAPTER 6
KNIFE'S EDGE

As the sun broke through the clouds like a fire on the eastern horizon, the boundary riders headed on home to Wolf Town. It was the end of their twelve-hour watch, and both were looking forward to a good hot breakfast and some sleep, when they spied the buzzards a little way off to their right.

They exchanged a glance, did not speak. They only changed their direction, cantered their mounts slowly toward the dang buzzards. They expected to find a dead sheep, perhaps one that had strayed. There are moments in life when we fear something bad — then later, wish it had been the very thing we had feared to begin with.

Gruesome sight at any time, a man hanging by his neck from a cottonwood. But this, this was worse, so much worse. You can't be any deader than dead, yet somehow this was worse.

For some reason known only to the killers, they had taken off all of his clothes. That wasn't nearly the worst of it. They had pushed the man's head back so it looked to the sky, and arranged his arms out to the sides — they had let him go cold, stiffen into that shape, before putting the rope 'round his neck and stringing him up.

It was a ghastly, ghoulish, unearthly position to bend a body into. Lent the whole scene an eerie wrong feeling. Ghostly, but worse. Unnatural.

He looked like a man who'd been nailed to a non-existent cross.

The two men came to a halt, twenty yards from the tree, and looked up at that terrible sight.

"Keep your ears open," said the older man, Wally, as he looked around nervously. But whoever done this was long gone, he quickly decided. Then he cleared his throat and, barely getting the words out, he added, "I believe it's Matt Roach."

"You can't see the face from down here," said young Tim, shifting uneasily in his saddle. He was just seventeen, and felt sick — but he wasn't about to let on. "You're loco, old man. Can't be Matt, you know he run off with..." He sighed deeply then said, "Can't be Matt, he's back East, half a year gone at least, you know that."

"Well, I'm tellin' you, boy, that's Matt Roach," said old Wally. "Gabe tole me Matt was due 'nother week or so, and to keep a sharp lookout for him. Reckon he never quite made it."

"If it's even him," said Tim, his head moving slowly sideways in the manner of a man who's certain of his own correctness.

Wally took off his hat with his left hand and ran his

fingers through his thinning gray hair with his right. "Aw, Matt. Hope you repented them sins o' your'n. Why'd they have to go hang you so high for? Ain't gonna be easy, gettin' you down from up yonder."

With all the bluster and impatience of youth, Tim slid his rifle from the scabbard and commenced to take aim at the rope. "Just watch this, old man."

"Hold your horses, young feller," said Wally, reaching for the rifle barrel and turning it to the side. "No sense gettin' folk all on edge by firin' shots. Gabe and every other man we got'll come a'runnin'. You need to brush up on our rules and procedures, I reckon. No, we'll do this the smart way. You climb on down from that hoss and shuck off your boots."

Tim looked at him like he was loco, but there wasn't no changing the mind of a crazy old man, so he did as he was told. In the meantime Wally tied a blanket around the lower half of the naked dead man, best he could. Couldn't rightly expect the young feller to do what he had to with the body that way — not all shucked and bloody as it was. Blanket would help some at least.

Wally steadied Tim's horse while the younger man climbed on. Then Tim leaned against Wally's shoulder, got up onto his feet and stood on the horse's back. Then, champing down on his knife with his teeth, he clung to Matt's body as he stood to full height, and reached up above his head to cut the rope.

You can say this for sheep men, they sure do keep a sharp edge on their knives.

Matt Roach weighed the best part of two-hundred

pounds. Gravity don't make exceptions for dead men — when the blade cut the rope, he sure fell. Spun just a little, hit the horse on his way, then crashed to the dirt in an awkward tangle, stiff-limbed.

The overconfident youngster had not been quite ready — he'd ignored Wally's warnings, and the suddenness of it surprised him. The rope had spun slightly as the blade sliced on through it; the spinning Matt's stiff outstretched arm slapped Tim sideways, knocked him right off the horse; he landed hard, sprawled on the ground, turned toward the body beside him — and finally found himself looking directly into two gaping black holes of nothingness, two deep cavernous sockets where Matt's eyes used to be.

Above that was maybe an inch or two of white bone, then a whole lot of nothing, where the top of Matt's skull should have been.

Young Tim was still spraying the weeds a half minute later.

CHAPTER 7
OUTLAW'S WARNING

Cleve rode into La Grange in mid-afternoon, earlier than he really needed to. He wasn't the only one with that same idea — but most of those others had used the Cattlemen's Meeting as an excuse to head to the Saloon, get an early start on some drinking.

Cleve rode right on past the saloon without hardly looking — he didn't drink much no more, and besides, it was Sam Perris he wanted to speak to.

He looked around, made sure no one was paying attention to him. Seemed quiet enough, and the whole town more or less normal.

But when he rode up to Perris's Clothing and Millinery, he could see that the front door was bolted. Unusual, that — Sam Perris and his wife generally stayed open until it got dark. There was yet two hours of daylight.

Gave Cleve an uneasy feeling, that bolted front door. He stayed on his horse a few moments, looked around. Watched a few children play at *Cowboys and Injuns* a minute, then wheeled his horse around and headed for the tonsorial parlor, just a half dozen storefronts along.

He tied his horse out front and went in just as one of the local cowpunchers walked out.

"Cleve," said the barber with a friendly nod. "Glad to see you all in one piece. Any chance you can come back in fifteen minutes? Wanted a word with you anyway, but I got a quick errand to run."

"Howdy, Lucius," said Cleve. "Had my hair cut in Denver while I was away. Just dropped by to see if you know why Perris's store's closed. Figured you of all people'd know."

There was always some good-natured joshing between them regarding the barber being such a good spreader of news.

"You better not be callin' me a gossip, young Cleveland!" Lucius Swan looked sternly at Cleve a second or two, then broke into laughter. "You know me *too* well, I reckon."

Cleve had always liked the old barber. "Wanted a word with Sam was all. We was in that stagecoach together when it got robbed. Never knew him before, but he seemed a good man, and I wanted to check on his welfare. Maybe ask if he'd heard anything."

"Bad business, all that," said old Lucius. "Well, truth is, it ain't really an errand I'm headed for, but rather to pay Sam a visit. Sure he won't mind if you tag along, in the circumstance. Let's get going quick, before anyone else needs shaving or cutting. Been flat out in here most the day."

Lucius locked the door and turned the sign in the window around — *Back in 15 minutes,* it read.

They walked through the back door of the barber shop, then down along the hallway through the house. Then Lucius called out, "Off to see Sam a minute," to his wife, but she didn't call anything back. "Never answers me," he said. "She could be dead a week before I ever found out, exceptin' I'd starve before then."

They stepped out the back into the lane that ran along behind there, and the old barber checked there was no one about before locking the door behind him. They turned left and moseyed along a minute — barber speed — 'til they came to the rear of the Perris place. Lucius knocked at the back door, then walked back a few steps and looked up at the window, shielding his eyes from the glare of the sun with his hand. Mrs Perris appeared, and old Lucius raised a hand in greeting.

She returned the wave and disappeared from the window. Fifteen seconds later Cleve heard her unbolt the back door and the woman opened it.

She was perhaps forty-five, still a handsome woman of attractive bearing and shape — and the worry on her face didn't suit her. Such wrinkles as she usually wore were of a sort made from smiles and laughter, but today she looked all wrong somehow. She cast a suspicious glance at Cleve, then looked back to Lucius.

"This is Cleve Lawson," said the barber. "He's a good man, Mary. He was—"

"There too, in the stagecoach," she said. "I know it. Quick, get inside then, the both of you."

"I ain't told Cleve what happened yet," said Lucius, but she didn't answer, only jerked her head sideways to tell him to hurry on in.

They squeezed past her, then she put her head out the doorway and cast worried glances in both directions. She closed and bolted the door, turned and said, "Go on up while I get him some soup. Go on, it's alright, he's awake now. Doc says the old coot'll survive."

"Old? Ha," said Lucius. "Spring chicken of fifty he is, half his life ahead of him yet." But his usually jovial voice lacked conviction. As they climbed the stairs Lucius told Cleve, "Happened in the middle of the night. It ain't good."

When Cleve followed the barber into that room, it was a grave thing he saw. Sam Perris was sitting up in bed. His head was bandaged, and one of his arms, and he was bound up tight 'round his ribs. He was pale too, so very pale.

"Lucius," Sam said between uncomfortable breaths. "Cleve. Glad you're here."

Cleve did his best not to look horrified. Failed on that count for sure. "Who did this, Sam? Why, I'll—"

"No one," said Sam. Then he winced from the pain before going on. "Fell down ... stairs. Cleve?"

"Don't give me that, Sam. You've been—"

"Let him speak, Cleve," said Lucius, placing a hand on Cleve's arm, and looking at him urgently. "Let him speak."

"Alright. Sorry, Sam. I'm all ears."

"Stairs," said Sam, with a sort of finality. It clearly hurt his ribs to speak, but he went on, brokenly squeezing the words out a few at a time. "Cleve, listen. Don't tell ...

Sheriff. Don't trust ... anyone. Or you'll ... fall down ... stairs ... too."

It was all Cleve could do not to fly into a rage at that moment. But it sure wasn't Sam's fault — not his wife's either, and not the barber's. When Cleve spoke, it came out quiet and deadly. "Who did this, Sam? Who? It was ... *his* men, wasn't it?"

The pale shopkeeper only shook his head a little, then said, "Don't trust ... no one. Don't ... tell."

Cleve could not now contain his outburst. His hands balled up into fists as he growled, "The Sheriff? Whipple's mixed up in this? Why, I can't believe—"

"No," said Sam quickly. It was clearly the truth. "No. Not ... not him. The ... others."

That was when Mary Perris came in with a steaming bowl of chicken soup and apologetically said, "You best leave now, he needs his rest."

"Don't ... do ... anything, Cleve."

"They warned him," said Mary.

"About the stairs?" said Cleve, a tight smile on his face. "Maybe they need to fall down a dozen or so stairs themsel—"

"Don't, please," Mary said. "It's not worth it. Please. If they come back..." She looked into Cleve's eyes, searched them, and her own eyes asked him to promise.

"I won't say anything," he told her. "But if they come after me, the place they end up in will be deeper than any set of stairs I ever heard of. I'll send them filthy bushwhackers down below where they belong."

Back at the barber's shop, Lucius told Cleve all he knew. Wasn't much.

"All I know's this, Cleve. That new Deputy took Sam aside for a talk, while you were in seeing the Sheriff. Whispered something to him, I know it for a truth, not some rumor — my wife never says much, but she told me that for a true fact. She was on her way past and seen it, didn't like the looks of it somehow, come right home and told me."

"Sam never said nothing to the Sheriff? About who might have robbed the stagecoach?"

"He didn't know. Told the Sheriff as much."

"Unfortunately for Sam," said Cleve, "he maybe *did* know. And he let something slip in front of that damn banker and the other slimy passenger. Dobson it was — you know *him*, of course."

"I know both of them skunks. Him and that banker's about half what's wrong in this town." The barber looked thoughtful a moment, then said, "Cleve, you and me been friends a good while. You're a man to mind your business, always have been."

"But?"

The old barber's brow creased as he slowly shook his head. "No buts at all, Cleve. That's just what I'm gettin' at. This ain't the time for a man like you to be changing. Whatever's going on here, best you don't get in the middle. Keep out of it, friend, is all I'm saying. I like having you around the town. Be a shame if I had to go visit you out at the boneyard, just for a chat."

"Just to spread the gossip, you mean!"

"If that'll make you listen, I'll admit to it, Cleve, I'm a gossip, a *terrible* gossip." The old barber looked Cleve in the eye, made certain he knew its importance. "So you listen now. Don't let my next piece of choice gossip be about *you* — about how Cleve Lawson was killed for sticking his nose in where it wasn't needed."

Those were the words that still rang in Cleve's ears as he walked into the Saloon for the Cattlemen's Meeting.

It was about to get underway as he walked through the doors. They creaked as they swung shut behind him.

Should have been earlier, he thought. He scanned the room quickly, half expecting to see the road agent who'd pulled the trigger in the murder of Matt Roach. Half expected to hear his voice — even see a blue paisley bandana maybe. And he could not help wondering if *that* was who'd beaten Sam Perris.

But if the man was there, Cleve didn't recognize him. Still, the place was overfull, and not everyone could be seen from where Cleve was standing. He kept his eyes and ears open. As he looked around, a few men nearby greeted him with respectful nods.

Cleve was held in high regard around these parts, not that he ever thought about that. He mostly minded his business; he did not suffer fools; and he surely could use his fists if the situation called for it. Knew cattle too; and good with horses. Most of all, he was straight from beginning to end — always did whatever he said he would, never once went back on his word. Any two of those things was enough for a man to earn respect — Cleve had them all in abundance, and yet, unlike some highly talented men, not a hint of swell-headedness to go along with them. Not a wonder most of the locals liked him, even those folk he barely knew.

He nodded back to those who'd greeted him, didn't say anything more than a *Howdy*. There was nowhere left to sit, so he stood nearby the doors.

Not a woman to be seen, was Cleve's next thought. *Again.* There had been no women at the first meeting either. It was unnerving somehow.

The La Grange Cattlemen's Association was relatively new. There had been a little talk around town that the Wyoming Stockgrowers Association did not care about La Grange and its problems — talk that something more needed to be done, especially about sheep ruining the range. The first meeting was two weeks ago, then there'd been one last week while Cleve was in Denver to visit his youngest sister and meet her new husband.

When Cleve went along to that first meeting, he had

not minded what he'd seen. It was just the local cattlemen talking business, and there had been no particular leader of the group. Just forty or so men discussing problems, and an expert — so-called — a supposed Professor of some sort, who spoke about how the secretions from sheep's hooves ruined the pasture for cattle.

Seemed more like sixty men here tonight — and several of them strangers to boot.

It was the Deputy, Vinton Waits, who opened the meeting. He stood about a third of the way up the stairs, all by himself, from where he could just about see the whole room. He was handsome, maybe too handsome for his own good — but dull as a dishful of rocks. And though that hadn't changed, there was *something* different about the young Deputy — he'd grown somehow more full of himself while Cleve was away.

Men don't just change like that in two weeks — takes some sort of happening to change a man in such quick time.

"You all know me by now," the tall young man said, brushing some dirt from his sleeve. "I'm Deputy Vin Waits, and while I don't yet own a ranch, I'm a cattleman like the rest of you here." There were murmurs of appreciation, then he went on, with an edge to his voice. "Anyone here who *ain't* a cattleman, you best leave now, you ain't welcome. Well? Anyone here don't belong?"

"I'm no cattleman," announced the feller working behind the bar. "Guess I better take my leave and see all you boys later."

"Your boss give his special permission," said the Deputy with an arrogant laugh. "You ain't gettin' out of work that easy, Frank. You just keep them drinks comin', and never repeat a word you heard here, less'n you want your pourin' hand stomped into fifty-five pieces." Deputy Vin Waits then cast an eye over those assembled, and the men in the crowd all looked at whoever was close by — but it seemed there weren't no one in the room who shouldn't have been.

Cleve had got a bad feeling when the Deputy said, "Your *boss*," to the barman. The man who owned this saloon was just the type to wear over-tall, special-made boots, to bolster up his short height for reasons of vanity.

"Bolt the doors down there," said Deputy Waits then. It was more than just a murmur went up, but no one outright argued against it.

Two rough looking newcomers — bearded, unwashed, and hard men the both of them — bolted the doors, then turned around and stood guarding them, arms folded across their huge barrel chests.

One caught Cleve looking at him and growled, "Got yerself a problem there, friend? Ain't polite y'know, starin' that way at a man. Leads to trouble, starin' generally does."

"Not me," said Cleve. "Just never seen them sorta doors bolted before, and had an interest in how it worked." Then he added, "But my eyes ain't the best," and he squinted a little.

Wasn't much all that, as excuses went, but it was enough for Cleve to get by without using his fists. Might almost not have been, but the Deputy was speaking again, so the feller growled a cuss word under his breath and let it go.

"Same goes this week as last," Deputy Vin Waits announced in a self-important manner. "Any man repeats Association business to *anyone* not in attendance, will be dealt with severe and painful. You don't tell your wives. You don't tell your friends who ain't members. You don't even tell your damn *horse,* if he ain't a paid up member of this fine Association."

"And if you're the damn Deputy," called one of the hard men who guarded the doors, "you sure as hell don't tell your *boss!*"

Some of the crowd laughed it up then, and Cleve got an uneasy feeling. His suspicions were fitting together a little too well.

"First up we got elections for office," said Vinton Waits. "We need a President and a Treasurer."

Norris Ricks — his ranch was right next door to Cleve's, slightly closer to town, and the pair were close friends — called out, "What about a Secretary for the minutes?"

"I'll just use my watch," the Deputy answered.

"I didn't mean *time* minutes," said Norris. "Are you taking the...? Minutes. You know? All associations have got to keep minutes. It's the notes of what's said and decided at the meetings."

Deputy Vin Waits, despite having gone to school for six of his twenty-two years, was not the sharpest arrow in the quiver. In fact, as arrows went, that boy was more feathers than head. He looked sorely perplexed now, unsure as he was whether Norris Ricks was serious or not. "We'll get to all that nonsense once we vote in the President and Treasurer. Any nonnimations?"

"Any *what-did-you-says?*" said Norris Ricks. "I believe you must mean *nominations.*"

That pompous damn banker, Romulus Hogg, had raised a fat finger in the air before Norris even spoke, and Cleve was enjoying the way he was being made to wait.

"I meant what I said," growled the Deputy then. "Nomna ... non-ma ... well dammit, now you got *me* all confused, Ricks, and you double-dog-done it on purpose. It's time for nom ... nom-ni-nations, like I said in the first place, and no more'a your tricks."

The banker had kept his finger in the air the whole time, and without any further hesitation, he seized his chance and spoke up. "I, Romulus L. Hogg the Third, nominate the most prosperous and knowledgeable cattleman in Wyoming — not to mention owner of this fine establishment — the greatly esteemed Pinckney Barron."

Despite the *prosperous and knowledgeable* part of that being a baldfaced lie — and also the *greatly esteemed* part — there was plentiful applause, and several men loudly endorsed the candidate, as the Deputy called out, "I second it."

Cleve was just about sick as he looked around — the result had already been decided, he realized now. *This ain't good.*

"Come on up, please, Mister Barron, Sir," said Deputy Vin Waits. "Anyone fool enough to go up against him?"

Cleve knew no one would speak then. The air itself seemed dangerously charged, as if lightning might tear through the room and burn up any man who spoke. He looked helplessly at his friend Norris, who looked back at Cleve, shrugged his shoulders.

Pinckney Barron had been standing with Hogg at the bottom of the stairs — a very short man next to a very wide one — which was why Cleve hadn't seen either one of them.

He sure did see Barron then though, as he made his way up the stairs — seemed taller than usual. Taller by several inches, as he clip-clopped up those few stairs.

A thought went through Cleve's mind, and a dangerous thought it was too — but as he went to say what he'd thought, the words spoken by the barber came back to him, stopped him in his tracks. *'Don't let my next piece of choice gossip be about you — about how Cleve Lawson was killed for sticking his nose in.'*

Evidently, though, Norris Ricks hadn't lately heard any such wisdom — and he spoke some words of his own. "Nomination doesn't count. That damn banker Hogg ain't got no cattle at all, and therefore should not even be here!"

CHAPTER 9

A MAN HAS TO BE WHAT HE IS

When Norris Ricks spoke up that way, the whole room went quiet as a man at his burying.

The ensuing two seconds of silence seemed to stretch out a long lonely time — long enough for Norris Ricks to think better of having spoken, by the look of him. Now Norris was plenty tough, but he wasn't a big man — and right now he looked smaller than Cleve had ever seen him, he reckoned. But done was already done, and it was too late for Norris to change it.

He had always been a quiet man, Norris Ricks, but when he felt strongly about things, he could be impulsive — still, way Cleve saw it, that did not seem a fault, but a virtue.

A man has to be what he is, or he's nothing at all.

When them stretched out quiet moments ended, they did so with a bang, not a whimper. For the moment, that bang was only words — but later, it might be bullets, Cleve knew it right off.

"Who the hell are *you* to decide who's a member and who ain't?" cried Deputy Vin Waits at the top of his voice, so loud it cut through all the rest of the shouting. "Why, I've a strong mind to—"

"Ha," exclaimed Norris Ricks just as loudly. "Why, you ain't got no mind at all, Vinton Waits, let alone a damn strong one."

The Deputy's face all contorted with rage, and he made as if to set off toward his smiling tormentor — but the tall-booted Pinckney Barron beside him placed a hand on the deputy's shoulder, and in a voice that didn't match his tiny stature, he simply said, "Stop."

Whenever Cleve had heard Barron speak, he always wondered if that was the man's real voice, or if he was putting it on. It was like he'd swallowed a mouthful of sharp stones, and the aggravation it caused him made him speak from the depths of his throat, and the finer gravel that got sifted down got all mixed in with the sounds. There are men who have gravel voices, but their vocalizations sound natural — this voice was different to those, and it sounded all wrong, always had. Halfway between graveled and hoarse, it was. Whatever way you described it, it must be downright painful, Cleve reckoned — and he imagined Pinckney Barron's throat must be damn red and sore whenever he'd spoke.

Real voice or pretend, it sure worked on Waits. He did just what Barron had ordered — stopped right there in his tracks and went silent, with not the slightest moment's hesitation.

Knows who his real boss is, Cleve realized right then and there.

Whole place hushed now as Pinckney Barron put his pudgy little hand up to quiet them. Fingers like fat little sausages he had, like a butcher had made them all wrong. "Friends," he said, *"please.* We're all of us on the same side here."

"Hardly seems so to me," said the ever pompous Romulus Hogg. "Why, the gall of that man!"

"No, no," said Barron, "calm down now, Romulus, and I'll sort this out once and for all. It's a fair point Norris Ricks has raised, and I'm very happy he did so. As a member, Norris has every right to know who his allies are — and his enemies too."

"The gall," muttered Hogg once again, but he quieted down quick.

Barron raised up his hands to the crowd again. "You see, Norris — you don't mind me calling you Norris — Romulus L. Hogg is indeed a valued member of our fine association. In his capacity as the proprietor of the La Grange City Bank—"

There were titters of laughter from a few of the drunker men when he said that, and one slurred, "La Grange ain't hardly a town, let alone a damn city."

"Quiet down now," said Pinckney Barron, "and don't worry none on that. I have big plans for La Grange, and we'll all be prosperous men when the seeds of my plans all bear fruit."

"Thought we was cattlemen," said Deputy Waits, "not damn fruit-growin' orcharders."

Pinckney Barron looked the younger man in the eye — even in his tall boots, that was only possible because he was standing one step higher up the stairs — and said, "Deputy Waits. How about you don't speak again until I request it, hmmm?"

"Yessir," said Waits, hanging his head a little, before shooting a mean look at a drunk who had openly laughed at him.

Barron looked behind a moment, stepped up one more step higher, tottering a little on the over-tall boots. Cleve could see the boots now, and the anger rose up within him — no doubt at all, they were the very same boots he'd seen at the robbery. He saw Barron's gaze rest upon him, and Cleve remembered then to squint some and blink, pretend there was something wrong with his sight.

Pinckney Barron faced them all and opened his arms good and wide. "Men. We're all in this together. And the esteemed Mister Hogg, as owner of the bank, holds mortgages over a good many of your properties — yours included, if I'm not mistaken, Norris Ricks."

Norris's eyes flared, but he did not utter a word.

"Now, the man who holds the mortgage, is indeed the rightful part owner of all that he holds that mortgage on. Not just your property, not just your home — but all the stock you own too. As such, Norris my friend, Romulus Hogg is your business partner, and you're lucky to have him. Indeed, if Romulus suddenly needed ... for *whatever* reason ... to call in your loan, why, you'd be out of business,

I guess. First thing you'd have to do is sell off your cattle. So you see, our good friend Mister Romulus Hogg is a vital component in the welfare of this fine city we're growing. Any more questions on that? Or shall we get on with the voting?"

All eyes were on Norris Ricks now. And despite the obvious anger that bubbled within him, he only said, "Thank you for the explainin', Mister Barron."

"No problem at all," Barron said with a smirk. "Now, Deputy, get on with the voting, we've other important business to get to once it's done."

"Yessir, Mister Barron, Sir," said the young fool. "So, no more nom-ni-mations? Then we best get to—"

"I nominate Cleve Lawson," Norris Ricks called out with conviction, and a great stir went through the crowd. "He's a top man with livestock, and we all know how straight and honest *he* is."

What Norris *didn't* add at the end was the words *Unlike Some* — but there were men who somehow heard them words anyway, Cleve himself being one of them.

"I'll second that," said someone down toward the front, and suddenly the room seemed divided into two camps. Cleve found himself being stared at — in ways both friendly and less so — and he had a decision to make, but not much time to make it.

He looked at the eager faces of some of the men nearby; he looked at the pleading eyes of Norris Ricks; he looked at the *very* tight, *very* annoyed smile worn by Pinckney Barron. And again, old Lucius's words rang strong in his ears — *'Don't let my next piece of choice gossip be about you*

— *about how Cleve Lawson was killed for sticking his nose in.'*

And right in this moment, Cleve knew he had more than trouble enough, without adding fuel to a fire that was already burning. And he said, "I'm flattered you thought of me, Norris, but I'd be hard pressed to organize a dung fight in a corral. Reckon Mister Barron's our man, what with him havin' both education and inclination for the job — my vote goes to him."

Norris Ricks looked disappointed, but he shrugged his shoulders and nodded, as if to say, *'Worth a try.'*

"A fine speech," said Barron from the steps. "Thank you indeed, Cleve — you don't mind me calling you Cleve — for lending your weight to my leadership. I won't let you down."

And as much as it went against all that Cleve Lawson valued and believed in, he kept his mouth shut, trapped his tongue between his teeth — and he did *NOT* say, *'Damn you, Pinckney Barron, you murderin' no-good tall-booted snake, I sure DO mind you callin' me Cleve.'*

Didn't *say* it, but he sure did *think* it.

Then he voted along with the others, for that damn flannel-mouthed Pinckney Barron.

CHAPTER 10

"ANYONE ELSE CARE TO DANCE?"

The Deputy called for the obligatory show of hands, then Barron leaned forward and whispered into his ear. Then Deputy Waits announced, "Mister Pinckney Barron is official voted in as President and Treasurer."

"*And* treasurer?" It was Norris Ricks who'd spoken up again.

Barron spoke his next words with a smile. "Problem, Norris my friend?"

"Not exactly," said Ricks. "Just wasn't made clear the vote was for both."

"It's just easier this way," said Barron. "I'll write the notes up myself too, so I won't need a secretary. No sense complicating a simple job with unnecessary extra discussions — I can easily do this job myself, and am happy to do so, for the good of us all. No objections?"

Every man in the room looked at Norris Ricks. He had always been a quiet sort of feller, kept to himself same as

Cleve. It was part of the reason the pair had become such good friends. Just wasn't like Norris to speak up so much — but now he said nothing, only gave a quick shake of his head, and Barron got down to business.

"As you all know from our initial gathering, sheep will completely destroy the graze wherever they're allowed for any length of time. In as little as a week, sheep can destroy land forever. The sticky substance they excrete from—"

"Mister Barron," called Norris Ricks, "I been reading up on that, and some time back I wrote away to the top known expert on pasture. Took him a good while to reply, busy man as he is, but I received a detailed summation of it from him last week. Turns out it simply ain't true, that stuff about the toes."

A loud stir erupted in the room, and it took Pinckney Barron to raise up his hand to put a stop to it. "Norris," he said. "You were here when a *real* expert gave us the facts, in this very room two weeks ago. A man came to face us, not hide behind the pages of books, or scribbled down letters. Perhaps you've forgotten that *real* expert, my friend. You losing your memory, Norris? We all of us saw Norris here for it, didn't we, boys?"

There was a whole lot of laughing, and a little good-natured ribbing about Norris maybe getting a touch of the Oldtimer Disease, then Barron quieted them again. Seemed like that pudgy little hand of his worked just about better'n magic for quieting folk down.

"Oh, I was here and heard it alright," said Norris. For a small man, he sure had no fear to speak out, and he did so now. "Hard to forget a man who lies right to your face, and smiles sly while he does it. That feller spoke fallacies and falsities and fraudulences, piled each of 'em up on the other. It simply ain't true, what he told us."

"Now, Norris—"

"I'll say my piece, Mister Barron, then you can say yours. Fact of it is, sheep and cattle can share the range just fine, long as the numbers ain't too great. There's a whole lot of good graze around here, all these fine creeks and valleys, and never no shortage of water. It's my strong opinion there's room for the sheep men as well, and we should let 'em be, they ain't doing us no harm at all."

Pinckney Barron laughed then, loud and long. "You think they're living on maggot-ridden mutton up there, in their little damn shantytown? Beef and more beef, I'd warrant, all of it stolen from us. Why, I heard a gang of them drove a hundred cattle to market in Sidney. How many are you missing, Bill? And you, Reed, you've had some losses, you told me. It's these thieving maggot-farmers alright, and they won't get away with it."

"I've lost a few too," said Norris Ricks, "but Cleve Lawson's place is closer to the sheep town, and he's had no losses at all."

"That splits fair," said Cleve. "No losses for me from 'round home."

"Full of tricks those scab-herders," cried Pinckney Barron. "And now they've robbed the stage too."

Cleve's blood just about boiled right then. "Robbed the stage? I was *there*, Barron! Were *you?*"

It came out more accusing than Cleve would have liked — and while Barron's, "Of course not," didn't sound too convincing, Cleve knew he had to tread careful, and did not press the point.

Instead, Cleve only said, "Well I was there — and while I don't know *who* they were, I know what they done. Damn road agents killed a sheep man, and made it clear why. Explain that away, will you now?"

"A personal dislike, no doubt." Pinckney Barron waved his arms about like a damn politician trying to gather up votes. "No easier way for the maggot farmers to cast suspicions elsewhere. Why, we should have known right off that was what it was about. We'd best tell the Sheriff now we've worked it out, so he can take care of it. And if the damn Sheriff won't do his job, we'll hire a man who will. Like young Vinton Waits here — young blood's what we need, and I'm betting *he'd* do the job properly!"

Norris Ricks wasn't having it at all. "When my stock were stolen, the tracks I found led me to believe it was experienced cattlemen. Locals, I'd reckon. The cattle thieves are here in this room."

"That's a strong accusation," said Barron, as some angry mutterings started up here and there. "Any proof to back up those words?"

"Not yet. But this past few months, some of the bigger spreads — we all know who they are," Norris said, staring at Barron, "— have employed a lot of new men. And *some* of those new men clearly ain't to be trusted."

"Them's fightin' words," said a huge unwashed feller standing nearby to Norris. That massive-muscled fool worked for Barron, everyone knew. He'd come just three months ago, and was already known for fighting — known for *winning,* more like it — and tonight, he was all roostered up, overly full of the courage cheap whiskey provides.

That gargantuan man must have weighed two-fifty at least, and was maybe six-four. He put his great calloused fists up before him, and his bloodless lips curled back in an ugly, toothless, kind-of-a-smile that meant exactly the opposite.

Norris sure did look tiny compared to that overgrowed feller. But he just smiled up at him and said — good and loud so everyone heard it — "I'd advise you against what you're thinking ... Stink-boy."

It was true, that big man was at least two, or maybe three weeks, past being just whiffy — but the huge stinking feller had about as much interest in Norris's advice as he had in regular bathing. Without any warning, he rushed forward and threw a wild haymaker at Norris's head — it was a style that usually worked for him, and he sure got some power behind it. Indeed, that punch would just about have knocked a head right off its shoulders — *if* it connected.

'Course, *if* is a fair stretch from *maybe,* and *maybe* a long hop from *fact.*

Norris Ricks wasn't hardly a big man — he was just under five-six, and would not have weighed even one-forty, ringing wet in his boots — but he'd done some serious boxing ten or so years back, and at forty, was still in good shape. He'd won fifty-two fights and lost three, then retired still in his prime, his heart no longer in it. Won a few titles even, not that he much spoke of it now — in fact very few of the locals even knew of his pugilistic past. Anyhow, way it turned out, it wasn't much of a contest, between him and that lumbering giant.

As the brawny colossus came at him, Norris's feet moved a little — *shuffled,* you might say. Or *danced,* a better word for it. Well, whatever name or term you applied to the movement, it was pure pleasure to watch, for Cleve anyway.

Norris's body moved backways and sideways and downways in one fluid movement — then his right arm moved so fast that most men close by did not even actually see it, as Norris drove his fist upward into that feller's jaw, just the once.

They might not have seen *how* he did it, but they saw the result clear and plain. Strangest thing was, those few who actually seen it all swore six ways to Sunday that Norris barely moved the fist at all. "Just sorta tapped him on the jaw," was how old Cal Weedle described it. "Almost like he had no wish to hurt him."

Seemed like the courage that huge feller had got from the whiskey hadn't worked in his favor at all — caused him a slowness and clumsiness he could ill afford, and he crashed to the floor, already out cold when he got there. Then those all around just sorta blinked and looked at him down there unmoving. Nobody helped him — seemed like everyone figured he'd rightfully earned what he got, and it wasn't like as if he was dying. Probably. There was even some smiles in that room, mostly appearing on the faces of that big stinky feller's recent victims.

Norris Ricks looked around him, and in the calmest of voices, enquired, "Anyone else care to dance?"

Never saw so many men find such sudden interest in lookin' at the floor, or the walls, or the ceiling, or the bottom of their glass. Anyway, weren't even one man in attendance got a hankering to go up against Norris Ricks toe to toe.

Quietest saloon in Wyoming it was, those few moments.

It was Pinckney Barron who finally spoke — must have felt mighty safe on the stairs, in his tall boots, with his gunmen nearby. Still, his usually tough-sounding half-hoarse and half-gravel voice sounded like it had caught a bad case of the wobbles.

"We, ah, don't need to fight among ourselves, men. Now do we?" More hoarseness than gravel it was, all of that, and Barron cleared his throat before going on. "Norris has voiced his opinion, and he has every right to do so. That's the good thing about a democracy — we can always put things to a vote. Sure, the decision is mine to make, as you've already voted me your leader. But I'm a fair man. If anyone *else* here believes sheep are good for the range, do speak up now. If not, I'll get on with explaining how we're going to deal with the problem these sheep men have caused us."

Cleve looked around him. Seemed like, while every man in attendance had gained a goodly respect for Norris's fists, no one much believed what he had said about the sheep. Or if they did, they weren't ready to go against the group. As for Cleve himself, he was beginning to suspect that Norris was right. Matt Roach had tried to tell Cleve the very same thing the other day in the stagecoach — and while Roach had been far too quick-tempered, he was clearly an educated man.

I'll talk some to Norris about all this later, he decided. But for now, Cleve needed to be seen to go along with things, and not be rocking the boat. *Rocking boats gets a man drowned, if he rocks the wrong one.*

"Norris, my friend," said Pinckney Barron now. "I'd have thought you of all people would want rid of these maggot farmers. Your place is one of those closest to the valley we've forced them back into. Perhaps you're a sheep lover, like they are. Are you, Norris? *Are* you a sheep lover?"

CHAPTER 11
BLOOD ON OUR HANDS

I
t was a filthy damn insinuation — and while the words had gone only so far, everyone knew what Pinckney Barron had meant by them.

Cleve saw Norris Ricks' hands curl up into fists, and he held his breath — but Norris only said, "I'm happy running cattle for now. I don't have sheep, or want them. I just don't believe they do harm. And I reckon we can all get along. There's plenty of range for us all, including the sheep men."

He looked down at the floor a few feet away, where the man he'd knocked out cold was beginning to stir, and mumbling something about *"whiskey,"* and *"run down by a bull."*

"Well, I'm sorry you see it that way, Norris," said Barron, matter-of-fact. "This is a cattle town. Our fortunes will ride on that fact as we build our future. My plans for this fine little town are visionary in nature. Two months from now, we'll elect a new Sheriff, a new Mayor. I plan to *be* that new Mayor, and guide this town onward to glory. There's no reason we can't build this little town into the biggest metropolis in Wyoming. The capitol, that's my aim!"

"Hoo-wee," exclaimed Deputy Waits amid the cheers. "The capitol!"

Pinckney Barron put both hands up for quiet before going on. "But there is *much* to be done, friends. We cannot allow a few miscreants to undo all our good work. Those damnable sheep men could bring our entire economy to its knees. They have proven obstinate about leaving. Various of our members have tried to persuade them to get their filthy sticky-toed beasts off our range — why, we've even tried being friendly."

"*Real* friendly," said Deputy Vinton Waits, as if it was the funniest thing he'd heard in his twenty-two years.

There was plenty of chuckling then, and Barron smiled, then waited for the laughter to die down before going on. "Those of you in attendance at last week's meeting are aware that a regulator was hired to ... *speak* ... to the sheep men, persuade them to leave. Discussions are yet to prove fruitful, therefore further ... *persuading* ... will be necessary."

"Has to be done," cried the Deputy, in response to a slap on the shoulder from the small man behind him, and most of the crowd got behind it, shouting variations of those same words.

A real fervor, it was, that tiny man whipped them all into.

Then he got to where he'd been heading all along.

"We need the damn scab-herders gone," Barron cried. "But that sort of convincing costs money. Our man can get the job done — indeed, he has already put the fear of the devil himself into them, and believes them ready to crack."

More shouting, more rattling of tables, more glasses and bottles being banged down to show support for Barron and his "regulator."

"It's time we put an end to them. If they won't leave of their own volition, we'll drive them out with strength, with force, with whatever it takes. To do that will require *money*. Every man in this room must pay his fair share. A small monthly fee to go toward keeping sheep — and any new cattlemen that come too — off of *our* range."

More cheering, and one man cried out, "I got ten dollars right here to put in!"

"Bert," said Pinckney Barron, fixing that man in his gaze. "Your heart's in the right place, but things cost more than you know. We'll pay what it costs, and such payment will distance us from any wrongdoing. It's a fee that keeps blood off our hands — and if there's ever trouble, it keeps the rope away from our necks. That costs real money, Bert. But think now, what is it worth? For a free range forever, and no chance of a rope around your neck?"

"I guess, put like that," murmured Bert, "a little more than I reckoned on."

"Clever man you are, Bert. Forward thinking." Pinckney Barron lifted his gaze and, forceful now, said, "Listen up good, we *must* get rid of these sheep men, lest they ruin us completely. For every hundred cattle — or part thereof — each man owns, a fee of thirty dollars is payable tonight."

It had been cheers before, but now it was unhappy mumbles — but still, no one complained very loud.

"Each man comes to our good friend Romulus Hogg before leaving, and pays him the fee. He'll record it all proper and give you a receipt. If you don't have enough money with you, you come to him and sign a note for it, then come back to town tomorrow and pay. Any questions?"

Cleve looked at Norris Ricks. Norris had been building a herd — more than three-hundred cattle were out there right now with his brand on.

Norris finally spoke. "You expect me to pay more than a hundred dollars, so you can give some part of it to this ... damn *regulator,* so-called ... and have him murder innocent folk in my name?"

"That's a strong accusation," Pinckney Barron growled.

"No," Norris answered, "it's a question, and I'd like an answer."

Barron sighed — a slow deep one, it was — and rubbed at his forehead. "Mister Ricks," he said then, before choosing the rest of his words very carefully. "It is not my belief, that the man the Association has hired to protect us, has harmed — or will harm — anyone. His methods are his business alone, and I do not tell him *how* to do his job."

"And if I don't want blood on my hands?"

"You've not been listening, Ricks. The point of us hiring this man, is that we *don't* have blood on our hands. If indeed any blood is ever spilled."

"You know it's been spilled, Barron," cried Norris Ricks then, and he thumped his fist on a table. "One sheep man murdered ten days ago, another this week in broad daylight. I won't be a party to it! I ain't gonna pay you one penny, and I'll see you hanged if this continues!"

Cleve's hand went to his gun — he sure wasn't the only one. And you could have cut the air in that room with a Bowie knife.

But as men started to look at each other with suspicion, and it seemed like battle lines might yet be drawn, Pinckney Barron raised up his hands, spoke to them all once again.

"That's alright, Norris," he said. "Everyone, please stay calm now. Norris Ricks has decided *against* being a member of our fine Association. That's his right. I won't have him persecuted for it. Norris, you're free to leave. So is anyone else who's not with us. We're a peaceful organization. Boys, unlock that door, allow our friend Norris to leave, he's no longer a member. Anyone else who's against us, you can leave too."

No one spoke, no one moved except Norris — and he walked through the crowd like a man preparing to fight. The men guarding the front doors unlocked them.

As Norris approached, he glanced at Cleve, read his eyes.

"Wait up, Norris," said Cleve quietly, and his friend stopped beside him.

Oh, Cleve knew how dangerous it was. Knew he had to take utmost care what he said now — not just what he said, but also *how* he said it.

When he turned toward Pinckney Barron, Cleve's words came out *sounding* respectful and sincere.

"Mister Barron, I don't have the money on me to pay my dues right now. But I'll be back in town in two days, so I'd ask that Mister Hogg writes that down. Other thing is, there's several men here I don't know, and therefore don't trust. And while I don't share Norris's beliefs on the matter, he's a friend, and my nearest neighbor — so I'll travel along with him now, and make it known that any man who follows is asking fair enough to be shot. I'd ask that you keep these doors locked fifteen minutes after letting us out. Any objections?"

"No objections at all, Cleve," said Barron. "Indeed, I was going to suggest it myself. I won't have any man taking things into their own hands. Norris Ricks might be against us, and as such, will be an outcast that no member of this Association will be permitted to have *any* financial dealings with. But he does have a right to his safety."

So did Matt Roach, thought Cleve, as he walked out the doors — backward, with his hand on his six-gun — to join Norris Ricks and head home.

CHAPTER 12
"I SEEN A PIG FLY ONCE TOO..."

C leve and Norris kept a sharp eye out as they mounted their horses.

"I don't trust a word comes out'a that skunk's mouth," Norris said as they got moving.

"Me neither," Cleve said. "But with him running for Mayor now, he'll make sure he's *seen* to keep his promises. He'll keep them doors locked fifteen minutes — but you need to be careful, Norris. Maybe come stay at my ranch tonight."

"I'll be fine," came Norris's answer. "But thanks for the offer."

A voice came out of the darkness then — Sheriff James Whipple, from his porch. "Trouble, boys?"

They pulled their horses to a halt, peered down at the Sheriff as he got to his feet from his rocker. He was cradling a rifle, Cleve noticed.

"Not much time to talk right now, Sheriff," said Cleve.

"Norris here spoke out against the new Association, and some of its practices and beliefs."

"It ain't right what they're doing," said Norris. "I refused to be part of it, and there was some unfriendly chatter. Cleve offered to accompany me home, and requested they keep the doors locked fifteen minutes."

Whipple sighed a deep one. "Come to that, has it? Bad business, all this. Maybe I should ride along with you."

"No need," Cleve told him. "Best you're not seen to take sides. I even made out I was with them, so they don't come after me too. You-know-who has hired a damn regulator — but you didn't hear it from me."

"They already know what side I'm on," said the Sheriff. "The side of law. Barron tried to put me in his pocket when this all started. I told the man what I thought of him — didn't take long. Anyway, he'll be Mayor soon, and I'll be out of a job."

Cleve found it hard to believe. Sheriff James Whipple was straight as they came, a man to ride the river with, and everyone knew it. "But surely—"

"Elections are less than a month away, Lawson. That'll be it for me, it's been made clear enough. That fool nephew of mine'll become Sheriff then." He spat on the ground in disgust.

"That chucklehead Deputy?" Norris shook his head in disbelief. "That's about the last straw. Maybe I'll sell my place, go on out to Montana. I've worked hard to build what I've got, but I don't see all this ending well. Hardworking men being murdered for greed. Ain't right."

The Sheriff's eyes widened at that. "Don't guess he said

anything we could convict him for? If enough men heard him implicate himself—"

"No such luck, he says all the right words," said Cleve. "Makes things clear enough to get the men to pay, but says the regulator's only here to negotiate peaceful-like. You know how tricky he is."

"Y'know," said Whipple, "Matt Roach's body was gone when I went out to look. They hid their tracks well enough too. I done my best, but I'm no Injun when it comes to tracking."

"Must have hid them tracks well," said Norris. "You're the best tracker I know."

"Bad business alright," said Cleve. "You go out to the sheep town?"

"Not yet. Don't want to go stirring things up any worse than they are. Hoped to find the body first at least, give them something to bury. Given what's gone before, I don't much fancy going out there. When the previous feller got killed, I tried to go out there, but they run into me out on the trail, and I never got close. Thing was, they accused me of being Barron's man. Can't blame 'em, being angry, I guess."

"We better be getting along," Norris said as his horse got impatient and shifted some sideways. "If you want these streets to stay peaceful, that is. I already had to persuade one under-bathed, overgrowed feller to sleep off a fit of vexation."

"That giant of Barron's," said Cleve. "One-punch specialist, you know the feller by now."

"Liked to have witnessed that for myself," said the

Sheriff. He had seen Norris Ricks box in Kansas years ago, and knew just how it would have gone.

"You'd have enjoyed it," Cleve told him. "I sure did."

"One last thing before you go," said Sheriff Whipple. "Didn't remember nothin' else about the robbery, did you, Cleve? If we could cut the head off the snake … well, you know how it works."

"Knowledge of who's guilty ain't enough," Cleve replied, as he wheeled his horse around. "Certain men seem always to have alibis, no matter *what* honest people see with their own truthful eyes. I'd reckon some men would have to be caught in the act — I'll be keeping an eye out myself, just as you will. I'll be back in town in two days, Sheriff. I'll come see you then. In the meantime, keep an eye out for Sam Perris and old Lucius, will you? I got a bad feeling."

"Already on it," said Whipple. "Fell down some stairs, Sam reckons. I seen a pig fly once too. I'll watch over the town, you boys take care. And Cleve…"

"Yes, Sheriff?"

"Give ol' Jimbo a good pat from me, I've not seen him in too long."

"Only been a couple'a days, Sheriff."

"Seems longer I guess. You give him that pat, Cleve, and tell him that one's from me. He's a good dog alright — shoe-related lawbreaking notwithstanding."

Cleve and Norris didn't waste any more time. They talked as they rode, kept an ear out — but nobody followed.

Norris told Cleve what the pasture feller had said in his letter, and what the books said as well. The sheep did indeed ooze a sticky substance from their feet, but that's the only truth there was in all that other business.

"All lies," Norris said as they came to his place. "Lies rich men tell to get richer. You'd think they'd be happy — seems like plenty just ain't enough for some men."

"My wife was that way," Cleve told him. "Always at me to make extra money. Had a place down in Texas then. Big place." He raised his eyebrows and his eyes opened up big and wide. "I actually *thought* she was happy."

"She wasn't?"

"I don't believe she knew how to be," Cleve said, looking up at the stars. He waved a hand back and forth across the sky. "Wouldn't even come outside at night to look at the firmament. Imagine that. What sorta person cannot see the beauty in the stars and the wind and the dark? Nothing inside her I guess — except maybe want. She run off with some rich feller she met, who come out on an adventure. Last I heard, she was still makin' him miserable over in Boston. Well, me and her never got married up legal anyway. Sure you won't come to my place, just for tonight, Norris?"

"No, Cleve, I'll be fine. Drop in when you're headed to town next, I'll talk to you then, let you know if I'm going to stay. Right now, Montana sounds good."

"Might even come with you," said Cleve. "Never been to Montana. See you day after tomorrow, we'll talk on it then."

CHAPTER 13
A YELLOW DOG

Norris Ricks woke several times during that night. Uneasiness, that's all it was. Around about four, he heard his dog bark and commence to chase something. Norris climbed out of bed, picked up his fully loaded Winchester, went and sat by the window awhile, but he couldn't see nothing untoward, or hear nothing unusual either.

That dang dog was always off after something. Wonder he'd survived as long as he had. Served Norris right, he reckoned, for getting a yellow dog in the first place. He'd always been a sucker for a friendly yellow dog, even though he knew they weren't worth a tinker's cuss. That fool canine was a fine companion, excepting that he would go off after things and not come back home for hours — one time, he was gone two long days, and Norris feared the worst. But back he had come, a little worse for wear, but with that funny dang dog-smile all across his face.

Norris wasn't surprised when Dog didn't come back.

Wasn't surprised when he couldn't hear him no more — and after ten minutes, he went on back to bed.

He dreamed of his boxing days then, and the dreams were of that fulfilling type, the ones you wish you could just keep on dreaming, instead of getting up in the cold and doing your chores. But as always, Norris woke with the first sign of daylight — it was less a *sign* of the daylight, more like a general idea that the day would eventually arrive. He stoked the fire, put the coffee on and went out to pee off the porch.

Steam rose off the stream, and he knew the warmth of it would be melting the frost on the ground. But it was still too dark to see that.

Cold this morning. Quite enjoy the cold. They reckon Montana's freezing. Still, they reckon a lot of things. Man's always best served to go find things out for himself.

No sign of the dog. Norris went back inside, commenced to cook up some bacon and an egg and a biscuit, then sat down to a meal fit for one of those English Kings he had read all about.

He always drank one cup of coffee while cooking his breakfast, and a second cup after he finished. He would end up more full up than normal today, on account of the dog not being home.

"Serves you right, Dog," he said as he ate the animal's share.

As always, once Norris finished his second cup of coffee, he picked up some reading material and headed for the outhouse. Seemed like that second cup always sent him straight there — suited Norris fine, for he was a creature of habit.

Did do one thing different today. He took his Winchester with him. Norris Ricks didn't really believe anyone would come after him — but he *had* said more than he'd meant to last night, and he still felt a little uneasy.

Ten minutes later, he stood up, tucked his book under his left arm, pulled his gallowses up over his shoulders, picked up the Winchester, and commenced to walk back to the house.

He heard the slightest noise in the trees back behind him and thought the dog had returned. But before Norris Ricks even turned his head to look, two bullets tore him to pieces — one ripped through his back, through his heart, out his chest, hit a post at the top of his stairs, and fell down onto the boards.

He never felt a thing though, not a pain, not a worry, not so much as a simple regret — for the other bullet had arrived a smidgen of a picayune of a quarter-moment earlier: had exploded through the back of his head; had carried the thoughts and the hopes and the future of Norris Ricks out into the ether as it smashed through his forehead, and spilled what used to be Norris all over the ground.

At least that yellow dog Norris loved was waiting for him in Heaven when he arrived.

CHAPTER 14
DULL AS AN OX

Sheriff James Whipple was hardly one for religion. Never had been, not really — not even when his wife had forced him to start attending church when they got hitched back in Kansas.

But since she'd passed on, there was something he liked about the ritual. The getting dressed up in his best; the shining up of his already shiny once-a-week shoes; the straightening of his tie as he looked in the mirror; the walking up the street when the bell rang out through the town; and the greeting of other people, not as the Sheriff, but as a man, a citizen of the town, same as everyone else.

The sermon, he could mostly take or leave — leave for the most part, if he was honest with himself. It wasn't that he didn't believe in goodness and righteousness, it was more that he didn't think of the Lord as so much of a punisher as was usually made out by these preachers, who all yelled so loud while their eyes bulged half out of their heads.

Seemed like most of them preachers was having some

sorta conniption fit, not spreading neighborly friendliness, the way James thought they should do.

Still, this one don't tell me how I should do my job, so I won't tell him how to do his. And this place is so dark, he can't likely see I don't listen to one word he says.

Sheriff Whipple sat in the church now, thinking fondly of his wife, rather than listening to the overly fiery sermon. He suspected that was the real reason he still came to church every Sunday — he felt close to Gertie somehow, while he was here. And for an hour or so, he could let himself relax — no one asked anything of him in here, or brought him no trouble to deal with.

It had been his dear Gertie's idea, that for one day every week, the young Deputy was in charge.

"Never any real trouble on the Sabbath," she'd said. "Go on, it'll be good for him."

Might not be so wise now, he reflected, as the preacher's voice rose to a crescendo — *but how much harm can the young fool do in one day? And besides, he's under strict orders to fetch me if there's trouble.*

One of the last things his wife had asked of him, was to let her sister's son come and work for him here in La Grange. Young Vinton Waits had fallen in with a bad crowd back in Kansas, and got into some sort of trouble. They all figured that James would be a good influence, get the boy back on the straight and narrow — and what better way than becoming a lawman himself?

Sheriff James Whipple had reluctantly agreed — *that dear girl of mine always did have me wrapped 'round her finger.* He'd remembered the child as a whiny-voiced, snot-nosed boy who was always pretending to shoot horses and dogs and cats — even people sometimes — with a wooden toy gun his grandfather had whittled just before the old man passed on.

Vinton Waits had arrived in La Grange just two weeks before Whipple's wife finally passed. The boy had seemed respectful and decent enough — though "dull as an ox," according to the soon-to-be-dearly-departed Mrs Whipple.

It was maybe too kind to describe him as *dull as an ox.* Not to mention, unkind to the ox.

The boy's own father had described him more truly accurate. "A dunderhead of biblical proportions," he had adjudged his only son to be. And if you go by the old adage, *It takes one to know one,* Vinton's Pa was something of an expert, when it came to dunderheadedness. No sir, that man wasn't *nearly* the sharpest sword in the regiment, having ended his own life by accident, while tutoring young Vin in the correct way to clean and oil a gun.

His very last words had been, *"Always check it ain't loaded 'fore you begin, as it could cause you a injury if pointed at your fool skull in this ma—"*

Consequently of that, Sheriff James Whipple had made it a strict condition that young Vinton didn't clean guns nowhere near him.

"Apples don't fall far from trees," he'd explained to his wife. "He can come, and I'll teach the boy what I can — but if he ever points a gun in my direction, by accident or otherwise, I reckon I'll just shoot him first, before he trips on his trigger."

Things had gone not so bad the first year. The boy had

even been something of a comfort to James when his wife passed. Gave him something to do, teaching that boy some sense.

For a while, it seemed almost like Vinton had growed a few licks of sense.

But six months ago, Deputy Vinton Waits had started up talking about what a fine feller Pinckney Barron was, and how the man was now helping him with advice on how to become a big cattleman like himself.

"He tole me I'm gon'a be be rich one day, not just be some stinkin' broke lawman. There's easy ways to riches, Uncle James, so he reckons. And he's took a right shine to me, on account of I'm clever."

James Whipple's brain had argued some with his ears then, and he'd said, "Did the man use that exact word, Vin? Clever, did you say?"

"Yessir, he did. Tole me he knowed right off when he seen me, that I was a feller'd go far. Said it takes a clever one like me to seize the bull by the tail and invest when he's young. I ain't missin' out, I'm no fool. Why, Uncle, you should invest too."

Despite Whipple cautioning him against it, the young Deputy had borrowed money from the bank to buy cattle. Vinton had even asked his Uncle to put up his house as surety for the loan, but James Whipple had not come down in the last rain shower. He'd put on his eyeglasses, looked at the loan agreement and said, "Vin, this contract's no good. Way this is worded, Romulus Hogg can call in the loan any time he chooses. If you don't pay the lot within forty-eight hours, he can seize the mortgaged goods — in this case, the comfortable home I worked for my whole life. I wouldn't sign this if an honest man asked me to — let alone Romulus Hogg. Nosiree. It's a flat no from me, and I *strongly* advise you not to trust Hogg *or* Barron, they aren't scrupulous men, either one."

In the end, Romulus Hogg had given Vinton his loan with no other surety than the cattle he bought with it — twenty head to get him started on his way, and at a cheap price from Pinckney Barron himself.

Even the rate of interest seemed too good to be true — it was a much better deal, James knew, than what other local ranchers were getting. And that worried him.

Then three months ago, young Vinton had moved out of their home. "Mister Barron reckons a man should have his own quarters, if he's to become someone big. Reckons no one will ever respect me while I hide behind your shirttails, Uncle. I reckon he's right."

Pinckney Barron had rented him a room at his own saloon, and at a mighty cheap tariff.

Ever since then, James had seen less and less of his Deputy — and what he *did* see, he didn't much like.

Just like Kansas all over again. Seems like the easily led will always find someone to lead them. Just like that ox, James thought. *The one the missus reckoned was young Vinton's intellectual equal.*

Sheriff James Whipple smiled at the thought of his wife saying that on her deathbed. Even with her body all ravaged by the consumption, her mind had stayed sharp and funny right to the end. The words she'd said might have sounded cruel from someone else's mouth — but somehow, that dear woman had said and meant them lovingly. She always laughed *with* folk, not *at* them.

And as foolish as that boy was being, he was her kin — so, as the preacher finished up with his sermon, James Whipple decided he'd try harder to help get that boy get back on the straight and narrow path.

He's just a kid, and there's hope for him yet. I only hope it ain't too late.

CHAPTER 15
A REAL BAD FEELING

When Sheriff James Whipple walked out of that dark little church and blinked his way into the sunshine, he knew right away something was wrong.

It wasn't unusual that his nephew was right across the street watching — the boy liked everyone to see he was keeping an eye out, as they walked outside from the sermon.

No, it was some other thing that felt wrong. To begin with, James's brain didn't know *what* it was. But sometimes a man's brain don't need all the answers — it's enough that he *feels* something's wrong, and can work it out from there. He had been alive sixty years. Been a lawman or soldier more than half of it. Not unusual for a man with that much experience to *feel* a wrong thing before any other of his senses inform him of what the thing is. Can save a man's life, such a feeling, if he pays due attention.

It's Vinton, he realized then. *Something's up, way he's*

carrying himself. Prideful — and not in any way might be good for him.

The Sheriff kept one eye on his nephew as he shook the hand of the preacher, and complimented the bible-thumper on an excellent sermon.

Preacher laughed good-naturedly at that one. Then, quietly, he told James, "The day you actually *listen* to one of my sermons, is the day I'll drop dead from surprise, James Whipple. It was neighborly of you to flatter me though, and I'm glad you still come along every week."

"It's not you, Preacher," he replied. "I spend the whole time I'm in there thinking of Gertie, I guess. When I close my eyes, I fancy I can feel her beside me, holding my hand as she used to. And I thank you for helping me do that, whatever your part in that is. There's more to preaching than words, and you do a mighty fine job."

"You're too kind," said the preacher, but anyone could see he was flattered.

"See you next week," James said, patting the bible-thumper on the back as he moved away. Then James Whipple put on his hat and walked across the street to where Deputy Vin Waits sort of lounged, cupping his chin in his hand, while his elbow leaned on a hitching rail.

"Uncle," said the young feller with a dismissive half-nod — both nod and voice lacked their usual respect, and he kept on leaning on the rail while he spoke, a little slower than usual. "Walt Smith came into town awhile ago. Reckoned he heard shots north of his place this morning."

"Norris Ricks' place?"

"Could be." The younger man paused, stood to his full

height and stared lecherously at the pretty Williams sisters as they crossed the street. Then loud enough so the girls heard him, he said, "They's a shapely pair'a fillies, ain't they? Might just take one for a wife one'a these days." Then in a lower voice he added, "Or try both of 'em out anyways."

The girls scurried away, fear in their eyes as they glanced back behind them, and James Whipple had to fight down the urge to slap his fool nephew a good one across his leering face.

The Sheriff's eyes blazed, and though his words came out quiet, they were fraught with meaning. "You been keeping bad company, Vin, speaking that way to decent young girls. Not to mention they're barely fourteen. Don't you *never* speak that way again. Now quit gawking that way, boy, unless you want to be taught some good manners right here where the whole town can see."

"Sure, Uncle ... whatever you say." The young fool seemed not to understand the danger. "But before you raise a hand to *me,* you best remember what you tole me 'bout how we *lawmen's* a'sposed to act out in public. Just wouldn't do, would it? The Sheriff attackin' his Deputy? Then gettin' the daylight beat out of him for it?"

Whipple looked the young chucklehead in the eyes. Vinton Waits actually seemed to believe himself capable of winning, if it came to a fistfight. "We'd best discuss all that later in private," James said, a sad smile on his face. "Now what about these shots?"

Deputy Vin Waits smiled a languid one, took his time before answering. "I was gon'a take a ride out there and check. Then I remembered, Norris Ricks upset quite a few men last night in the saloon — beat some poor feller unconscious at one point. Fair fight though, I figured, so I had Mister Barron lock the saloon doors and allow Ricks a fifteen minute start. Just in case, you know? Thing is, I'm worried Ricks might think I'm one'a them men he angered, maybe even start shootin' at me."

Whipple knew the truth about the previous night, had heard it from two good men, not just Norris Ricks, but Cleve Lawson. But he didn't let on that he knew what had *really* gone on. All he said was, "Where's Walt? I'd speak to him myself."

"Well, Uncle, that's a complication right there. Meant to be a secret, it is. But he'd be plowing the widow Langley's field right about now, I'd reckon."

"But she lives in town, Vin, doesn't have any fields to ... oh, I see. Never mind."

"I can go check on Ricks," said the deputy. "But if he shoots at me, won't be my fault if I have to kill him."

"I'll go out there and check myself," Whipple said. "Norris Ricks ain't the sort to shoot without reason — but anyway, he knows my horse, if we're playin' it safe."

"It's what you always drummed into me, Uncle," the Deputy smirked as he pushed away from the hitching post. "Play it safe. That's why I better go with you."

The Sheriff was about to tell the whippersnapper to stay in town, but something made him change his mind. A *feeling* was all. "Get the horses," he said, "while I have a quick bite and collect my guns."

CHAPTER 16

THE PROBLEM WITH HORSESHOES

Sheriff James Whipple *wanted* to trust that nephew of his — for the sake of his wife's family, if nothing else. But the boy made it less and less easy.

James thought some about the situation as he chowed down a quick piece of pie, then he carefully chose some guns from the rack. His trusty Winchester, and the old Sharps he never had much call for.

Just in case.

He wasn't sure what it was just in case *of*, but whenever he got such uneasy feelings, they turned out to be for good reason.

If his instincts had told him to paint his boots pink, and wear a flower in his hair, well, he would have done both — lucky for him, his instincts just said *Take the Sharps, the Winchester, your six-gun and extra ammunition.*

He was a man unsuited to wearing flowers, and he had no damn pink paint anyway.

By the time Vinton Waits went to the livery, saddled

the horses, and arrived out front, the Sheriff was ready to go, and loaded for bear.

The Winchester was a short one, and he wore it in a special-made scabbard on his back. Comfortable and easy to get at, compared to most others.

The young deputy cast a scornful eye over the old Sharps. "That useless ol' thing even fire? You know there's no buffalo 'round here, don'tcha, old man?"

"Just figured I'd bring it along, see if it still shoots straight," said James, cradling the beautiful weapon in his arms. He knew perfectly well that the Sharps was in top condition, but there was no need to tell his fool nephew anything else.

He slid the Sharps into the saddle scabbard and checked the cinch strap on the horse — funny thing, even at sixty, he still heard his father's advice from when he was a child. *"Never trust no other man's saddling of horses, and neither his loading of guns. Either thing done wrong'll kill you. Anyone touches your gear, always check on their work 'fore you use it."*

He had been a good man, and it always warmed James's heart to hear his father's true voice in his mind.

Vinton suggested they race out to Norris Ricks' place, but James told him he could just stay in town if he didn't have a mind to behave.

"We'll take our time, not waste our horses, just in case we have need of their speed and stamina later."

Vinton looked at him funny a moment, Whipple thought. But maybe he just imagined it. This trip would most likely be for nothing — that was how these things usually went. But he had to be sure.

They rode along side by side, not speaking much. James was enjoying the sunshine, the fresh air and big sky, the feeling of sitting on that wonderful, powerful horse. Cranky, that big bay gelding's name was, and sometimes he earned it — was known to bite folks he took a disliking to, without any hint of a warning — but he was a fine horse to be sure. Cranky wasn't much of a looker, but he was unafraid of gunfire, surefooted as a mountain pony, and could dance side to side on command — why, that big ugly horse could dance almost like Norris Ricks could, when the man put his fists up.

A few minutes out of town, and Vinton's impatient nature got the best of him. The boy urged his horse into a trot, but James Whipple just let him go without saying a word. He'd known that boy since he was filling a diaper, and wasn't about to allow him to dictate terms now.

Man has to earn such a right.

Soon as the deputy rode ahead, the sheriff noticed the tracks weren't quite right. Whipple had told young Vinton a week ago, that the boy's horse had a broken shoe. Wasn't missing the whole thing, but about a third of the left hind shoe was missing, and the horse's gait showed he was favoring it ever so slightly.

Wasn't enough of a change in gait that he'd have noticed, he only saw it because of the missing bit of shoe.

James never lost sight of his nephew, and the boy eventually stopped and waited in some shade for him to catch up.

"You didn't get that broken shoe fixed," he said as he reined up beside the young feller.

"Had more important things to do, old man."

James took off his hat and wiped his brow with his sleeve. "Can't think of what such things might be. Horse is beginning to go lame already, for the sake of just a few minutes. Too good a horse to waste, that nice gray."

James had gifted the gray to his nephew a year ago. He was a nice horse, but not quite as good as Cranky. Less prone to foul moods though for sure.

"Ain't hurting him none just for now," said the deputy in a dismissive tone. "I'll get him to the blacksmith when I got time."

"It's not easy to find, a good horse. When you got one you should look after him." Whipple put his hat back on and added, "Let's go."

"Reckon I'll get a better horse soon," the young deputy said under his breath, casting an eye over Cranky's powerful rump. "Another month or two, I'll be takin' whatever I want."

CHAPTER 17

A REAL BAD BUSINESS

There's something about this boy today, thought James Whipple, as Norris Ricks' neat house came in sight. *Something too eager in his actions, and overly confident in his speech.*

Nothing looked too unusual 'til they got close.

He pointed across the yard with his head. "Drag marks," he said — half to Vinton, half to himself.

The experienced sheriff knew what it meant right away, and his senses went on full alert. He motioned to the deputy to climb down from his horse, and he did so at the same time. Both horses were trained to stay right where they were let go, and that's just what they did.

He raised a finger to his lips for his nephew to stay quiet, as he studied the signs.

The markings started halfway between the porch and the outhouse. A large man, heavy in his boots, had dragged a body across the yard from that point, all the way to the stairs.

"This is bad," he said to his nephew. "We best go look inside. Get your pistol out, look through the window. I'll keep you covered."

Vinton Waits smiled. "When did you become so damn afeared, Uncle? I used to look up to your bravery, now you're sendin' me ahead to do the real work."

Whipple ignored the taunt and stuck to his plan. "Go on," he said, drawing his own six-gun.

The younger man sidled on up to that window like he already knew there was no one there to be afraid of. He cupped one hand against the window and peered through the glass best he could. Then he looked around at his Uncle, half-smiled and strode to the door.

He threw that door open — gun still drawn — then relaxed some, turned about and called, "Walt Smith was right, Uncle. Someone's done for Norris Ricks." Then he put his gun away in its holster and walked on inside.

No mistaking, James Whipple's heart dropped a little when he heard those words. Norris had been a fine man, one of the best he had known.

Bad business, all this.

His thoughts went to that damn Pinckney Barron — he sure had a strong feeling about who had orchestrated this death, and the deaths of those sheep men.

But feelings and hunches are one thing, solid proof is another.

As he walked up the stairs, he noticed a book laying out on the porch, and knew someone else must have put it there. Norris would never risk ruining a book by leaving it outside that way. Whipple stepped through the door, but was unprepared for what he saw.

Norris Ricks had been hanged from the rafters — and as James Whipple entered the room, his nephew reached out a hand toward the completely naked body, pushed it a little so it spun slowly around.

"Don't," said James. "Don't touch him again."

Vinton Waits withdrew his hand, but he didn't move none. The young deputy's eyes sort of studied the body all over with a strange fascination.

The sheriff's gaze went from his nephew back to Norris Ricks' body.

Wasn't being hanged that had killed him. That fact could not have been clearer. The top of that good man's head was all gone — he'd also been shot in the back, the hole there was small, but the one in his chest surely wasn't. And his throat had been cut, ear to ear — there was blood down the front of him from it, but not so much as you might think.

Dead before that was done.

His clothes had been thrown on the floor next to a blanket that had dirt and blood on it. There was no blood spatter inside the house — just a small pool under the body.

Sheriff James Whipple had to push himself hard to keep thinking — to work it all out, as he must. Was no easy thing, but he did it. Forced himself to.

Whoever had done this to Norris was no ordinary man — he was a man gone wrong in the head. He — or they — had shot Norris Ricks outside, when he was coming back in from the outhouse. Then put him on that blanket — his feet still hanging off the end of it — and dragged him across the yard to the stairs, before wrapping him up and carrying him inside. That's why there was no blood on the porch. Then they'd strung him up right here — would have taken two men for certain, way he was strung — and cut his clothes off him, before taking to his throat with a Bowie knife.

But why? Why all this, once he was dead?

"Don't touch him," said James to his fascinated nephew, whose hand had reached out toward the body again. Then Whipple walked to the bed, picked up a blanket, came back and wrapped it around what was left of Norris Ricks.

"We should go tell the undertaker to deal with it," said Vinton.

The boy's eyes shone in an odd way, James noticed now.

"You have your knife on you, Vin?"

The deputy's eyes went wide, just a fraction of a moment — then he settled and said, "Sure, Uncle, right here." He kept it in a small scabbard, left side of his belt. He took it out now, and it flashed as the light from the window shone on its sharp blade.

"I'll take his weight, while you cut the rope. Not right to leave such a man hanging this way."

So Vinton Waits cut the rope, and Sheriff James Whipple lowered Norris Ricks down onto his shoulder, carried him to his bed, laid him out with his head on the pillow.

"Wait outside," he told the deputy then. Vinton hesitated a moment, then walked on out. Then James took the last spare blanket and placed it over poor Norris's head, before saying, "I promise you, Norris Ricks, I'll find the man — the *men* — responsible for this, and I'll make them pay. Good man like you earned that much. I swear it, Norris. They'll hang or I'll kill them myself, every last man involved."

CHAPTER 18
FEAR, NOT REMORSE

When Sheriff James Whipple walked outside into bright daylight, his nephew had already mounted the gray horse.

"Hold up there, Vin," he told the boy. "We best look around, see if we can't work out who done this."

Vinton Waits wheeled his horse about, looked down at the older man and laughed a mocking one. At twenty-two, he believed himself a great font of knowledge — and was such a damn chucklehead, he thought his Uncle a fool.

Youth is wasted on the young — they sure don't know what they don't know.

The young spooney tapped the side of his cheekbone with one finger as if to indicate James had gone loco. He spoke slowly, eyes wide, and moved his head from side to side, as if he was speaking to a lunatic in an asylum. "How you gon'a do that, old man? Ain't likely they's writ you a note of confession. We should get on back to town, get the undertaker out here, 'fore that body gets to stinkin' up the place any worse."

"Vin Waits," said James then. "I was young once, like you are now, and I said and done my share of fool things. Makes me somewhat forgiving, remembering just how damn stupid I was at your age. And I promised my dear Gertie — and your poor mother too — that I'd do my best to help you along the right path. But if you keep up disrespecting folk, I *will* sit you on your behind, you hear? Enough."

"If you can't take a joke, Unc—"

James Whipple leaped forward, dragged that arrogant flannel-mouthed boy off that horse down into the dirt, and dragged him ten feet across the hard ground before Vin knew what was happening. Then James pulled him up onto his knees, held him tight by the scruff of the collar with his left hand, bunched his right fist and recoiled it ready to knock that boy into next week — but he didn't throw the punch.

Instead, he looked down into his nephew's shocked eyes and said, "You damn fool. A good man is *dead*. You ain't fit to lick that man's boots, and you think it's a time for jokes and jests? You disrespected them young girls in town, and for all I know, you're somehow mixed up in all this, way you run around doing that damn Pinckney Barron's bidding. Give me one good reason not to ram this fist down your throat 'til it comes out your—"

"I'm sorry, Uncle, I'm sorry." The sniveling coward's eyes were blinking fit to burst their lids, and there was fear in his voice.

But not remorse.

"You're not really sorry."

"I am, Uncle James, I am. I just ... I'm sorry. I didn't mean nothin' by it, I..." His eyes shifted this way and that, then he looked right at James and said, "I was shocked by the sight of it, Uncle. Never saw such a terrible violence done to a body. Upset me it did, is my best guess. I know you liked Norris Ricks, and I'm sorry he's dead — but Aunt Gertie wouldn't want you to beat on me, just 'cause of this. I miss her, Uncle, don't you?"

James Whipple had been through things even worse than this one. It was not the first mangled corpse he had seen — but he thought back now to when he saw his first one, and again made excuses for the boy.

"You need to stay away from Barron, Vin." He relaxed his grip on the collar, let his fist open, stretched out the fingers. Then he smoothed down his nephew's collar before offering him his hand to help him up.

"I'm sorry, Uncle," said the boy as he took James's hand and got to his feet. "Maybe you're right. Mister Barron was talking strong at the meeting, it's possible he could be tied up in all this I guess."

"Let's go see what we can find, son," said James, patting Vin on the shoulder. "Sorry I pitched a fit. Was a terrible shock for me too, seeing Norris Ricks done for that way."

They walked side by side to where the dragging had started. There was blood soaked into the dirt in two places where the body had fallen.

"Head and chest," James said, pointing at each spot in

turn. "Must have been coming back from his morning trip to the outhouse."

"But that doesn't tell us anything."

"Norris Ricks wasn't the sort to get sneaked up on. Most especially after what happened last night at the meeting. That tells us that whoever shot him was waiting back there in them trees. And that's maybe seventy yards. Shot with a rifle — no, two rifles."

"Two?" Vin's eyebrows were raised. Looked like a quizzical dog, he did. An ugly one, kinda stupid, the eyes lacking normal intelligence.

"Both bullets hit from behind. But either shot would have killed him."

Vin Waits looked at his Uncle, then quickly away toward the trees the shots had come from. "Maybe the feller shot him through the head from back there, then came and put one in his back here. He messed the body up other ways too, with the cutting and hanging and such."

"No. Size and shape of the holes are from good rifles fired at a distance. Both bullets hit pretty much the same time. Two shooters, both guilty of murder."

Deputy Vinton Waits looked away again, to the trees. "Well, that still don't help, I guess. Reckon it was them sheep fellers?"

"Come on," said James. "Let's go take a look."

Vin seemed to hang back a second, then came along when James turned to look at him. They walked side by side down to the trees.

"Look around," Whipple said, "they were likely here a

good while, the ground'll be tramped down some. Once we find it, we'll see if they left any clues."

"Clues? What sort of clues?"

"Here we are," said James. "See how the grass is all flattened. Look around, if luck's with us we'll find something useful. Packet of bible papers. Tobacco pouch, maybe the cartridges so we know what sort of rifles they used."

They searched awhile, but there was nothing.

"Well," James said after he'd given up on it, "let's go find where their horses were tied."

"What?" Vin's look was blank.

"They didn't ride in on a storybook magic carpet, now did they? There was moonlight enough for riders to see by, and they had to be in position before the first light. But they wouldn't bring the horses all the way, in case they made too much noise and Norris heard it. So the horses will have been tied up back further a ways."

"But that won't help either."

"They might have dropped something there. Worth a look."

Vin kept wandering away, but James kept an eye out, told him they should stay within sight of each other while they looked. "Have to be methodical when searching," he said. "No use wandering about willy-nilly, best to know you covered a whole area so you don't miss any out."

Took about fifteen minutes, but James finally found it — a clearing, best part of an acre in size, where two horses had been ground-tied and eaten down all the grass within reach.

And off a ways to one side, unmoving with blood at his throat, that fine over-friendly yellow dog Norris Ricks had raised from a pup. Must have run right up to the killers, wagging his tail in greeting.

Poor good feller.

Whipple was about to call his nephew over when he noticed the hoof-prints. One of the two horses that'd been here this morning — one of the horses belonging to the killers — was missing a piece of its shoe.

Vinton was one of the men who murdered Norris Ricks.

CHAPTER 19
DEPUTY DAMN DOUBLE-CROSSER

Maybe James Whipple saw something, or maybe he heard it — but it's much more likely he sensed it somehow in the ether, man like James Whipple.

Whatever it was made him jump to one side in that moment, it saved his life.

The big forty-four Winchester bullet Vinton Waits fired at his Uncle whistled past him and into the trees as he launched himself through the air. He hit the ground, rolled and jumped sideways again, but the second bullet tore through his shirt — he felt it, sensed the drag of it somehow, the closeness — and for half a moment, Sheriff James Whipple thought he'd been hit.

Must have missed his flesh by a beaver hair — he half-ran, half-limped, half-staggered, and then he was into the trees and safe behind cover. He'd had to release his Winchester when he rolled, but he was alive, wasn't shot, and had some good cover. He sat with his back against a sizable cottonwood, evened out his ragged breathing, took out his six-shooter and listened.

"Damn you, Uncle," called the treacherous Vinton Waits. "Fool old man, why couldn't you leave it alone?"

James could not see his nephew at all. But for certain, the boy had the advantage, where he was situated. James was on the wrong side of the clearing, further away from the horses. The trees were thinner to one side, and Vinton would certainly see him if he went that way. But the other way around was longer — further from Norris Ricks' house.

And crossing the open clearing would be suicide — that damn kid was lazy and stupid; had never been much use for anything; but the one skill he had was that he could shoot straight with a rifle.

Biggest problem was, the Sheriff's foot was beginning to throb. *Must have landed wrong on it. Old bones ain't what they were I guess.*

He couldn't hear any movement, but the deputy was at least forty yards away, other side of the clearing. An experienced man could sneak quietly, but Vinton Waits was clumsy as a mule on a tightrope. James called out, "Why'd you do it, Vin?" He knew his best chance was to keep the boy talking, while he maybe came up with a plan.

"I'm goin' places, old man. I ain't gon'a be a broke no-count lawman like you. Mister Barron's got plans, big ones. Clever feller like me can go all the way with him, he reckons. And Norris Ricks was a fool. We'll do them same things to you, if you's fool enough to come back."

The Sheriff wasn't too worried — for now — about Vinton being able to shoot him. Not now he had decent cover. James Whipple had survived far worse situations than this, up against better men, and more of them.

"Think of your poor mother, Vin. You getting hanged'll kill her. I can get you a deal, I'm certain. You testify against Pinckney Barron, they'll go easy on you for sure — just some time in the hoosegow, no hanging. Think of your mother, Vin!"

There was no answer.

The Sheriff knew he needed to stop the boy from getting back to La Grange. Once he got back to town — Whipple knew it now for certain — Pinckney Barron would send a trained killer to hunt him.

Whoever the other killer is, he knows what he's doing. The killing of Norris Ricks was done by a professional.

"Vin? Talk to me, son, we can fix this."

The deputy answered with his Winchester, the sound of the shot partly dulled by the trees — and the bullet didn't come through the clearing.

Could be a trap. Maybe. But is he that clever?

Sheriff James Whipple listened close then, and he heard it. The boy was moving away — careful at first, then with no care at all, only haste.

That damn Vinton Waits crashed through the undergrowth, getting further away by the second, going back to the horses.

James was on his feet, thinking to follow — but not for long. *Damn foot. Ten years ago I'd have been fine. I'd be on his trail right now, shoot him off of his horse as he tried to escape.*

The thought of it chilled him a little.

Could I do it? He's kin after all.

The sounds the desperate young killer made were distant now. James found a stick to lean on, used it as a crutch, limping his way across the clearing, back into the trees again.

Then the sound of the deputy's voice came floating toward him. "You're a dead man, Uncle James. If you don't ride away and never come back, you're gon'a be dead 'fore the day's out."

Then he heard the sound of the gray horse galloping away — a sound so sweet to his ears, he could barely believe it.

Damn young fool's ridden away, but he's left me my horse.

CHAPTER 20
FRIENDS IN HIGH PLACES

C leve Lawson hadn't slept well the previous night, on account of his worry for Norris Ricks' welfare. And since waking at daybreak, he'd considered riding over to Norris's a half-dozen times.

But every time he thought of it, the very same answer came to him. *Norris Ricks is a force to be reckoned with — and he'd just be insulted, same as I would.*

Cleve knew that was foolish of Norris, but he also knew that was just how things were. And he wasn't about to ruin their friendship by trying to molly-coddle the man.

Still, Cleve wished he'd told everyone he planned to go back into town Sunday, rather than Monday. *That would not have worked either,* he realized, *Norris would have seen right through it.*

Thing about that was, Cleve had never once attended church since he'd lived here. He was sort of against it, ever since he lived down in Texas, where certain churchgoers had ostracized him and his wife 'cause they hadn't got married up legal yet. Leaping the book was frowned upon there, and things weren't no different in these parts.

The punch in the nose didn't help, now he thought some about it. *But if that preacher hadn't stuck his nose in where it didn't belong, I would not have punched it. Just because a man has friends in high places, don't mean he ain't bound by the simple rule of minding his business.*

Cleve was inside the barn, rubbing linseed oil into his spare saddle when his dog commenced barking. He wasn't much of a one to yap for no reason, ol' Jimbo — big sleepy spotted thing he was, but he came right to life when he had a good reason, and was good with cattle as well.

Cleve wiped his hands on the old towel, picked his rifle up from where it leaned against the bench, and walked out of the barn. "What is it, Jimbo?"

The dog, twenty yards up ahead, turned to look at Cleve a moment, turned back toward the road and barked again.

"Good boy," Cleve told him. "Come away now back here." He was mostly obedient — when he wanted to be — and he wagged his tail a moment, then did as he was told.

Cleve and Jimbo waited by the barn doors a minute, and soon Cleve heard the horse coming too. *One rider. Norris, I guess.*

The dog commenced wagging his tail again.

Norris.

Cleve still didn't put down the rifle, but he felt more relaxed. Then the horse and rider came into view. They weren't exactly galloping, but were moving at a good steady canter.

Trouble.

But it ain't Norris.

"Who is it, Jimbo, you know him, boy, don't you?"

The big spotted dog wagged his tail, barked once and spun a full circle. But he was well trained, and he stayed right by Cleve's side.

"Ah, it's the Sheriff," Cleve said to the dog, and he put down the rifle. "I shoulda known, way you carried on like a Nancy. You're a dang traitor, Jimbo, y'know that?"

There was something about the Sheriff and the dog, that had always seemed strange to Cleve. That dog didn't much care for most people — not exactly unfriendly, but not over-friendly way Norris's dog always was. But whenever he saw Sheriff James Whipple, ol' Jimbo was happy as a frog with four extra legs. He'd rub up against him, wag his tail like nobody's business, even stand up on his hind legs and kiss the man on the face.

Seemed downright unseemly to Cleve, but James Whipple never minded at all — *no accountin' for taste,* Cleve reckoned. Truth was though, he maybe even felt a bit envious, way that dog behaved with the Sheriff. Seemed almost like that pair was in love with each other's company.

"Sheriff," he said with a nod, as the man rode up to the barn and the dog whined with pleasure. "Stay, Jimbo."

"Good dog," said Sheriff James Whipple, "you stay like he says." Then he winced a little and added, "I'll need a hand down off the horse, Cleve. Hurt my foot some dodging a bullet."

Cleve Lawson looked at the Sheriff's old eyes, and in them, he saw the worst. "Norris?"

Whipple's nod was brief, and the tightness of his face told the story. "My damn nephew and some other man. Professional."

"Blue Bandana," said Cleve, as he helped James down from the horse. "Did you get either one?"

"Only Vinton was there when I injured myself. When I come out of church he told me Walt Smith had heard shots out at Norris's place."

"Dammit," said Cleve. "Never heard a thing. Sound of shots don't carry there to here, even though I'm closer by travel time."

He left Whipple leaning against the barn, went inside and came out with two chairs. James sat himself down on one, then Cleve put the other in front, helped him lift his foot up on it. Whipple had already loosened the boot, and was clearly discomfited as Cleve took it off, gentle as he could manage. He was a man unused to needing help, and it irked him some, this situation.

"It's swelled bad, Sheriff," Cleve said. He threw the boot across the yard in frustration, then his fists curled up, and he just about spat the words, "Damn them. If only I'd..."

He walked around in a circle, ran his fingers through his hair, wiped something out of an eye. Then he stood quiet awhile, facing away from the Sheriff, looking out in the direction of Norris Ricks' place.

Damn them.

CHAPTER 21

"DEAD BEFORE HE HIT THE DIRT…"

Sheriff James Whipple understood shock and grief — what they did to a man. Even a strong man. *Especially* a strong one.

Maybe that spotted dog understood too. Jimbo whined just a little, sneaked over and sat by the Sheriff, extra well behaved. James reached down, stroked the fur on his head some.

"Good dog you are," he said quietly, and the dog licked his hand. Then as Cleve turned around, the Sheriff looked up at his stricken face. James Whipple spoke softly, but clearly then. "You'd have been too late anyway, Cleve. It was over in a second. He never even knew."

"Through the head?"

Whipple nodded that tight nod again. "I went out there with my damn nephew. I never twigged he was part of it — I should have, he'd been acting strange. I blame myself for that, *wanted* him to turn out alright, despite all the evidence saying he'd been going wrong. But even if I'd known, I could not have saved Norris. They ... they made an example of him, Cleve. When he opened his mouth at that meeting, he signed his own death warrant."

"I should have..." Cleve didn't finish the sentence. He did not know how.

They ain't no use, *Should Haves,* when there's nothing you could have done.

"They'd have only murdered you too, Cleve." Whipple let the words sink in a moment before he went on. "They went out in the night, hid back in the trees, killed his nice yellow dog. Then they waited. Two shots at once, certain of it. He was on his way back from the outhouse, took one in the back and the other through his brain. Dead before he hit the dirt."

"What was he reading?" The words had just sort of fallen out of Cleve without him choosing them. He looked at the Sheriff, waved a hand dismissively and added, "Creature of habit, good ol' Norris. I'd arrive early sometimes to collect him, go into town. But he weren't goin' nowhere 'til he'd finished his breakfast and his second cup of Arbuckles, then headed off to the outhouse with a book for ten, fifteen minutes. Whole lot more readin' than action in there, I reckoned — but he always said that's how long things took, and I sure never followed him to check."

"He did love to read," James said with a smile. "It was a book on Montana. It's right there in my saddlebags. I brought it along — reckoned he'd want you to have it."

"Oh, Norris," said Cleve, then he sighed a deep one before explaining it further to the Sheriff. "He was of a mind to sell up and start afresh out there. Up 'round the

Breaks maybe. Invited me for serious, just last night. We was to argue it out tomorrow over a meal. Guess we ain't goin' now."

Under different circumstances, the two men might have spoke fondly of Norris for some considerable time — but the truth of it was, time was a luxury unavailable to them.

"I'll go fetch Norris's body," said Cleve.

"There isn't time." There was a finality to James Whipple's words. He looked a little guilty and sad, but the truth of it had to be stated. "If I hadn't hurt my dang foot, I'd have been able to bring him. But now it's too late — Vinton'll nearly be back to town by now, and they'll be comin' after me. We got forty-five minutes, I'd reckon, and none of those to waste. The best we can do's go back later, bury him proper."

"If there *is* a later," said Cleve. The men exchanged a meaningful glance. "Gives us one thing extra to fight for, I guess. I ain't dyin' before I know my friend's proper buried."

Cleve fetched a bucket of cool water for James to soak his swelled foot in, and tended to the Sheriff's horse while they nutted out what they should do.

They didn't completely agree, but they came to consensus on one thing — they would not be safe here, just the two of them. Cleve told James Whipple of the tall boots the bossman had worn when those men robbed the stage, and murdered Matt Roach in cold blood. Told him he then saw those boots on Pinckney Barron at the Cattlemen's Meeting.

"I seen him stumbling around town on the fool things," said the Sheriff. "Like a foal that ain't learned to walk proper yet. Things a man does for vanity's sake." He shook his head slowly before going on. "Well, there's no doubt Barron's in charge. And we know he's got at least six other men on the payroll."

"Five," said Cleve. "It was him and *five* others robbed the stage."

"But Vinton was with me in town at that time," Whipple reminded him. "So there's seven at least, including Barron, that'll come after us soon. And one at least knows what he's doing."

"And the others well disciplined too," Cleve said. "They all knew their jobs at the robbery, and not a one spoke. Army background, I'd warrant, they worked as a unit. I agree, if we stay here, we might not survive it." He looked around at all he'd built, then his gaze went back to James Whipple's. "You know, Sheriff, I reckon you should consider doing what your damn nephew suggested."

Whipple's eyes hardened. "You'd have me run?"

"I'd have you *live*. Look at Norris. That's your future if you stay. I'll be alright, most likely — because I ain't spoke out against 'em yet. Reckon they won't kill me, not unless I speak up. But you ... you're a dead man soon as they find you, no matter the circumstance. You could take some food, head out from here through the hills. Stay away from the main trails, go to Cheyenne, maybe Sidney. Sell your house to someone once you're there, go somewhere else, live out your life. This ain't your problem, 'less you keep makin' it so."

"I'm the Sheriff. That makes it my problem. I'll go to the sheep men, ask them for help. I tried to help them before, but there was no proof what was happening — so they might not be happy to see me. But they're my best chance now. Up to you if you come with me, Cleve. My honest opinion, you should just stay here and say you never saw me. Be the sensible thing."

"Bad business, Sheriff, beginning to end. I've never been a man to stick my nose in. Right or wrong, it's how I was made. How I was raised. But this whole thing's been a challenge to that — bad enough what they done to Matt Roach, but now Norris too. He got killed standing up for what's right, while I minded my damn business, stayed out of it, way I always have done." Cleve looked away, took a deep breath, absentmindedly reached down and stroked one of ol' Jimbo's ears.

"I need to get going," James Whipple said. "But first I'll say this. Cleve. I heard from Sam Perris what you said and did in that stagecoach — *all* of it — both before *and* after Matt Roach's death. Seems to me you got choices to make. You can choose to live your own true nature or not. That's up to you, and I won't say one more word on it. But me, I know what *I* have to do." The old Sheriff lifted his foot from the bucket and commenced to dry it off with the towel. "I'll be needing my boot."

Both men looked across the yard to where Cleve had thrown the boot. It had been a mighty throw, fueled as it was by frustration and anger and grief.

Cleve smiled and nodded. He left Whipple to finish drying his foot and pull on his sock, while he walked across to the boot, picked it up and brought it back, shaking out the dirt as he went.

"Wonder Jimbo never et it," he said as he handed it over.

Whipple rubbed the dog's ears and said, "He wouldn't do that to a friend, would you, old boy?" Jimbo whined with pleasure as he looked at the Sheriff adoringly.

Cleve shook his head at the overt display of affection. "I'll get a few things from the house and saddle my horse. Only right I should tell the sheep men how brave their friend died."

Cleve and the Sheriff rode on up toward the sheep town, took the dog along with them. Cleve suggested the sheep fellers might frown upon them bringing the dog, but James Whipple had refused to hear a word of it.

"If Pinckney Barron's men think you're helping me, Cleve, they'll shoot Jimbo here out of spite."

Cleve had hoped James would make him bring the dog, and it set his mind at rest some.

They rode into the valley side by side, the dog scouting off to the left of them, but still within sight — dang dog chose Whipple's side, Cleve noticed. *No accounting for taste.*

At the mouth of the valley they brought their horses to a halt and quietly stared at the signs. Three of them, there were, wooden boards painted bright white: big enough no one could miss them; the huge letters red enough to catch any eye; each of them clear enough worded that no man could say he weren't warned.

~ **Private Land** ~
~ **Keep OUT** ~
~ **Trespassers SHOT** ~

Even if a man was unable to read, the drawing of a skull with a pair of crossed rifles painted through it would have sent a clear enough message.

After several seconds ol' Jimbo came over to read the signs too. Seemed to think about the words a few moments before making his mind up. Then he barked once at the Sheriff, once at Cleve Lawson, spun an impatient circle, and went running forward into the valley.

"You heard him," said Whipple. "We ain't got all day."

Cleve raised two fingers to his right eyebrow in salute. "He can't really read you know, Sheriff, he just pretends. Made me read the Cheyenne newspaper to him when I got back last time."

"You wouldn't think he'd care," said the Sheriff. "Mostly the bad news is what they print anyway. Could even make a dog unhappy, newsprint these days."

Both men gave their horses some rein, and they followed their four-legged friend up the valley at a comfortable trot. It was a pretty place, this one, and Cleve almost chose it when he first came here — had to toss a coin in the end to decide, he liked both places so much. "Come on back," he called to the dog before Jimbo got too far ahead — no sense letting a good dog go get himself shot, even if he *was* a bit of a traitor.

Sheep men's just as likely to believe dogs can read, for all I know. Might be I could teach him someday. Cleve chuckled some at the thought, then pictured ol' Jimbo sitting up in a chair by the fireplace, wearing eyeglasses as he read the newspaper.

It was a funny old thought, and something of a pleasure to his mind, after all the recent bad happenings.

He was in the process of adding a pipe and a nice glass of whiskey to the picture when the first shot rang out and disturbed him from all of the fun.

Here we go again, he thought, and he noticed that big ugly horse of the Sheriff's had jumped to his left, quick as some circus tumbler.

"Stop right there," came a voice from their right.

"Unless you'd rather be dead," came a voice from their left.

Not wanting to be dead, they all stopped right where they were — even ol' Jimbo stopped right there in his tracks, with his right front paw in the air.

They'd never even said, *'Stick yer paws up!'*

"Stay, boy," Cleve said, just to make sure ol' Jimbo didn't change his mind and get himself shot.

Cleve could not see either of the men who'd called out, so he just kept his hands well away from his guns and let James Whipple do the talking, as they'd agreed.

"I'm the Sheriff of La Grange," he called good and loud.

"Thought Sheriffs should be able to read," came the voice from the left. "Turn around and leave now, or be considered trespassers, and suffer the consequence of it."

Whipple let go of the reins and slowly raised his hands to the sky, both his palms clearly open and empty. "I can read just fine," he called. "Important business I'm here on. I need to speak with the man in charge. One of your people was recently killed, and I need your help to arrest the men responsible."

"Heard that one before," the reply came. "Who's that you got with you? I don't trust men with dogs. Bounty hunters and regulators, that's who ride 'round with dogs. Who's that dog tryin' to catch?"

"This dog couldn't catch cold, Mister," said Cleve. Even knowing there was rifles trained on him, he couldn't stop himself speaking up. "And I don't appreciate the insult, Mister — I sure ain't no damn regulator, I *work* for *my* living."

"Then who the hell are you?"

"I'm your closest neighbor, Cleve Lawson. I was with one of your men on the stagecoach a few days back when..." He struggled a moment with the words, had to swallow down his upset and anger before he got going again. "... When six damn road agents robbed us, and murdered your friend in cold blood."

"How do we know it wasn't *you* killed our friend?" This time it was the voice from their right.

"You don't," said Cleve. "But we'd be a right pair of chuckleheads to come here if we had, all things considered. We look like chuckleheads to you?"

"Reckon you do," called the voice, "but we'll see. Now — *one at a time* — climb down, lay down your guns, ground-tie your horses, and walk forward 'til I say stop. You first, Mister Cleve Lawson."

They did what they were told. And ol' Jimbo stayed right where *he'd* been told, still with his paw up. Watched Sheriff James Whipple the whole time, his eyes gleaming with what looked like love, as the man limped his way forward.

"Face each other and hold hands now," said the voice on the left. "Both hands."

Cleve's eyes narrowed some. "I ain't—"

"Just do it, Cleve," said Whipple.

A minute later the two sheep men were standing ten feet away, guns pointed at them and laughing.

"Such a pretty sight," said the tall one who'd been on the left. "This dog likely to bite? I like dogs a lot, but I'll shoot him if he tries it."

"He's my dog," said Cleve, "and he's never bit no one before. But I reckon he'd likely bite *me* if the Sheriff here told him to. Got a thing goin' on, these two."

"Dog'll just follow along," said Whipple. "Please don't harm him, he's about the best friend I got."

"Damn traitor's what he is," said Cleve.

The tall sheep feller chuckled and shook his head some in sympathy. "That's a sad story, Lawson. Happened to my friend here once, but that was only a wife, weren't it, Bill?"

"True enough," said that Bill feller. "Not sure I coulda moved on from it, if it was my *dog* who loved another."

"Go get the horses, Bill, and don't forget to pick up

their guns," said the tall feller. Then he laughed one more time and said, "Follow your noses up the valley, we'll go see the boss."

CHAPTER 23

A LONG SLOW WALK

I f that damn young fool Vinton Waits ever listened to his Uncle, things might have come to a head a bit quicker than they did.

Sheriff James Whipple had told him three times to get that horse to the blacksmith — told him the horse would go lame if he didn't look after it.

Galloping hell for leather out of Norris Ricks' place had finally done it. A mile down the trail, with Vinton still using up the horse like the chucklehead he was, the horse's leg gave way a little. He was lucky that horse was as good as it was, or it would have fallen to the ground underneath him, instead of pulling up how it did.

He had cursed the horse roundly the whole way back to town — took a good while to get there as well, having to walk as he did. Indeed, it was even a little slower than ordinary walking, as the fool Deputy wasn't about to carry his gear — he left the horse fully laden, and tried to make it walk faster, but it was slow going.

When he finally trudged into town, dusty and thirsty and tired — he had forgotten to take any water — he dropped the horse at the livery, guzzled a bellyful of water himself from a horse trough, then headed for Pinckney Barron's saloon.

Despite it being the Sabbath, there was no shortage of drinkers inside.

Soon as he walked in, Waits asked a rough looking feller, "Where's the boss?"

The man pointed the way with a raising of his ugly bent nose. "Upstairs in his office. He said to send you right up."

Deputy Vinton Waits tramped up the stairs, went along a corridor and knocked on the door with the fancy lettering on it — **P.B.**

"Come," called the voice from inside. More gravel than hoarse at the moment, Barron's voice was.

Vinton took his hat off, held it in front of him, opened the door and went in.

Pinckney Barron was sitting behind his big fancy mahogany desk. His small hand held a massive six-shooter, the butt of it sitting on the table as it pointed at Vinton in the doorway.

Barron smiled at Vin, way a cat might smile at a bird, and said, "My boy, how are you? Come in and have a cigar. Sheriff believe the whole story?"

He opened the cigar box, and after Vinton took one, Barron indicated he should sit.

He sat. He fiddled with the cigar. He looked nervously at his boss. "It ... it didn't go so well, Mister Barron."

"What? Spit it out, boy, what are you waiting for?" There was a tell-tale twitch underneath the tiny man's right eye.

Vinton tried not to look at the twitch, but it was distracting. "I'm sorry, boss, it weren't my fault, honest it weren't. My damn Uncle, you don't know what he's like, how thoroughly thorough he is. Damn old man stuck his nose in things, one end of Norris Ricks' place to the other. Found our tracks, somehow knew it was me."

"Damn," Barron growled. "You killed him. Tell me you killed him." He stared so hard into Deputy Vinton Waits, the boy felt just about burned from it — and the twitching under Pinckney Barron's eye only got worse, and harder to look away from.

"I shot him, I reckon, Mister Barron. But he's so full'a beans for such a old man, he was already jumpin' as I fired — like he somehow sensed I would do it, it was, never saw such a thing in my life."

"Damn. Didn't you go after him? Where did you get him? Dammit, boy, what *happened? Tell me!*" He smashed his little fist on the table, grimaced from the pain, then blew on his fingers the whole time Vinton was answering.

"He was havin' trouble with a leg, boss. I reckon I got his leg, or maybe a foot. But he's quick too, for such an old man. Got in the trees, then I couldn't rightly find him, and he's crafty, been in some wars, knows how to sneak on a man like you wouldn't believe."

"So you ran like a coward?"

"Not right away. And I weren't no coward, I was just bein' smart like you tole me. You tole me, Mister Barron, you tole me, no matter what happens, I should always get back here and tell you if somethin' goes wrong. You tole me that, so I done it, I done what you said."

Pinckney Barron stared at the young Deputy, enraged but thoughtful. He made a fist, but did not bring it down on the table. "Alright, Vinton, alright. Good boy — at least you got that right."

"Thank you, boss. I'll do better next time."

"So, what happened when you left? Did he chase you?"

"I heard him comin', long way behind me, in the trees. But by then I'd sneaked off, was already back at my horse. So I jumped on and galloped away, but the damn thing went lame. That's why I'm late, Mister Barron, had to walk nearly most of the way. Wonder he never catched me up — but I'd made sure he knew, if he ever come back, we would kill him."

"You told him that?" All the gravel was gone from the voice now, it was hoarseness and worry and fear.

"Yessir, Mister Barron. Yelled it out at him when we was hid from each other, and tryin' to find each other to shoot."

"You didn't mention *my* name?"

"I ... I think I ... I don't think..."

"No. You don't, do you?"

"You tole me not to, Mister Barron, if you recall. Said it weren't my job, and to leave the thinkin' to—"

"Yes. Yes, alright." So where would he walk from there? And how long would it take?"

Deputy Vinton Waits' eyes seemed to go all strange

then. He found himself blinking, and looking away, and his breathing went funny too.

"Wait," growled Barron then. Then he groaned and ran his fingers through his hair and said, "You damnable fool. You left his horse for him, didn't you? Didn't you?"

"I ... I didn't really think ... I mean I—"

"Of all the chuckleheaded spooneys in Wyoming Territory, I had to get lumped with you." Barron shook his head slowly as he sighed — or maybe it was more of a groan. "What am I to do with you, Vinton? It's going to go very badly if your damn Uncle lives. Whatever are we going to *do* about that, Deputy Waits?" His eye had stopped twitching, and for such a small man, he sure showed off a whole lot of meanness.

"I ... Mister Barron, he won't get far, I promise. He's friendly with Cleve Lawson, and it's Cleve's place he'd have gone to, it's the only place near enough. If you want, I could go on back out there, kill the both of 'em — but I'll need a little help to make sure. Real good shot, my Uncle. Heard Cleve Lawson was too, but maybe not now, with his eyes so bad like you said. Still, no sense takin' chances, Mister Barron."

"Finally making some sense, Vin, there's hope for you yet. Go out to the cabin, get the others. *All* the others. Go track the damn Sheriff down—"

"But how, boss? I ain't no tracker."

"Jenkins is. You think I keep him around for his looks? He'll find your damn Uncle, *wherever* he's gone — and when you find him, make certain Sheriff Nosy Damn Whipple doesn't survive to tell any tales."

"So we take *all* the men? Even the ones who's a'sposed to be hidin' out?"

"All of them, Vinton, my boy." Pinckney Barron smiled now, lit his cigar and leaned back in his chair. "And tell my dear friend Prosper Peterson I'll be paying him double for this one."

"Yessir, Mister Barron, I'll go right away, get it done, I won't let you down."

"You're going to make a fine Sheriff, Vin. Has a nice ring to it, doesn't it? *Sheriff Vinton Waits of La Grange.*"

"Yessir, Mister Barron, that rings real nice."

"Clever, that's what you are, Vin. Clever enough to know *not* to return until Whipple — and anyone else he's spoken to since this morning — are dead, and properly buried where no one will find them. Now go make it happen."

CHAPTER 24
GABE ROACH

Sheriff James Whipple struggled to walk, his limp getting worse by the second. They'd not gotten far when four men came riding down the valley toward them, all of them heavily armed.

"Sheriff from La Grange," the tall feller told the leader, "and this other one's our closest neighbor — so he *says* — come to pay his respects."

"Right neighborly of him, after only two years," said their leader.

"Mister Roach," said the Sheriff to the man, nodding respectfully.

Cleve was taken aback some hearing the name, but then he remembered the stories about how these sheep folks all was related.

"Sheriff Whipple," said Roach. "Given our recent discussion, I'm guessing this visit's a necessity." He turned to the tall feller then and said, "You boys can go back, well done. Give these men back their horses, we'll take it from here."

"Good luck with that unfaithful dog," the tall feller said with a laugh, while the one called Bill handed Cleve and James the reins of their horses. Then those two sheep men turned and commenced walking back to wherever they came from.

"I'm sorry to bring more bad news," Whipple said to Roach, "but one of your number is dead. Murdered."

"There's a surprise," Roach replied, his voice thick with irony. He stepped down from his horse, took three steps toward Cleve, looked him square in the eye as he offered his hand to shake and said, "We've not met. I'm Gabe Roach."

As Cleve shook the offered hand, he met the big sheep boss's gaze just as square and said, "Pleased to meet you — not pleased by the circumstance of it. I'm Cleve Lawson."

Gabe Roach's hand was as rough as it was strong. He seemed educated — like Matt Roach had been — but they didn't look much alike. Not their faces anyway, though they both had dark hair. He sure had Matt's size though, and even a little more maybe. He was probably forty, well muscled yet light on his feet.

Must be Matt's older brother.

He stood and moved different to Matt though — there was something about him that brought Norris Ricks to mind, and Cleve winced a little as he thought of his friend lying dead, and as yet unburied.

Gabe Roach turned back toward the Sheriff and said, "You've come about Matt." It was a statement, not a question.

"Yes," said Whipple. "I'm sorry. But how did you know?"

Gabe Roach leaned his head back and studied James Whipple a moment, then turned toward Cleve and did the same. He seemed to be considering something. He turned back to the Sheriff again, and his eyes, his stance, his very being, all issued a challenge. "There's something more to this visit, isn't there, Sheriff? We've been blamed for something, and you've come to lean on us."

"Damn you, Roach," said James Whipple. "I'm sixty years old, and I've been an honest Sheriff so long it's a stumper how I'm still alive. But you still don't trust me." He took off his hat, slapped his leg with it, and his voice sounded pained. "Dammit, I sure can't blame you, after all that's gone on. But we need each other, you and me — and if you don't start listening, we'll all of us here end up dead."

"Alright," said Gabe Roach, nodding slowly. Thoughtfully. "Get on your horses, we'll all ride on up to town, talk over a meal."

"You might want to put out extra sentries," said Whipple as he mounted his horse. "I'm sorry — but I might have brought trouble on my trail, and it may not be long catching up."

Gabe Roach stared at the Sheriff, smacked his lips, and shook his head slowly. "Full of bright news today, aren't you?" Then he turned to the men behind him and said, "You all know what to do."

"If they follow us here," said Whipple, "it won't be no fiddle-faddle, they'll—"

"They won't get in as easily as you did. My men are well trained, and those going out now are my best."

Cleve and the Sheriff rode up into the valley with Gabe Roach, ol' Jimbo off to the left a little just like before. Took but a few minutes to get where they were headed, and Cleve was most pleasant surprised by all that he saw.

All the talk in La Grange regarding the sheep men, was that they lived in tents, did not bathe, and were more akin to animals than people. But the sight that greeted Cleve put all that to the sword, every last twisted word and untruth of it.

On the grassy slope above the creek rose the makings of a picturesque little town. Its buildings were neat, well constructed of logs and straight boards and split shingles — some even had pretty colored curtains hung in the windows, and flowers growing in neat rows in front of their porches.

There were signs announcing some of the buildings:

~ Livery ~

~ Mercantile ~

~ Schoolhouse ~

Others as well.

This was not thirty or forty unwashed scab-herders scratching about in the dirt — this was a well ordered town of perhaps a hundred people, industrious and hardworking, good honest folk who had built up a place to be proud of.

And if they looked at him and the Sheriff with too critical an eye, Cleve could well understand why, and easily forgive it — they had been sorely treated at best, by the folk of La Grange.

By me.

The thought made him uncomfortable. Oh, he had done nothing really *against* them — but he had done nothing *for* them either. Had never once spoken up when he'd heard they were being made unwelcome by some in La Grange. Had never introduced himself as a neighbor, way he had to Norris Ricks when he came.

There had been no signs either, back then.

No sign that said **Private Land.**

No sign that demanded **Keep OUT.**

No sign that warned **Trespassers SHOT.**

The signs had not been there that first year — Cleve knew that, he had passed this way hunting, or looking for stray cattle. No, the signs had been a response to how these folk were treated.

Busy minding my business, he told himself. But that thought too, rang out hollow in his mind, and he deemed it a damn poor excuse, now he knew more about them. He had seen something of himself in Matt Roach — and something of Norris Ricks here in Gabe.

They're just honest folk, trying to survive, living the best way they can.

And Cleve Lawson felt damn ashamed.

CHAPTER 25
A GIRL NAMED FRED

"We'll talk up at my place," Gabe Roach told them, as they rode between the buildings, and past the accusing eyes of the townsfolk. Not just men, but women too, looked up from whatever they were doing to watch them go by. They wore expressions of distrust and anger, in about equal parts. Most even looked suspiciously at ol' Jimbo.

"We generally don't trust any dogs but our own," Gabe said by way of explanation.

"Don't trust any people but your own either, by the looks," said the Sheriff — before quickly adding, "Understandable on both counts."

Gabe and Cleve dismounted, tied their horses to a hitching rail out front of a medium sized house — it was higher up the hill than the others — then Cleve helped Sheriff James Whipple down from his horse.

Gabe watched as James leaned on Cleve, then stood by the horse, favoring one foot. "You're hurt, Sheriff?"

"Getting too old for dancing, I guess," he replied.

Cleve looked up at the house. It had a deep porch, the whole length of it. A table, perhaps eight feet by two, ran along the porch's front rail, a little like a saloon bar, but not quite so tall. There were four chairs set up behind the table, all overlooking the entire town.

Cleve turned his back on the house, looked down on all the buildings, the creek, the neat log and branch fences that kept the sheep away from the houses. He sure enjoyed how those sheep made such pretty white dots on the green of the pasture they fed on. "Pretty view from up here," he said with a broad sweep of his hand.

Gabe seemed surprised, turned to look at it. "Guess you're right," he said. "Never thought about it before. Yes, now you say it — it is pretty, isn't it?" He took the view in, a deep satisfaction on his face for a few quiet moments, as he let his gaze wander from one side of it all to the other. Then — as a man with responsibilities must — he cast aside the enjoyment, set his mind back on serious matters. "If you're still here in fifteen minutes, someone'll come take your horses and see they're looked after. Just so you know, he's not thieving them."

"Good to know," said the Sheriff with a smile. Then he turned his head toward the door of the house as it opened, took his hat off, nodded politely and said, "Ma'am."

Cleve turned too, looked at the woman, surprised. She was small, yet strong-looking somehow. She was dressed like a cowhand, more or less — red bandana tied at the throat, neat blue calico shirt, brown canvas britches. And on her feet, a pair of top quality shop-mades, with good riding heels and well-oiled soft leather uppers. Cowhand clothes perhaps — but she filled them out in a way no cowhand ever could.

Pretty, was Cleve's first thought.

No.

Beautiful.

Her blue eyes were shot through with red, was the next thing he noticed. The blue and red both, such a contrast to her alabaster skin and her raven black hair — and her jaw stuck out forward, defiant.

In Cleve's experience, most Western women were always happy for visitors — *not this one.*

She was not the least bit happy to see them. Her eyes blazed at him now, almost pierced him — and Cleve realized he'd been gawking at the woman like a fool.

Gabe had not seemed to notice. "Sheriff and his friend here to discuss some matter of importance," he told her. "Bring some coffee, will you, Fred?"

"Don't call me that," she replied. "You know..." She clenched her hands in front of her, smiled tightly. "Don't, Gabe. Please."

He huffed some, annoyed. Then said, "Alright. Alright, I'm sorry." He still did not introduce them to the woman properly, but Cleve could forgive the man that, given the circumstance.

She turned her head a little, looked coolly at the Sheriff, then down at ol' Jimbo beside him. The dog was smiling at her, but it didn't seem to make her no happier. She aimed her critical gaze next at Cleve, looked him all the way up and down, slow and accusing, before saying, "I don't trust men who bring dogs along to see strangers."

"I'm sorry, Ma'am," Cleve replied. "I don't trust such folk neither — but in this case there's good reason, and I promise it ain't what you're thinking."

She looked into his eyes like she wanted to slap him right then, and her words came out colder'n the deep part of Bear Creek in winter. "You have no idea what I'm thinking."

"No, Ma'am," Cleve said, hanging his head some. He fiddled with his hat-brim in front of him, looked up at her again a mite sheepish. "I'm sorry, Ma'am, you're quite right, my apologies."

Then the woman turned to Gabe Roach, stared him down too, and her words came out clipped closer than a sheep in early Spring. "I'll need to make the coffee fresh, it will take a good while. If that's alright with *you!*"

His eyes widened, but he gave no answer. Then she turned and disappeared back inside, slamming the door closed behind her.

"Women," said Gabe once she'd gone, with a shake of his head. "Each one should come with a book of instructions, warning how not to tread on their toes." He shrugged his shoulders and sighed a deep one. "Still, not easy for her. She's not always like this. Mixed up emotions, I guess. Take a seat, gentlemen, please, and explain why you're here."

Cleve and Gabe stood one each side of James Whipple — he put an arm around each of their shoulders and hopped up the stairs. The three of them settled into the chairs, and they got down to business.

Right up front, the Sheriff told Gabe that the men who'd murdered Matt Roach had killed Norris Ricks too; also, that he knew who some of them were; and, that they were now trying to kill him as well.

"You? They'd risk killing a lawman?"

"Already tried once," Whipple answered. "My own damn nephew it was — it gets worse, he's my deputy too. I saw the tracks of young Vinton's horse where Norris Ricks got shot in the back from — damn fool kid was watching me, knew I'd caught him out. Didn't waste no time either — tried to put a bullet through my brain."

"Nice family," said Gabe.

"We all have our black sheep," said Whipple, raising his eyebrows.

"I'll drink to that," said Gabe Roach. Then he seemed almost guilty, glanced around toward the house, winced a little. "If the coffee ever arrives, anyway. Our chances are about fifty-fifty, we'll see how it goes."

"Anyway, that's how I hurt my dang foot," said the Sheriff, to get back on the subject. "Leaping out of the way when my nephew shot at me, no warning. Old bones ain't what they were, I guess."

"Sheriff," said Gabe, "I'm sorry you've got trouble, I am. I misjudged you, that day you informed us of Ernie Moore's death."

"Understandable."

"Well, I'm sorry, regardless. But I don't understand what you want from me. We've had our hands full up here, just trying to protect our flock from these..." He cast a glance at Cleve then. "...these cattlemen. And now, our men are being killed too, and you *told me* — you *told me,* Sheriff, there's nothing you can do."

"There was no evidence, Roach, no leads to who'd killed Ernie Moore — *that's* what I told you. But *now* there are witnesses. Witnesses to one murder, and one other attempted."

"Someone saw Matt killed? Saw what they did to him? Stood by and allowed such atrocities?" Gabe Roach jumped up from his chair then, all six muscular feet of him, and he thumped his fist on the table so hard it shook. The bearish man's next word came out, not like a word at all, but a guttural growl. "Who?"

Cleve took a deep breath, got to his feet, and faced that wrathy, impassioned, angrified man. Then he looked Gabe Roach right in the eye, and he said, "It was me."

CHAPTER 26
WRONG END OF THE STICK

Gabe's first punch was wild, filled with fire and indignant fury. Lucky for Cleve, he managed to move just a little before that punch landed. Still, that big fist crashed against his left ear with such brutal ferocity, Cleve Lawson saw stars — but not the nice-looking sort that he liked.

Cleve fought back, the way a man must, landed a booming left uppercut on the advancing Gabe Roach's chin. Would have stopped a bull, punch like that — but it didn't stop Gabe. Indeed, it just added fuel to his anger, and threw a lit torch on his bloodlust.

As ol' Jimbo jumped out of the way and hid behind the Sheriff, Gabe moved forward, jabbed twice with his left; Cleve blocked and countered with a vicious right to the ribs; and Gabe Roach's eyes showed surprise. He knew now, knew it for a wall-to-wall truth — Cleve was no ordinary man, but one to be reckoned with, and respected.

Gabe backed away some, kept his hands up, taunted Cleve into a mistake. "You damn lickspittle—"

Cleve lurched forward, unleashing a flurry of powerful punches. He figured he had the upper hand, as he drove the slightly larger man back — but the sheep man wasn't done yet, far from it. Light on his feet, and now thinking clearly, Gabe dropped his guard to draw Cleve in further, then danced to his right as his adversary came — and he launched the full force of his body through his giant right fist. Like a blacksmith using a hammer, Gabe Roach smashed that ironlike fist into Cleve's unfortunate jaw.

Cleve awoke — more or less — a few moments later.

He was in a dark dream, all blackness and pain, and ol' Jimbo was whining about *something*.

Cleve's eyes fluttered open — and he looked up into the lovely soft eyes of a woman. She was on her knees, leaning over him, her raven hair falling forward, and some of it brushing his face.

Soft.

Soft and nice.

He halfway remembered who she was. The bandana she'd worn earlier was now missing — the milky skin of her throat was completely exposed.

Pretty, he thought.

No.

Beautiful.

She reached down, touched her hand to his cheek, a look of concern in her beautiful eyes. If Cleve had been much of a one for churchgoing and such, he might have confused her for an angel, right there in that moment.

As it was, he half-hoped he was dying. *Be a nice way to go, seeing that.*

When she spoke, it didn't quite sound right — he only heard the words through one ear, for his other was ringing, he realized now.

"Are you alright?" she said.

"Oh, sure," he answered, recalling now what had happened. "We was just havin' a discussion. But I reckon it's over by now."

"It's over alright, cowman," growled Gabe, stepping closer and looking down on Cleve now. "You can leave as soon as you can stand."

The girl sprang to her feet, and as she did, her left hand surely flew — and the slap she delivered to Gabe Roach's cheek sent out a great ringing sound. That sound the slap made was a good one, but it weren't hardly nothing, compared to the wrath in her voice. "Always *fighting!* Why? Why, Gabe? Why this time? Why last time? Why *always?* You think it's the answer to *everything* — this is half the reason we're having all of this trouble!"

Gabe's right hand had shot out, grabbed her wrist after she hit him — and still he stood holding it tightly, met her furious gaze as she poured all her outrage upon him. And when she was done he said quietly, "That's not nearly the truth, and you know it, Fred."

"Don't ... call me that!" She wrenched her hand away from his grasp, defiantly looked up into the big man's eyes.

She was fire and fury and passion, beginning to end. All five-foot-two of her. Cleve had never seen anything so beautiful in all of his life — and yet, sudden-like now, he felt ashamed to be watching.

Such moments between a man and a woman should surely be private.

"We'd best be gettin' going," Cleve said, pushing himself up a little and leaning back against the logs that made up the front wall of the house. He was still some lightheaded, he realized. But he tried not to let on, and added, "I apologize for such troubles as I caused you good folk."

"Wait!" It was Sheriff James Whipple who spoke. "Gabe Roach, you can tell us to leave, and you have every right. But first, you listen to me. While you boys was testing each other out, I was using such small brains as I got, and I put two together with two, and I reckon I come up with four."

"What the—"

"Calm down, Roach," said Whipple, "and just hear me out. By the time I got to see the corpse of our friend, Norris Ricks, it had been *sorely* treated by the men who had killed him. I won't say what was done here and now, in front of a lady — but whoever done it is a sick sort of man, there's no doubt. Were any unusual barbarities performed upon the body of Matt Roach? Things done to him *after* he died, is what I'd be getting at."

Gabe stared at the Sheriff a long second or two, then he turned to the woman, and his face looked more than some stricken. "I..."

Her own sweet face fell a little, then she got up her courage and spoke. Strange, how her voice come out soft, yet somehow still full of strength. "That's why you buried him without letting me see the body."

"Yes," Gabe answered. "I'm sorry. I just didn't want you to see what was done. Didn't want you to know — or *any* of the women, for that matter."

Now, Gabe had been angry with Matt a long time — truth was, he'd looked forward to giving Matt a well-deserved beating upon his return — but no man, no matter how sinful, deserved such atrocities as had been committed upon his poor carcass.

And in the mind of Gabe Roach, Cleve had seen all that happen, and not lifted a finger to stop it.

Of course, that was just one of several misunderstandings, each of them leading to a little more trouble and confusion. Some of these had already occurred — one in particular, to do with identity. But that would all come out later, with surprising results.

For now, the Sheriff adding up two and two, was about to fix *one* of their problems.

James Whipple spoke quietly, but firm. "Mister Roach. Missus Roach. All Cleve saw was the single shot that killed Matt. He was inside the stagecoach when they done it — and the driver hightailed it out of there, lickety-split. Not a thing Cleve here could have done. And he had no idea about the terrible things they did to Matt's body after — indeed, he still doesn't know what they were, and for that matter, neither do I. But when you mentioned atrocities, my mind went to what them fellers done to Norris Ricks, and I put it together."

The woman spun quickly, looked down at Cleve

rubbing his jaw. She spoke so softly he barely could hear it, what with his ringing ear and all. "You were with Matt when he was killed?"

"Yes, Ma'am," he replied. "I seen them cowardly hard cases kill him, and I hope to see 'em all hang — two in particular."

She didn't speak, only nodded. And though her eyes looked wet, not a single tear escaped them.

Gabe Roach looked down now. Cleve stopped rubbing his jaw, commenced tapping three fingers against his ear, and looked up at him with raised brows.

Then Gabe said, "Please accept my apologies, Mister Lawson. I believe I got the wrong end of the stick." And he reached out a hand to assist Cleve in getting to his feet.

Cleve smiled a little, gripped the offered hand with his own, allowed Gabe to pull him up, and stood there on his hind legs. Then he smiled a wider one and said, "You got the wrong end of the stick alright, Roach — but I reckon I'm the one got the wrong end of the fists. Where'd you learn to fight like that anyway?"

Gabe's eyes did the smiling for him, as he looked at Cleve, then at James, then the woman, before looking back at Cleve again. "Reckon that's best explained over an excellent meal. You like mutton, Mister Lawson?"

"Call me Cleve."

"And you boys call me Gabe, please. Now, about that mutton..."

"Gabe, this ain't no time for lies, so I guess I'll leave out the politeness and tell you the true of it. I can eat mutton when I need to, but it weren't never my favorite. But there's nothin' so good as a fistfight to work up an appetite — and besides, I always find that good company improves any meal."

"Well, you might yet be surprised, Cleve."

"Wouldn't be the first time since I got here," said Cleve, rubbing at his jaw once again.

"Listen, Fred..." Gabe sure hushed quick when he said it, then put both hands in the air in apology, as he backed away from her and said, "I'm sorry, just a slip of the tongue, I'll try to remember. Fact of it is, *Winnie* here makes a mutton stew you'll remember the rest of your life. For *good* reasons, not bad, to be clear." He smiled and winked at the woman, then added, "Set two extra places, won't you, Winnie? And we'll see if we can't work together to get justice done."

The scruffy band of outlaws on Pinckney Barron's payroll were, for the most part, lazy, stupid men who were down on their luck, and didn't have the work ethic to do something about it. Such men weren't too hard to find in the West. Life being what it is, men with an aversion to hard work will often seek ways to make an easier living — and while such men were not clever enough to stay alive long, they suited the purposes of men like Pinckney Barron.

He paid most of them very little, and treated them as disposable assets — no more or less valued than his cattle.

They were like ammunition, something to be fired at targets of Barron's choosing — but he needed other men too, men more capable, men who could act as the guns, to direct all that cheap ammunition.

This was how Pinckney Barron saw things — *he* was the mighty brain who thought up the plans, and moved the hand that held the gun that would get him all that he wanted.

Some of the men he employed were more clever than he thought — but seeing himself like a great General, he could not stand the notion that some men had more smarts than himself. Still, that was just a small part of his problems.

Biggest problem with Barron was, there are two paths any man can take, and he'd chose the lesser. Many men are born with problems that thrust difficulties upon them — other men acquire such problems during their childhoods. These problems are no fault of the individual men — but some choose a *decent* path to rise above the problems, while others choose evil instead.

Pinckney Barron was nowhere approaching average height — that was the long and the short of it. Mostly the short. Tiny build he had too. Wasn't a dwarf or any such thing, he was just a small man. There are small men who don't let that stop them, and work hard until they become great — history is awash with such men. And the West, despite being an environment suited to physical strength, has always had its share of small men who excelled in their own chosen field. Still does to this day, and that fact ain't likely to change.

But Pinckney Barron, he was a tiny man with a gigantic chip on his shoulder, and it weighed him down sorely, to the point where the man was unbalanced. He resented his own lack of physical strength, yet he never did nothing about it — nothing useful, or personal, at least.

What he *did* do, was surround himself with men who

were vicious — the meaner the better, way he saw it. Had his lackeys keep an ear to the ground, in the hope of recruiting such men. So when Bat Jenkins set up a meeting between Barron and his friend, Prosper Peterson, a match made in Hell was born — to coin a phrase not used so much as it should be.

There was nothing about Prosper Peterson that Barron didn't like. The man was a vicious killer; there was nothing he wouldn't do for money; not only was he willing to kill and to torture, he was truly a man who enjoyed it; the nastier Pinckney Barron asked him to be, the happier he became; and finally, he was wanted in so many places he could not show his head in a town, so was easy to control — easy to control, anyway, for such a volatile man.

When Deputy Vinton Waits arrived at the secret cabin, Prosper Peterson, sitting on a log just outside, licked his lips in anticipation.

He had previously told Pinckney Barron it would be best to kill the Sheriff too — but Barron hadn't wanted that, not yet. So Peterson had killed Norris Ricks, played some with the body, then gone back to the cabin to wait for his next opportunity.

The moment he saw Vinton coming, he knew that opportunity had arrived. "You messed things up with your Uncle." It was a statement, not a question, and his eyes were eager.

The young Deputy climbed down from his horse, tied it to a rail. Wasn't the gray horse, of course, but a little bay gelding he'd rented from the livery. After seeing what Peterson had done to Norris Ricks' body, he chose his words more careful than usual. "Yessir, Mister Peterson, I'm sorry, I messed it all up. But Mister Barron said it's alright, and that he shoulda let *you* deal with it, and to get you to do so now."

"What happened?"

"My Uncle worked out it was us, Mister Peterson, who done—"

Prosper Peterson slapped Vinton Waits so hard it knocked him to the ground. As the youngster looked up in terror, the furious outlaw clenched his fists and growled, "*Us?* Your damn Uncle knows I'm here? I'll kill you, boy, spit it out."

Deputy Vinton Waits had to think quick — wasn't his strong suit. But somehow, as he cowered on the ground, looking up at the killer, he managed to yell, "No, no he don't, Mister Peterson, sir, no he don't."

"What then? Say it clear, kid, say it quick," The outlaw's gun was out now, and he thumbed back the hammer, pointed it into the face of Vin Waits.

Young Vin swallowed hard in his terror, looked into the barrel of the gun, only inches from his eyes. Then the words all spilled out of him, faster and faster as he went, and the pitch of them rose higher too, 'til he sounded like a young girl. "Please, Mister Peterson, sir, it's just *me,* he worked out it was me. I tried to kill him, but I only got his leg, maybe, I mean I reckon I did, but he got away into the trees. I rode away hard, but my damn horse went lame, but I got there and told Mister Barron and he sent me here. Said for you to take us all with you and kill my damn Uncle, please don't kill me, Mister Peterson, sir."

"That it?" He still had the gun pointed at Vinton, and by now, all the others had come out from inside and were watching. "Slow it down now," Peterson growled, "and speak like a man, or I'll blow your damn privates off so you got an excuse for such squeaky high-talkin', boy."

"Yessir," Vin squealed. Then he swallowed hard again, set his voice back to somewhere near normal before going on. "Mister Barron said we should go kill my Uncle, and anyone else he's spoke to since he went to Norris Ricks' place. And he said to tell you he'd pay you double this time."

Vinton Waits had been just about messing his britches — but now, the man pointing the gun at him busted out laughing. Vinton relaxed a little and said, "That alright, Mister Peterson?"

"Sure, kid," said the outlaw. "I was just playin' with you a little, been on a streak'a boredom out here since this morning." He clicked off the hammer and holstered the gun, much to the young feller's relief, before turning to the others. "You heard him, boys. We got at least one man to kill, maybe a whole passel of 'em. Bring plenty of cartridges, and you, Slim, bring a goodly amount of explosives, I've a mind to enjoy myself."

"Mister Barron said not to—"

"Not to *what,* kid?" Peterson's eyes looked some sorta crazy, but Vinton Waits knew he had to convey the message anyway.

"Sorry, Mister Peterson," the young Deputy said, "but Mister Barron said to dispose of any bodies quietly this time, is all. He said only to kill 'em and bury 'em, and not leave no evidence."

"Well, ain't much fun diggin' graves, is it, young Deputy Waits? You enjoy diggin', do you?"

"No sir, Mister Peterson, not much. But Mister—"

"Me neither, young Vin." Prosper Peterson laughed it up big then, a great belly laugh that rang out through the forest around them. "And the best way to avoid all that diggin', and still leave no evidence — is blowin' a body to pieces, with lots of explosives. Enjoyable too, and a great satisfaction it is, to see a man torn asunder. And the wolves and coyotes, they got to have *somethin'* to live on, don't you think so, young Vin?"

Deputy Vinton Waits weren't about to argue. He just nodded his head, smiled a weak one and said, "You're the boss, Mister Peterson, sir, and I'm double-dog sure you know best."

The sheep town's livery feller had arrived just in time to see the fight between Cleve and Gabe. He'd stood by and enjoyed it from a safe distance — just out of earshot — and waited 'til things was all settled before asking if he should take the horses and feed them.

"Sure, Tom," said Gabe Roach. "Feed them well, and put them in the stables. Our guests are staying the night."

"How's Selma?" Winnie asked the man.

"Doing better today, Missus Roach," he replied. "Reckon she'd be up to a visit tomorrow. She said to thank you for the soup."

She smiled and said, "I'm glad she's feeling better. Tell her I'll come tomorrow."

That Tom feller turned toward Gabe then and pretended to throw a few punches, and he wore a huge smile on his face. Thing was, that feller was to the sheep town what Lucius Swan was to La Grange — to be clear on that, not a barber, but a dab hand at spreading the gossip. And the story of the fight was certain to spread a little joy through the town.

Wasn't too long after that, the food was all ready, and the men washed their hands and their faces, went inside to eat. Whipple's foot was some better now, and he was getting around not too bad, though a little slow maybe.

"Wolf Town, we call this place," Gabe said as they sat down to dinner. "Kind of a joke among ourselves, is all. Everyone knows the fairy tale, of course — and when the folks of La Grange leaned hard on us, we had to fight back. Suited us then to think of ourselves as wolves in sheep's clothing, you see?"

"I didn't like it then, and still don't," Winnie said, as she leaned in to put the big steaming pot of mutton stew in the center of the smallish round table. "It's needlessly aggressive."

The inside of their home was well kept, Cleve noticed — even pretty, with colorful fabrics and paintings of flowers adorning the walls. And two closed doors that must lead to bedrooms.

Wonder if they got children.

It seemed unlikely, for the sun was now setting, and no child had come home from the schoolhouse.

"That sure does smell good," said Cleve, as Winnie filled a bowl for him.

"I know you had troubles when you came," said the Sheriff, "but I thought it had all settled down up 'til just lately."

Gabe was the sort of feller who pointed his fork a lot

while he explained things. "Early on things weren't too bad. The usual trouble here and there, when we'd go into La Grange, and a cowhand or two had partaken of too much whiskey. We'd settle things with our fists — way you do in the West — and most men respected us fair, and we went on our way."

"You should not have fought them," said Winnie.

"This stew is delicious, Ma'am," said Cleve, "best I ever had, that's the truth. But I must disagree with you there on the fighting. If your fellers hadn't fought back, they'd a'got no respect in the town, which always leads to more trouble."

"Exactly," said Gabe, pointing his fork at Cleve. "We ran the sheep on open range at first. Not just this valley but others. Nobody seemed much to care. Our dogs are well trained, never bothered the cattle, there weren't any problems at all. But then one of the bigger ranchers started throwing his weight around — not that he had much to throw."

"Pinckney Barron," said Sheriff James Whipple in disgust.

"That's him," said Gabe, tap-tapping his bowl with his fork. "Three feet tall in his hat, and substantial as two chickadee feathers. He'd have to be tied to his horse if a slight puff of wind came."

In truth, the despised rancher was around about five feet two inches — but not one person present was the sort to let facts deplete a good story, long as no harm got done by the telling.

"Barron warned us to get off the range. Suggested —

almost politely — we'd do better further West. Montana, he reckoned, for sheep."

Cleve winced when he heard the word *Montana,* and the Sheriff patted his shoulder and gave a slight nod.

"After that," Gabe went on, "a few sheep began to go missing. Natural losses to wild beasts, we assumed. Back then, we were still going into La Grange for our supplies — a year and a half ago now."

"You know, Ma'am," said the Sheriff, "I didn't speak up before, only out of politeness, when mutton got mentioned. My dear wife, may she rest in peace, cooked it for me a time or two. In the end, I just had to come clean and beg her to stop — seemed me and the taste of it didn't agree, though she wasn't a bad cook at all."

"Oh, I'm so sorry," said Winnie. "I can make you something else if—"

"No, Ma'am, I'll get to my point now," said Whipple, raising a forkful of the meat up in front of his eyes to study it. "I don't know quite how you did it, but this mutton tastes better than the best antelope I ever had — antelope always being my favorite, at least until now."

"Well ... thank you," Winnie said. "I'm happy you like it. And I'm sorry about your wife. That ... can't be easy."

"Thank you, Ma'am." Whipple nodded to her, turned to Gabe Roach again and said, "But you were saying, Gabe?"

"After that, it became five sheep at a time. Always five; always shot through the head at close range; always hung by their necks from a tree, as if it were a lynching."

"I saw that sorry sight once," said Cleve, and he hung

his head some. "I ... I should have asked questions. Should have *done* something. I was always a man to mind his business — maybe too much so, I'm thinking. I'm sorry."

Winnie Roach reached out a hand, squeezed Cleve's shoulder, and he just about jumped from the shock of it. His head turned swift to look at her, and she smiled so nice her eyes crinkled at the edges, and his heart just about skipped a beat. Cleve looked 'round then at Gabe, but somehow he hadn't even noticed.

"We reported it, of course," Gabe was saying, "but as the Sheriff here said, there was nothing could be done without any proof of who'd done it. We herded all the sheep back here to this valley — had to sell a good many off so we weren't overgrazing it. And we posted sentries day and night at the top of the ridges. We first chose this particular valley because the sides are mostly steep — but still, there are vulnerable places. Matt made up a roster and ordered twenty-four hour patrols, and for a good while there was no further trouble — long as we stayed out of town."

Cleve was surprised. "Matt Roach was the leader back then?"

Gabe shot a look at Winnie, then he said, "Up 'til then, there'd not been any need for a leader. We were just several families who'd thrown our lot in together and come West to build better lives. Some knew sheep, some did not. Some of us were highly educated, others had never been schooled, but had more life experience. Many of us were from different backgrounds. But we were united in one thing — we all sought an honest living, and believed we would find it if we came out West and worked hard."

They'd finished their meals by now — all except Gabe, who'd been using his mouth more for speaking. He chowed down on his stew now though, left the speaking to others, and listened.

"Mister Lawson," said Winnie, "I wonder if you might tell us what Matt's final hours were like."

Gabe stopped mid-chew and stared at her a moment, then thought better of speaking. He filled his mouth with more food, and left Cleve to answer the question.

"It's ... it's not pleasant, Missus Roach."

"Winnie," she said. "Please, call me Winnie."

"Alright," he said. "Winnie it is. You call me Cleve if you like. And while we're on introductions, that traitorous hound there's called Jimbo."

"Hello, Jimbo," she said, turning toward him. The happy spotted feller wagged his tail, but stayed where he was by James Whipple. "I hope he likes mutton," she added. "He's waited so patiently to eat."

"He's a right fussy eater, Ma'am ... I mean, Winnie. Why, just for starters, that dog won't eat ... hmmm, let me see, must be somethin' I reckon. I know! He don't eat trees, ol' Jimbo — though he does like the bark."

"The *bark!*" she said with a laugh. "Oh, Mister Lawson, you're pulling the donkey's tail now. Bark indeed!"

"Woof woof," went James Whipple, and ol' Jimbo cocked his head sideways and barked once himself to get in on the joke.

"Glad you all found the humor in it," said Cleve, "but I

did mean it serious. Ain't nothin' much he *don't* eat, this dog. Eats bark off of trees, eats carrots and apples and peaches and beans — he can open the cans with his teeth, but he don't eat the cans. I was still makin' boots when I got him, but he kept on eatin' the leather, and it added up costly. Your mutton'd be wasted on him, Ma'am. Why, he'd just as soon eat the pot you cooked it up in."

She looked at him sideways — half-smiling, half-serious — and said, "I know what you're doing, Mister Lawson. And I thank you for it, I do. But I'd not be spared the details. Despite all Matt's faults, he was, after all..."

She was a strong woman, but right then, she couldn't go on.

And Gabe, who had just swallowed down his last mouthful, said, "Let's go outside on the porch, have some coffee, look up at the starlight. Cleve can tell us the story out there — I too wish to hear it."

CHAPTER 29
THE PROBLEM WITH DAVES

The sun had set blazing and fiery, and the moon that rose now almost seemed like it wished to compete.

As they stepped outside, Cleve was struck by the beauty of Wolf Town at night — the neat little buildings that dotted the hillside; the orange glow of warm fires seen in some of the windows; the wispy smoke that curled out from chimneys; and the shining glassy surface of the creek as it wound its way through the bottom of that pretty valley.

Far off came the mournful, primitive howl of a lone coyote — and it brought to mind the danger they surely must face sometime soon — yet for now they felt safe, ensconced here in this steep-sided valley, with each other for company.

If only they'd known...

As Jimbo demolished an oversized bowl of mutton stew, the Sheriff took a seat, rested his foot — but the others pushed their chairs out of the way, stood leaning against the table, looking out at the valley and the night.

They all four stayed quiet, listened to the night sounds a minute or two, as they sipped at their coffee. Then finally, Gabe simply said, "Cleve?"

As Jimbo lay down between Whipple and Winnie, Cleve reluctantly began to tell the sad story.

"First thing happened was the road agents shot the guard, and he flew through the air, hit the ground already dead."

"Before that," said Winnie. "Please, Mister Lawson. I'd know of what happened *before* the murderers came. We didn't know he was coming, you see, and ... perhaps he told you *why* he was coming back. It ... it makes no sense that he would, after..."

"I knew he was coming," Gabe admitted as her voice trailed off. Her head spun toward him, her eyes hot with accusation. "Calm down now, Winnie," he said, "I only mention it now in case—"

"You didn't tell *me?* Damn you, Gabe, I was—"

"Winnie! Language," cried Gabe, as Cleve thought, *Ahh, they were close, Matt was her brother-in-law, and perhaps lived here in this house with them. No wonder she's so upset.*

Her eyes blazed at Gabe. "Damn you," she said, and Cleve could not help noticing, her defiance only added to her beauty.

Don't look at her, he told himself then, for it would not be right.

Now, Gabe Roach was no shrinking violet himself.

"You just listen up, Winnie, for once in your life." He raised a fist as if he was going to thump it down on the table — but instead, he looked at it a moment. Then he let the big hand open wide, pressed his temples with it instead. He made a low sound of anguish, then pushed the hand back over his hair.

"Well?" She had said it like a challenge, and she put her cup down on the table much harder than she needed to.

Gabe did not turn toward her, but instead spoke his words out into the night. "I never asked to be leader here, but I *am*. It was my decision to make, and it wasn't easy, but I chose not to tell you. Matt wrote to me, said he would come, but what if he hadn't? His letter said he wanted to talk — set things right, as much as he could. It was only a visit, he had no plan to stay. But after what he did ... Winnie, I'm sorry. But you know as well as I do, the things he said weren't to be trusted. I ... I couldn't be sure what to..."

He stopped, looked out into the night, like as if some difficult answers might float to him on the night air.

"Alright," Winnie said — although clearly it wasn't. Then she added, "Please continue, Mister Lawson."

Cleve said, "Well, truth is, I'm a man who keeps to himself, much as I can. I was doing just that on the stage, when Matt started in on the banker, Romulus Hogg. Accused him of dealin' shady."

"He does," said Gabe.

"I know it," Cleve answered. "And Matt Roach was a fine speaker, an intelligent man, as I'm sure you're aware. Tore the banker to pieces with facts, was what he did. Was a downright pleasure to hear it, but I didn't join in. But then Hogg said some things about the way the sheep ruin the pasture, and Matt said some things that *I* didn't agree with — and finally, I said some things too."

"You argued?" Winnie's whole expression was a disappointed question, a look that demanded to be studied, stared into, deciphered. But the way the moonlight fell upon her, Cleve could not barely stand to look in her direction, fearful of what his own expression might convey.

"I'm sorry," he told her. "It's true. I guess me and Matt were alike in some ways — hot-headed is one way to put it. I told him he was a fool who didn't know the first thing about sheep."

"We had our differences," said Gabe, "but Matt was the most knowledgable sheep man I ever met."

"I understand that now," Cleve said, tapping his fingers on the table as he spoke. Then he laughed, a sad yet fond sort of chuckle it was, and he said, "Matt sure won *our* battle of wits. He told me he chose to farm sheep because they were stupid, and stupid's less trouble. Then he added that, having met me, he'd have chose to farm cattlemen instead, if he had his chance over."

"That sounds like Matt," Winnie said softly. "Always too clever for his own good — always too willing to prove it."

Cleve did not look in her direction. "We'd just agreed to give up on words, and settle things with our fists when the stage stopped instead, when the road agents shot dead the guard. Poor feller got shot right off'a the box seat, I seen him fly through the air on his way to the ground. Dead already he was, he did not make a sound as he flew. Well, with him gone, only me and Matt was left armed, excepting for Dim Dave the driver — sorry for how that sounds, Ma'am, it isn't an insult, Dim Dave's a real fine feller. That's just what he's generally called by, I'm not even sure why."

"I understand," she said, her voice small now and quaking a little.

"There's too many Daves around is all, so one's Big Dave — he's the short one, you see — and there's Wild Dave and Little Dave, though some call that feller Fat Dave, on account of him not bein' so little at all, and in truth, he's much bigger than Big Dave. And then there's Dim Dave, like I said."

"The story, Mister Lawson. Please?"

"Yes, Ma'am." Cleve nodded a sad one then and rubbed at his temples, not quite sure how to proceed. Seemed like it got harder by moments, the telling of this story to a woman. "Well, me and Matt was busier right then than a sinbuster preachin' in a cathouse." He realized what he'd just said, shot a look at the lady and added, "Sorry, Ma'am, it ain't easy tellin' this story, and I ain't got control of my words way I usually might."

"Well, it sounds like you *were* rather busy," she said helpfully.

"Yes, Ma'am, it was a bad situation, and me and Matt was well fired up as the moment unfolded. At such times, you see, men can lose themselves to the battle — and might say things they otherwise wouldn't, I'd just have you know."

The Sheriff — who had heard the whole story before —

tried his best to save Cleve from saying what he was about to. "They don't need all the details, Cleve, just move to the bit where the stage stopped."

"I want to hear it," said Winnie, insistent. "Please. I don't care *how* upsetting it is, I *must* know the truth."

Whipple started to speak, got as far as, "It's not—"

But Winnie gripped Cleve's arm, caught his eyes with her own, and said, "Please."

Well, there's certain tones of their voices women can use that render men helpless. Unable to reason, more or less. And right then, if Winnie had said, *'Please walk through the town wearing your socks on your ears, and nothin' else but your hat held in front,'* Cleve would have done it without even questioning why.

Fact is, *all* women, at certain times, can get men to do any old thing of their pleasing. And right now, Cleve was as helpless as a fish out of water surrounded by big hungry bears.

He completely forgot what the Sheriff suggested, went right on and told the whole story, every sad detail.

"Well, Ma'am," he said, "we got all charged up and threw a few insults — good-natured — about how useless the other was with their guns. We was on the same side by then, see? And men *will* say things to help fire each other up, if you get the gist of what I'm sayin'."

"That's certainly true," Gabe said to Winnie.

"Men are foolish, but do go on, please," she said.

"Problem is," Cleve said then, "in the heat of such a battle — and I don't mean at all to excuse my behavior —

but the fact is, things slip out we never would say other times."

"Don't," said James Whipple, but Cleve never even heard him, and went on.

"And I said ... well, that is, I *repeated* what I'd heard in La Grange. I ain't proud, but I said what I said, and I'll own up to it honest. What I said was, '*Roach by name, Roach by nature.*'"

"Here we go," said the Sheriff, and he put a calming hand on the head of ol' Jimbo.

"That's not nice, Mister Lawson, not at all," Winnie said very quietly.

"That weren't the bad bit," said Cleve, unable to meet the woman's gaze. After that I told Matt, '*I heard you maggot farmers is all blood-related to your own wives.*' I'm so very—"

The punch Gabe Roach landed on Cleve hit him flush on the chin. And when he woke up two minutes later, he was missing a tooth.

CHAPTER 30
HIS BARK IS WORSE THAN
HIS BITE

Cleve Lawson had always loved a good fistfight, that's the plain and the simple of it. It's a fine way to settle some differences; to get rid of folks who ain't your friends; and sometimes, as had happened earlier, it can even be a way to make new friends.

On top of all that, it can be a downright pleasure to partake in, long as men just stick to fists and don't go gettin' nasty.

He was good at it too. He was no Norris Ricks, to be sure — but as everyday men went, Cleve was better than most. Before today, he'd lost only two fights in the twenty years since he'd left home and gone out in the world.

Losing two in one day would come as a surprise — once he awoke, and his wits came back to him, of course. Thing about being knocked out though, the wits don't always come back right away with the waking.

Still, this time it didn't go too bad — considering how good the punch was.

His first thought on waking — *Where am I?* — was quick enough replaced by a second — *That Gabe feller hits like a steam train.*

He remembered the blur of Gabe's flying fist; the moon seeming to jump through the sky; then a dark sorta darkness with a burning white light in the middle of it.

Cleve was lying on his side, more or less, with his head and neck awkwardly angled, up against the front wall of the house. He opened his eyes, hoping to see that pretty woman again — as it had gone last time this happened — but somehow he knew he wouldn't see her.

Sure enough, all he got was a sideways view of ol' Jimbo — and behind him, James Whipple's boots.

Though he could not see her, he sure did *hear* Winnie Roach — she was inside the house, and if yelling was punches, Gabe would have been unconscious too, perhaps even worse off than Cleve was.

"*Had* to say it, didn't you?" It was James Whipple's voice alright, but it sounded strange to his ears — mostly because it was not the respectful tone James usually used when speaking to Cleve. No, this sounded more like the way the Sheriff would speak to a drunk — perhaps one who'd just shot his own toes off while riding a mule backwards through town in his birthday suit.

"Sorry, Sheriff," he said. The sound of it didn't come out too clear, so Cleve spat out the blood from his mouth that was causing the problem. He noticed a tooth in the spittle, and he winced as he reached for his jaw to check if it was broke. It wasn't — but it hurt worth two damns and three top-notch curse words. But all Cleve actually said was, "I gotta stop upsettin' that feller, them big fists of his are like two slabs of iron."

"Well, I guess we best go get our horses," said Whipple. "You in a fit state to ride?"

"Give me a minute," Cleve answered. "I got trouble enough just tryin' to crawl for the moment. Next step after that'll be walkin' — reckon ridin' might come after that."

He managed to push himself up and lean against the front of the house for the second time in a few hours. Ol' Jimbo came over, commenced to lick Cleve's face. He tried to push the dog away, but he was persistent.

"At least *he* likes you now," Whipple said.

"He's just licking the blood," said Cleve. "Damn dog's probably planning to eat me. Get away from me, Jimbo."

"How's he taste, boy?" said the Sheriff, sure enjoying himself. "Ol' Cleve got some bark off him, has he? Don't worry, boy, I hear his bark's worse than his bite."

The shouting indoors raged on, but Cleve was in no condition to make out the words. "What's the argument?"

Whipple put a finger to his lips for Cleve to shut his cake-hole while he listened.

"She's saying they should help us, and that Gabe was wrong to hit you again. He's saying he wants to come out here and give you some more, because you damn well deserve it."

"So she's wrong again," said Cleve, "and he's right."

"Hope you don't expect me to argue," said Whipple. "You deserve what you got, for being fool enough to say it in the first place — but a man who repeats it, when he could have left that bit out? Well, I've a mind to land one on you myself. Might help knock some sense into you, Cleve. Come away from him, Jimbo, or you might catch a dose of *stupid* off of him."

A door slammed somewhere inside, fit to break off its hinges. Then there was silence.

Cleve and James looked at each other and waited.

Waited some more.

Weren't much fun waiting at all, but sometimes you ain't got no choice.

It was a long fifteen or so seconds, though it seemed a lot longer than that. Then the front door opened, and the shapely form of Winnie Roach appeared. She came out, closed the door behind her, smiled at Whipple, then turned and looked down at Cleve. She was carrying a glass in one hand.

He looked up at her, but could not make out her features, as they were completely in shadow. From down where he was, that beautiful big full moon was right in behind her, framing her wild untamed hair, and he heard himself make a small, involuntary noise.

Despite the inexcusable thing he had said, her voice was still kind. "Anything broken?"

He wondered how such a creature could even exist — she had such strength, this woman, and a fiery, vibrant beauty of spirit that set her apart from all others Cleve had gotten to know. And yet, she was gentle, forgiving, and set against violence of any sort, so it seemed.

Well, *that* whole concept was alien to him.

I'm a man, after all, he thought. *And a simple one at that.*

"I'm fine, Ma'am," he replied. "And I'm so very sorry."

"Again," she said.

He still could not make out her features, but somehow, it seemed that she'd smiled.

"Yes, Ma'am. Again. I did apologize most profusely to Matt when I said that terrible thing. We agreed to discuss it once the robbery was over. I believe the discussion would have turned out the same as the one I just had with Gabe's fist — but it would have been settled fair, and I'd have deserved it."

"Here, drink this," she said, handing him the glass of water she'd brought. "What else happened that day, Mister Lawson? Please."

Cleve thanked her for the water and drank some. Tasted of blood that first bit, but he could not very well spit it out in front of a lady. He took another mouthful, then held the glass in his hand as he spoke. "We done everything right, Ma'am. The road agent done all the talkin', and kept tryin' to goad Matt into taking a poke at him. But Matt bit it all down, played it smart. That feller — don't know who he was — kept lookin' to his boss. His boss was Pinckney Barron, Ma'am, without doubt — I promise you that — and that blue bandana-wearin' feller kept lookin' to Barron for instructions. He went over and spoke to him once, quiet-like. Then he come back and insulted Matt somethin' terrible."

"As badly as you did?"

"Roundabout so." Cleve hung his head a little further.

"It takes admirable strength for a man to admit he's done wrong, Mister Lawson," she said. Then she sat in a chair beside Whipple, but still facing Cleve. "I know you didn't mean what you said. And I accept your apologies."

"Thank you, Ma'am. Thank you very kindly. I thought ... I believed we'd got through the robbery. Matt done the right thing, never bit when they goaded him, and that took some doing, believe me. Then they told us we could get back in the coach and leave."

"They shot him then, didn't they?"

"He never even knew, Ma'am." Cleve took a deep breath then. He had not cried since he was a child, and the memory of that last occasion came to him now. He pushed that remembrance down and went on with his story. "I helped that useless banker Hogg into the stagecoach, then I climbed in and turned to face Matt. Offered him my hand, to help him up."

She made a little sound — not a word exactly, more a whimper — and she wiped a tear from her eye.

"He didn't *need* a helping hand, Ma'am — both of us knew that — he was one big strong feller, Matt Roach was. When I offered my hand, he looked into my eye, and he knew. Knew it was my true apology, you see? Better than words to men like us. I offered that hand as a friendship. He looked me right in the eye, and true as I sit here before you, he accepted, and I felt glad of it. He gave me a nod and he reached out his hand toward mine — and that lowdown snake workin' for Barron put a gun to Matt's head and he killed him. Ma'am. I am so very sorry."

And to his greatest surprise, a tear rolled down Cleve's face, hung off the end of his chin an uncomfortable second, before finally departing, and falling down on the porch boards.

Damn, was all he thought. *Damn.*

When Bat Jenkins had tracked the Sheriff to Cleve's place, then tracked the both of them to Wolf Town, it made Prosper Peterson happy as a blood-sucking lawyer with newly cleaned fangs.

While Jenkins did not know the area quite so well as Sheriff Whipple, he was a man of similar talents and interests — and he had been bouncing around the locality like a pebble in a barrel this past year or so. Consequently, he had not only learned the topography, he had spied upon the comings and goings of the sheep men, and worked out the best way to attack their town when the time came.

All of that was like pretty music to the ears of Prosper Peterson. Good thing there was *something* that pleased him that way, for he so disliked *actual* music, he once killed a top-notch musician with the man's own harmonica — shoved it so far down his throat, they could not remove it, and his family did not wish his throat cut in order to do so. Directly consequential of that, old Linwood Davenport was still making musical notes in the coffin when they buried him the following day.

"Settling gases," the doctor had said, but it sure did unnerve those few folk assembled for the burial. It was a rare and exquisite instrument, that harmonica, and built such that it could reach the high notes, all the way up to High C — which made the sounds that came from the coffin more plaintive than one might imagine.

And indeed, it is said to this day, that if you stand in a certain Colorado boneyard at night, when the wind starts to whistle through the cottonwoods, the mournful sounds of some top-notch harmonica — all the way to High C — can be heard as accompaniment to the wind.

Bat Jenkins could have done with some soothing music right now. He was a man not much suited to practicing violence himself. He was what you might call *the thinker* of whichever gangs he rode with. But the thinking he was doing right now, was that he had made a mistake when he introduced Prosper Peterson to Pinckney Barron.

A bit of violence and mayhem and disorder was a fair enough thing — but Barron and Peterson had took it a mile too far, by where Bat drew his lines.

Peterson shooting Matt Roach dead was *business* — shady business, and unpleasant, yes — but it still fell within moral lines, far as normal outlawing went. But all the mutilation that came after, well, that just weren't right.

Men should be buried respectful, by whoever killed them, or in a proper boneyard when possible. Not be twisted about, and bits cut from 'em fed to wild creatures. And lynching a dead man? What's that?

Seemed to Jenkins that Peterson and Barron were making each other worse. Feeding off of each other's sickness, somehow — and truly a sickness it was.

Problem was, Jenkins would need to pick the right moment to leave. He could not just say a friendly goodbye and ride out, way things had gotten. Peterson was becoming more muddled each day, and he had ever been a vindictive man, even when they served together in the Army.

No, I'll have to stick around until he's killed, or the right chance for leaving unfolds.

So Jenkins just did his job, tracked the Sheriff and his friend to the Sheep Town. He suggested they camp back a ways, ambush the pair when they left.

The eleven of them sat on their horses and discussed it, a half-mile from where the nearest sentries were surely patrolling. Deputy Vinton Waits and the others seemed to agree Bat's idea was the right one.

Prosper Peterson, had listened in silence awhile, fiddling with his lucky blue bandana while the other men argued it out. But now, he'd had enough. He got a wide crooked smile on his face and he snarled, "Our job's to kill anyone the damn Sheriff spoke to. He's been talkin' to the maggot-farmers, but we don't know which ones. Might's well kill the whole damn lot of 'em now, while we're here, to be sure we get the right ones."

"But there's children and women in there," Bat Jenkins said. Wished he hadn't, a half-second later, as he stared down the barrel of Peterson's old Army Colt.

"Woman *maggot-farmers*," said Peterson, his lips

curling back to expose two blackened side teeth. And with even more scorn, he added, "Child *maggot-farmers.* Thing about that, the children grows up to farm maggots as well. Becomes maggots 'emselfs, in a way. And the *women,* the women goes and breeds again, if yer fool enough to let any live. They raises up more maggot-farmers, 'til there's a damn plague of 'em. No, best way, we cut 'em down now, cure the problem. Don't you think so, Bat, my old friend?"

"Sure, Prosper," Bat Jenkins replied, convinced beyond doubt now of Peterson's madness. "That's the right way forward for certain." He moved slowly, put his palms out before him, spoke in tones of mild suggestion, without so much as a hint of confrontation in his manner. "All I was thinkin' of, Prosper, was that once the maggot-farmers are gone, Pinckney Barron will have no further need of our services. And this here's such a nice easy job, and he's payin' us well enough. But it's up to you, of course, Prosper. Your decision completely."

"You always was the clever one, Bat," Peterson said with a chuckle, then he holstered his gun. "But you ain't quite so clever as me now."

"Never was," Jenkins answered, happy to still be alive to tell such a lie.

"See, Barron told young Vin here he'd pay double for whoever we kill this time. That's a whole lot of willing corpses just waiting there in that town to be slaughtered, and it has to happen sooner or later. Why not now? Now when the price of 'em's double?"

Deputy Vinton Waits still had some learning to do, regarding keeping his mouth shut in tight situations. Spoke right up then, he did — let the thoughts from his head tumble right on out of his mouth, like he *wanted* to die. "Aw, Mister Peterson, I don't believe Mister Barron meant—"

"*Shut it.*" The tone of Prosper Peterson's words would have been enough, but the way he pulled that Colt so fast was a whole lot of extra encouragement.

The young Deputy just sat his horse and nodded, as he clamped tight shut every orifice he could control, for fear one would fail him. He sat there remembering the sight of what Peterson did to Norris Ricks' body. He did not want that to happen to him. He wished he weren't here.

"Should see your fool face, boy," laughed Peterson, gleeful in his madness. Then he held the Colt up so the full of the moon was behind it, and closed one eye while he admired it. His movements were wild and exaggerated now, as he forgot Vinton Waits and turned quickly in his saddle to face Bat Jenkins again. "What's the best way to get in there, Bat? Let's go have us some fireworks, and kill us some maggots."

CHAPTER 32

ATTACK ON WOLF TOWN

Winnie Roach had told the visitors to bed down in the parlor, which was fine by the Sheriff and ol' Jimbo.

It was Cleve who was having some doubts. Understandable, given there was a man in the bedroom with hammers for fists and an avowed wish to use them on Cleve again, next chance he got.

Cleve briefly wondered why she hadn't told them to sleep in the spare bedroom — but for all he knew, that room was full up with sheepskins.

Or man-skins maybe — the skins of men Gabe hit one time too many.

He was too tired to think much about it. He drifted off into sleep, one ear somehow yet listening for danger, but his eyes closed tight shut, and soon enough he drifted off.

Not for long.

It was just after eleven when he heard the first shot, and heard men raise the alarm.

He had taken his boots off and slept in his clothes — not much else you can do when you sleep in a fine lady's parlor — and Cleve jumped to his feet before he knew he was awake.

Right beside him the Sheriff yelled, *"Fire,"* and his senses weren't wrong.

Cleve heard a door flung open behind him in the not-quite-dark, and Gabe Roach came charging into the room, grabbed a rifle from the rack on the wall, and went swiftly to the front door, which he opened a crack.

"Looks like that trouble you mentioned's arrived," he said to the Sheriff. He flung open the door, but didn't run out into the night — instead, Gabe Roach did the smart thing, stayed behind cover as he looked out to see what was happening.

Well, things were happening alright, and no shortage of them — and there was moonlight aplenty to see it all by.

Cleve had already pulled on his boots, and he quickly went to the other side of the doorway — always helped, him being left-handed, when he had to shoot with a partner. There was fires in two of the houses well down below them, and folks being shot at as they ran out from the burning buildings.

Somewhere behind him another door opened, and Cleve was vaguely aware of Winnie Roach running across to the gun rack. A bullet came whistling right through the doorway, and Cleve's heart leaped, for he thought it must surely hit the woman.

But she was already safe at the window — other side of it from the Sheriff — and she knocked out the glass, stuck her Sharps rifle through it as she called, "They're across the creek near the sheep, come down through the windbreak."

They fired, all four of them then, almost exactly together — and the loudness of it inside Cleve's skull made him feel like those guns was all in there inside him, and the echo bounced all through his mind as it tried to find its way out. *Wob-a-bobbompa, wob-a-bobbomp,* was the sort of deep echo it made — only it seemed to keep going and going, going and going, going and going and going. He shook his head hoping to clear it.

He'd seen one of the men they were shooting at fall, as Gabe Roach cried, "They're out of range of our repeaters." Yet the three men all fired again, adding smoke and noise to the ruckus, as Winnie, with her back to the wall, reloaded the Sharps.

Surely that wasn't her bullet that shot the man down.

Might not have been, he decided. They sure weren't the only ones firing. Sheep men all over were swarming, protecting their town. And though there was carnage all over, Cleve understood ever more clearly — these were men well prepared, not the fools that some in La Grange had made them out to be.

"The Southies will flank them from the left in a minute," Gabe called, "but we three men need to get out of here, join the Northies. You keep at them from here with that Sharps, Fred, whenever one sticks his head out."

Cleve remembered the dog now, but didn't look for him, he just called, "Stay, Jimbo, stay." Weren't like he needed to though. That old dog knew what bullets could do, and he'd already run off to hide underneath Winnie Roach's bed.

"Out the door, one by one?" the Sheriff called over the noise.

"There's a back door," Gabe replied. "Follow me."

"Extra Winchester shells on the table, you men," Winnie called.

"Grab a box each as we go," called Gabe, and he ran for the doorway of one of the bedrooms, scooping up a box from the table as he went.

As he followed hot on Gabe's heels, Cleve could hear the terrible sounds of the fighting outside — shrieks of pain, anguish too, the panicked bleating of sheep and the barking of dogs mixed in with the gunfire. And as a backdrop to it all, the crackle of buildings aflame.

Cleve stumbled and very nearly fell as he jumped down the back stairs — and he realized he hadn't yet tied his bootlaces. He stopped, reached down to do so, and James Whipple almost knocked him over, steadied him with one hand.

"Hurry," said Whipple, and half-limped half-ran down the side of the hill after Gabe, who was waiting for them behind cover at the next building.

Bootmaker Forgets To Tie Own Laces
- Brought Undone By Mistake.

Cleve hadn't just thought those words, he'd seen them in his mind, like a newspaper headline. It was an odd time to laugh, but he did — men do strange things sometimes under pressure of battle.

Laces tied tight, he ran lickety-split, joined up with the others.

"Over there," Gabe said as he pointed the way with a nod. They were going to head for the Northern-most buildings of the town — a pair of long low buildings they were, with a lengthy log fence between. It was higher at one end than the other, over six foot in places. Perfect spot for men to take cover behind while they fired. A dozen men were already there waiting, though none were firing yet.

Cleve looked to where the outlaws were — their gunsmoke was coming from good cover, not too far from the creek, other side. The belt of trees had been left for a windbreak — it ran all the way down that side of the valley, ending perhaps only twenty yards from the creek. To go back through those trees was the only way for the outlaws to get out alive now — but Cleve saw there was no way to get in behind, cut them off.

Still, now both groups of sheep men were in their crossfire positions, there was no option left but for the outlaws to retreat. At least, that was how it seemed to Cleve.

As he watched, one of the outlaws ran out helter-skelter from cover, *zig-zagging zag-zigging zig-zooming* to the edge of the creek, a rag-lit bottle in his hand. Some of the Southies opened fire, a few shots went near him but missed, for he was a man fleet of foot — and as he hurled the burning bottle across the creek toward one of the buildings, a great boom came from where Winnie Roach was, the big

Sharps exploding into the night, and the man who hurled the flaming bottle was wrenched backways and sideways by the big bullet. He staggered a little and fell forward, face-down-dead, in the creek.

"Now," cried Gabe. And he, James and Cleve ran to join the others, the outlaws' bullets falling all short or wide of them — all except one, which flew past Cleve's head, only inches away, and kept going far into the night.

"Southies are already in place," Gabe said to the Northies already assembled — there were twenty by now. "We'll have them in a crossfire, they'll be forced to retreat or we'll cut them all down one by one."

"Wait," said James Whipple. "One thing. If they stay and fight, we must take some alive to testify against Barron. It'll help when I bring him to justice."

"The Sheriff's right," Gabe said sharply, "but keep shooting 'til you hear my command. If I'm killed, Wally's in charge."

"Don't get kilt then, young Gabe," came a gruff voice from down near the end. "I ain't suited to bein' tall hog at the trough, leastways not how you seem to be."

"Everyone into position," Gabe called.

Now Cleve was there, he saw the cleverness of it, for what looked like an ordinary log fence had been built as a battlement — there were narrow slots left for rifles to fit through, and he scurried to take a position along with the others.

But right then, in the top left corner of the valley, where the sheep had all gathered together, there came an explosion — an explosion that would have woke the dead, and busted their poor ghostly eardrums.

"The sheep," someone cried, the words followed by a long stunned second of stillness.

Then into that still eerie quiet, an outlaw fired a shot, and another explosion was heard, as a fireball erupted in one of the buildings — the schoolhouse it was — just this side of the creek.

It was a parting shot, that one.

The outlaws stole away through the trees then, leaving the stunned folk of Wolf Town to deal with the slaughter.

CHAPTER 33

JUST ABOUT DEAD IN HIS BOOTS

I t was a bloodbath alright.

Gabe sent ten of his best men after the outlaws, but they were gone into the night.

Sheriff James Whipple went along too. "I'm likely the best tracker here," he said. It was a simple true fact, not a boast — and when he insisted on going, Gabe had enough respect for the man to put him in charge.

Didn't take Whipple long to find how the damn outlaws got in unnoticed — they had killed all four sentries that were posted up there without ever firing a shot. Two of them died with their throats cut, but the others had been bludgeoned.

"They must have some men good at sneaking," old Wally said when they found the last of them. "Jimmy Moore here had ears like a owl, and eyes like a eagle. Poor Jimmy. You had the makings of a real good man. Well, you're with your Pa now, I reckon."

"Ernie?" said the Sheriff, and old Wally nodded a sad one. The outlaws had killed two from that family in under two weeks.

Sheriff James Whipple felt he owed a great duty to these men. He was not about to lead them into an ambush, and used all his skills and experience to make certain of it. He could have tracked the outlaws all the way back to wherever it was they were hiding — but he called off the search once he *knew* they were gone for the night.

He was a man who made maps for a hobby, Sheriff James Whipple — and no one knew the area better. Every cutback and shortcut was clear in his mind, and he'd have known his way even on a dark night. He was certain the outlaws had no way to double back on them.

"Two hours ride for them to go back around the other way," he explained to the men, when he told them it was safe to return to Wolf Town.

While Whipple and his small band were trailing the outlaws, those back in the sheep town didn't have it no easier. Somehow, only one man had been killed, but two others were shot, and a few people had minor burns.

It was the sheep who had taken the brunt of the attack — and sadly, some of the dogs.

"A sheep dog will lay down his life to protect the flock," Gabe told Cleve when they found one lying dead. "This poor feller must have attacked the man who came here to set the explosives."

The first thing that had to be done was put out the fires before they could spread to other buildings. It wasn't too bad — the buildings had deliberately not been built close together, and the fires were easily contained, there being no strong wind to spread them.

Only two of the outlaws had been left behind — both shots having come from the Sharps of Winnifred Roach.

"I won't allow *them* to be buried here on our land," Gabe told Cleve, as they dragged an outlaw's body up out of the creek. Then he turned to one of his men and said, "Build a separate fire for these two bad eggs. We'll burn their worthless carcasses, then carry out what's left tomorrow. They'll get no eternal rest here, not among us."

The other outlaw's body was lying face down, perhaps about twenty feet away, just outside the edge of the tree-line. "I'll go drag that one over," said Cleve.

"Thanks for your help," said Gabe. "Appreciate it. I'll give you a hand with the skunk."

But as they approached, the outlaw they had thought dead moved a hand a little, and groaned.

Gabe Roach's eyes widened, and enraged, he drew back a stiff-toed large leather boot, his plan being to kick the man's head.

Cleve leaped forward, crash tackled Gabe to the ground. Without losing momentum, he rolled and jumped to his feet, holding his hands out in front of him. And standing between the sheep man and the outlaw, he quickly said, "Woah, Gabe, let's all calm down now — this here feller's a witness, and we need to keep him alive. Much as he don't deserve it, it'll work in our favor when we try to get Barron convicted."

As he sat there on his hindquarters, Gabe's eyes flashed with hatred at the outlaw, then he looked up at Cleve in between them. He seemed like he was weighing things up in his mind — then he reached out his hand, and Cleve took a step forward and reached his out too, helped Gabe up to his feet.

"Alright," Gabe said, "alright. But I'm not touching him, I'd not trust myself to do so. Have someone else help you move him, and see if our doctor can't save him — *after* our own have been treated."

Cleve breathed a sigh of relief — half because Gabe had seen sense, and half because Gabe hadn't hit him with them iron fists again.

Only so many quality beatings a man can take in one day.

There was much to do, and mostly, it was sad work.

Some of the men built fires and cut wood to keep them going, while others dragged sheep carcasses over to burn them. Men and women tended to sheep who were injured — and to dogs and people as well.

Women made coffee and food, kept everyone fed. They consoled the grief-stricken families of those who'd been killed. It was only the children who slept, and even then, only the youngest.

By the time the Sheriff returned — leaving extra sentries strategically posted, as Gabe had ordered him to — most folk had settled into a calm resignation. A sort of *coming to terms* with all that had happened.

"I'm sorry, Gabe," James Whipple said, climbing down

from his horse. "It's my fault, all this. I should not have come."

Gabe Roach heaved the final sheep carcass onto the fire, and stepped back away from its heat before turning to face the Sheriff. His face was covered in soot and dirt, and his sweat had caused all the filth to run down in lines. He looked fifteen years extra worn than he had when James and Cleve had arrived.

"No. This wasn't your fault," Gabe said. "You didn't do it. But the man who did, he *will* pay."

Cleve turned to James Whipple and said, "You might yet have a witness to the murders."

"If I don't change my mind and beat him to death," said Gabe Roach, his voice dark and deadly. "Well, tell the Sheriff of the witness, Cleve — he looks like his head might explode, and we've cleaned up enough mess already."

"He's pretty stoved in," Cleve told Whipple, "but that first man Missus Roach shot's still alive. Doctor's treating him now."

James Whipple looked from Cleve to Gabe and back again. "If we can keep him alive, get him to Cheyenne..."

Cleve finished the stunned Sheriff's sentence for him. "He *might* just give evidence against Pinckney Barron — and against whichever man fired the shots that killed Matt Roach and the others."

Whipple could barely speak, his exhaustion now mixed with faint hope. "How bad is he, Cleve?"

"Lost a lot of blood, but the bullet went through his belly and out the other side. Ain't good, but he's all the chance we got. Doc declares a small hope."

Whipple nodded, took a deep breath, set his face hard against his tiredness. "I've seen men live through that. One had a hole in his back near six inches across — well, only lived two weeks, that one. It'd be enough for us though. If the man's still alive at daylight, there's an even money chance he'll survive the trip to Cheyenne. Can we borrow a wagon, Gabe? Pad it good so the trip doesn't kill him. Me and Cleve can get him there, I reckon."

"I'll have one made ready. I'll have to leave most of the men here in case those hard cases come back — but I'll bring three good men, and we'll all go together, make sure no one gets him away from you."

Whipple nodded his thanks, blinked hard against being overtaken by sleep. "Do his friends know he's still alive?"

"I don't believe so," Gabe told him. "They'd have taken him with them — or shot him dead before leaving. Now go get some sleep, will you, Sheriff? You looked sixty when you arrived, but you don't look a day under ninety, and I'd have you well-rested for the trip in the morning. Well-rested as three hours can do, anyway."

"Best go sleep some yourself," said the Sheriff. "I'm not the sort to cast aspersions on a man's age, but I've seen a few mountains looked younger'n you do right now."

With that, Whipple went off to check on the health of the outlaw, and then to his bed.

Gabe mumbled a sentence that had the word bed in it somewhere — but instead of heading toward the house, he went off to offer condolences to a newly grieving widow.

And Cleve — well, Cleve knew he would not be able to sleep yet, and he went for a walk through the town to help out where he could. But as he turned to walk back to the house for some sleep, he saw Winnie Roach all alone, staring up at the moon. And without even thinking — he was just about dead in his boots, after all — he walked right on up behind her and said, "Penny for your thoughts, Missus Roach?"

If Winnie Roach had accepted that penny, and given Cleve Lawson what he asked for, he'd have sure gotten more than his money's worth.

He would not have believed what she said though — would have put it down to him hearing her wrong due to tiredness — for one part of Winnie's thoughts were of Cleve, and other parts for her husband.

It's a terrible thing, the ruination of a marriage, she'd just thought *to herself. But how long must a woman grieve such a loss, before she can rightly move on? Don't I deserve to be happy? Doesn't he?*

"Penny for your thoughts, Missus Roach?" came the lovely man's voice.

If only you knew, she thought, as she turned to face him.

She saw him as handsome, in a rugged sort of way. Matt had been that way too. And like Matt, this Cleve Lawson could be quick to anger; he was prone to saying things he'd later regret; he preferred not to stick his nose in the business of others, even on those occasions when it was the *right thing* to do.

But unlike Matt, this Cleve Lawson was also quick to apologize; he did his level best to make things right when he'd made a mistake; and though he might indeed now be learning it's okay to stick your nose in other folks' business, where good reason warrants it — he did not seem the sort of a man who'd stick his nose in the business of a woman who he wasn't married to.

So only like Matt in the good ways — not in the bad.

As for Cleve's thoughts, he was so tired he wasn't hardly having none at all. The woman had turned, she had faced him and not said a word — only stood there under the moonlight, she did. And the sight of her, oh, she was a sight such as he'd never seen.

Dark beauty, silver light, and that smile. Oh, if only! Dammit, if only...

There — he was thinking again, and he smiled back at her.

"What do you hope for from life, Mister Lawson?"

Her voice had taken on an ethereal quality, magical somehow, he decided. He laughed at his own silly thoughts. *Tiredness does funny things to a man.*

The smile left her face, she looked puzzled. "Is it a secret?"

"Oh, no, Ma'am. I was ... I'm just so dog-tired is all, it's just hard to think straight, get my mind to tell my mouth to form words."

"It's funny," she mused, looking up at the shine of the

moon again. She had always liked the way it lit up the clouds soft and pretty. "Life has a way of taking some things away, Mister Lawson — then bringing new things to replace them. The good though, as well as the bad. I guess we too often forget that."

There was something in her voice, something wonderful, but he could not understand what it was — for Cleve's understanding of the woman, his assumptions about her, were wrong. He had jumped to conclusions, misunderstood something important, from the very first moment he'd met her. And still, he continued to do so.

He watched her as she watched the moon, never guessing at her true feelings, while he thought about her question.

"I guess I don't know, Ma'am," he finally said. "What I want from life, I mean. Maybe just to survive the trials of it somehow. I mean, what else is there?"

Winnie Roach spun back toward him so fast he almost jumped in alarm. "Why, there's love, of course, Mister Lawson," she said. Then she looked away just as quickly — at the shining creek this time — and added, "You don't have a family?"

"I have three sisters, Ma'am. Youngest just got herself hitched awhile back, she's down in Denver. I was comin' back from visiting with her when ... well, I just come back last week, it was real nice to see her. I guess, if I'm thinking about it, I might try to become a good Uncle to all of their children someday, maybe help the young'uns along when the time comes."

"But what about *you*, Mister Lawson. Why aren't you

married yourself? Surely a man like you — I'm sorry, I shouldn't pry, this has all made me ... I don't know ... a little wild and crazy, I suppose. I never killed anyone before."

"I did, more than once," Cleve said, and a little cold shiver ran through him. "The war, of course. Took a bit to reconcile it within me. Still ain't done so yet, that's the truth of it. But I *do* know this — it's different for you. You only done what you had to, and you saved innocent lives by the doing of it. Women and children maybe. That feller forfeit his life when he came here with all bad intentions. You done what was right, Ma'am, and there ain't no question about it."

She looked like she might cry, just a moment or two. Then she smiled, the tiniest yet most grateful of smiles, and she said, "Thank you. I needed to hear just those words — I know you'd never lie to me, Mister Lawson. And I'm sorry, please just ignore me, those things that I asked. I should not ask such personal questions, I'm not usually like this."

"It's alright, Ma'am, understandable, it's been quite a week. For me too. Not just what happened to Matt, but other things too. My best friend was killed. Good man he was, Norris Ricks ... when was that now? Seems so long ago, but it's not even twenty-four hours. Strange, it seems a lot longer."

"I'm very sorry," she said, and she reached out her hand, almost touched his face, thought better of it.

"I was, for awhile," he said.

"Sorry?"

"Married. I don't mind speaking of it."

"Your wife died?" Her voice was filled with sadness for him then.

"No, Ma'am, that hellcat's still alive, far as I know." He sighed a deep one, looked across at the fires still burning, watched those folk who'd not yet gone to bed, still working away, their lives hard, unforgiving this night. Then he said, "Seems like I always had better luck with cattle than women. It was lucky at least, that we'd leaped the book."

Her eyes filled with puzzlement then. "Leaped the book?"

"Just means we never got proper married, official," he said. "Good thing it was too. She run off with some rich feller, spends her days making *his* life a misery now, I don't reckon. I got the best of that deal, it occurs to me here in the moment — though I didn't much see it that way at the time. Saw only the loss to begin with."

She turned then toward him, her eyes shining like glittering stars were caught in them. He had never seen a woman so beautiful, and it hurt him somehow, someplace deep — someplace he was maybe afraid of.

She smiled then — not just with her mouth, but with her eyes too, and it seemed to Cleve like her whole pretty face got itself all involved in that smile.

"Not all marriages are meant to last," she said. "That's what I've learned. Haven't you?"

It was strange, how hopeful she sounded when she said it. He wished ... well, he just wished.

Dangerous things, wishes, he thought. And not wanting his wishing to get noticed, his mouth started speaking, way it did at such times.

"I envy you, Ma'am," was what came out. "And your husband, if I may say so."

I should not have said that, he thought, but it was too late, she was already replying.

"But why would you, my husband is—"

"I'm so sorry, Ma'am, please excuse that," he said in a hurry. He felt he'd crossed a line he should not have gone near, and he felt some ashamed, tried to explain it away. "I only meant ... I'm just saying, Missus Roach, I guess I'm lookin' to settle down soon. Reckon maybe it's time again. I mean, with the right woman, I believe I could do that."

"What sort of woman?"

Oh, that voice of hers, was his thought — and his mouth jumped right on in to cover his wishing again, and out popped the truth.

"Strong yet soft," he said, and the sound of those wistful words made him breathless, felt dangerous to him. "Beautiful, in all the ways that matter — and maybe some ways that don't. I reckon, maybe—"

And right then and there, Winnie Roach took a step, pushed her body against him, and her soft salty mouth was on his. And he felt it, his love for this woman, all the way through him, as her lovely hands gripped his shoulders, and she kissed him, crushing his lips with her own.

And just for a second, maybe two, he allowed it to happen, lost himself up to the moment — then he came to his senses, his hands pushed her slightly away, and he looked down at her, horrified by what had happened.

His words made almost no sound, but their meaning

seemed as harsh as if he had yelled them, top of his lungs. "What sort of woman...?"

She looked up at him then, the hurt of rejection so plain she looked like she'd been struck — then Winnie Roach pushed him away, and she slapped his face hard.

And it *hurt* — sort of *tore* something a little, in that place deep inside.

Winnie Roach turned from him then, strode away, wiping hot tears as they streamed from her eyes. She had no way of knowing how badly Cleve had misunderstood. No way of knowing that Cleve believed Gabe was her *husband* — and believed, too, that Matt had been her *brother-in-law*.

Cleve had gotten it wrong from the start — did not know that Winnie Roach had long ago married *Matt* Roach, her distant second cousin, barely even related. They had known each other two weeks before even learning each other's surname was the same as their own.

And Gabe Roach, well, he was a *most* protective brother — especially since what Matt had done to Winnie, running off as he had with her friend, and moving back East to Boston six months before.

Gabe had looked up from what he was doing just a few moments ago. He had missed the first part — the part where Winnie threw her arms around Cleve and commenced then to kiss him. What Gabe *had* seen, when he looked up, was that newcomer Cleve Lawson *kissing* his sister; seen her push him away; seen her slap him.

Gabe's anger rose up from within him, and he covered

the ground toward Lawson in no time at all, as Winnie stormed off in the other direction.

And Cleve thought, *What a thing for a husband to witness. Well, here we go again.*

But on this occasion — though he had time enough to try to defend himself — Cleve put his hands down by his sides, allowed Gabe the free shot he believed was deserved.

Didn't help none, that Cleve smiled a bitter one as the other man arrived — one of those fool imaginary newspaper headlines had occurred to him in his mind. It was strange, way he'd started to see them.

This one was:

Bootmaker Turns out a Heel
- Deserves a Good Lacing.

But Cleve's only words was, "I'm sorry" — and he truly meant it.

Gabe's face was contorted with anger — too much anger, he knew — and the punch he threw this time was not at Cleve's head, for Gabe felt he might actually kill him, and sensed wrongness in it. He stepped up to Cleve, stared him down a long moment, then he let fly a punch to the gut.

As Cleve doubled over in pain, Gabe Roach told him, "You're on your own, you and the Sheriff — *and* that damn outlaw you're trying to save. The wagon's out front of the livery ready — you'll leave here at daybreak and it better be the last time we see you. You ever go near her again — I'll kill you, Lawson."

CHAPTER 35

BROWN DERBY HAT, BLUE
BANDANA

No way Cleve was going back to the Roach's house after that. He went to the Doc's place instead, to check how the outlaw was doing.

Sheriff James Whipple was just walking out the front door as Cleve approached.

"Still alive, Sheriff?"

Whipple put on his hat and said, "Doc reckons he'll live if gangrene don't set in. Bullet missed most things that matter, and the bleeding's just about done with. He's a little awake, but out of his head from the laudanum."

"Think he'll testify?"

"Only sensible words he said sounded like anger at whoever left him there to die. Good sign, I reckon."

Cleve took off his hat, fiddled some with the brim. "He say any names?"

"Peter, maybe. Hard to tell, way he was splashing. Might hopefully make sense tomorrow."

"He'd better," Cleve said. "Listen, Sheriff, I can't go

back to the Roach house. Gabe's gunnin' for me again. Rightly so."

Whipple shook his head slowly. "What is it with you two?"

"Can't rightly tell you. I mean, I could do, but it wouldn't be proper. Bad enough what happened happened, without a man spreadin' it 'round for public consumption. Gabe ain't comin' with us now, after what I done to him. Said to tell you we're on our own. But he told me the wagon's all ready to transport our witness, so I reckon I'll go sleep in that."

If Whipple took the news badly, he didn't let on. "See you right here at daylight then, Cleve. You bring the wagon, I'll bring the dog. Some food too, if I can get some."

"Best we leave early," Cleve said, "just in case Gabe changes his mind and decides to take revenge on our witness. Must be hard not to."

"Half hour early then. Oh well — two hours sleep if we're lucky." Whipple sighed a deep one, and they walked off in different directions. At least the Sheriff was no longer limping.

Most likely so tired he forgot just how bad his foot is.

Cleve had gotten to that stage of tiredness where it gets near impossible to sleep. His bed itself was just fine. Warm and cozy a place as ever he'd slept, and the way the sky looked that night made him glad to be under it. He dozed now and then, but the sight and the sound and the smell of Winnie Roach kept invading his senses — the *softness* of her lips, the worst of it — and before he knew it, it was time to shake himself back to life and face the new day.

At least I had a comfortable couple of hours lie down.

He lay there a minute, just thinking. The moon was gone now, but the sky was clear, and dotted with beauteous stars. He felt bad about Winnie Roach — he realized now that she must have sensed how he felt; must have picked up on his reckless desire; and being herself overtaken with tiredness and grief after all that had happened, the woman had done a thing far removed from her usual character.

If Cleve knew one thing for a solid, it was that Winnie was a fine and upstanding woman, not given to honeyfogling, hornswoggling, rooking or roping, or any other sort of shenanigans.

It was my fault entirely, and I wish I'd not said that terrible thing that I did.

He knew it would bother him a good long time to come, what he'd said to the woman. But he had to put it out of his mind. Had to get his wits about him. He had to help Sheriff James Whipple get a man to Cheyenne.

The wagon was a good one alright. Smallish buckboard, built for fast travel, just long enough for a man to lie down in the back. It had high boards all around the tray — could have laid two dead men in it and nailed a top on, would have made a fine coffin.

They had spared nothing in making it comfortable for the badly injured man's travel — it was filled with clean straw, not just in the middle, but piled up thick at the edges as well. Two blankets of sewed-together sheepskins were in it — Cleve slept on one and under the other. Like sleeping in a silken cocoon, it had been — more comfortable by half than the bed he usually slept in.

He rubbed the sleep from his eyes, groaned like a bear as he stretched, and forced himself to sit up.

Wasn't easy.

Bet ol' Jimbo got plenty of sleep. Must be half cat, that hound, way he always lands on his feet.

Cleve climbed out of the wagon, walked off a ways and relieved himself, went back and hitched up the two horses. They hadn't skimped on them horses either — they were a proper span, he now noticed, a fine pair not only matched size and strength-wise, but of similar markings, both blue roans with white blazes.

These sheep folks don't do things by halves.

By the time he arrived at the Doc's place, the Sheriff was already there. Whipple and the Doc brought the outlaw out on a stretcher, and the three of them loaded him into the back of the wagon. Their breath still steamed in the crisp morning air as they climbed up onto the seat — Cleve at the reins, and the Sheriff beside him to his left.

Cleve looked around then, sudden-like, and said, "Hey, where's my dog?"

"Figured him safer here for the moment," said Whipple. "We don't want him under our feet if push comes to shove on the trail."

Cleve nodded and shrugged, murmured, "Splits fair I guess." Then out loud he said, "Best we get a move on then if we're going."

The Doc gave some final instructions, reminded Whipple of the laudanum dosage, then wished them good luck before watching them drive away.

They weren't yet out of Wolf Town when the feller

complained — reckoned it too soon for travel, him still being in a perilous state.

But he shut up right quick when Whipple said, "You can stay here if you want, but I'm headed to Cheyenne. The Doc's on your side, but he's only little, and got no gun either I noticed. Without any law here to keep the rest of these sheep fellers off you, I doubt you'd live out the hour. Up to you though, Mister Greene. What's it to be?"

"Put that way," said the outlaw, "guess I'll do what you want."

"What I *want*," said the Sheriff with anger, "is for men like *you* to stop killing innocent folk at the say-so of rich men. But right now, I'll settle for you coming to Cheyenne, and testify against that damn Pinckney Barron, and whoever done the atrocities upon all the men you snakes killed."

"'I'll testify against Barron, if you see I'm let off," the outlaw said, then he groaned in discomfort when the wagon hit a pothole in the still almost-darkness. "But I ain't sayin' nothin' official against Prosper Peterson. Plumb loco he is, and he'd just as soon—"

"Peterson? *Prosper* Peterson?" The way Whipple said it sure made Cleve pay attention. Shocked, Whipple sounded, and then some.

"Yessir, Sheriff," said Greene. "It was Peterson done them bad things, and don't you be blamin' no other. Rest of us is just regular fellers, tryin' to get by, make a livin' — though a'course, I'll admit, not a honest one. But him, he's a damn bad egg, and somethin' gone serious wrong with him, up in his head."

Cleve turned about and spoke to the feller. "Peterson's the man with the brown derby hat, blue bandana? The man who murdered Matt Roach?"

"That's him," came the answer. "Didn't just killed him, but done mutilated the body. I'd have you know for the truth — Peterson done every bit of the killin' himself, takes a pride and enjoyment in it."

Whipple's eyes gleamed. "You'll testify to that?"

"No, not that."

"But surely—"

"Sheriff, here it is. I'd just soon not have him tear *me* to pieces for fun, neither after he kills me or afore it. So no, while ever he's alive I won't go on the record on nothin' he did — but it were him alright, not the others. I'd have *you* know that afore I die, in case I'm gonna."

"It was all done on Pinckney Barron's orders?"

"True enough, Sheriff. Barron's your man. Rest of us is terrified we might be next, that's what Peterson's got to. Even ... even his one friend don't seem to trust ... grrrrr. Dammit Sheriff, I know I don't have no rights to complaint, but dammit, this sure hurts. I never been shot before."

"You stay quiet now, Greene, we'll get you to Cheyenne before the day's out, there's proper doctors there."

"Who was that feller stitched me up then?"

"Animal doctor, mostly," said Whipple with a laugh.

"Well, that shakes fair 'nuff I reckon," said Greene, "me bein' mostly animal anyways. Hell, I'm grateful he got me this far, 'stead of jus' lettin' me die."

CHAPTER 36
CAMP-FIRE PLAN

When they rode away from the attack on the Sheep Town, Prosper Peterson had been in a foul sort of mood. It had not gone all to his liking.

He had expected little resistance, despite all Bat Jenkins' warnings. Peterson had enjoyed sneaking up on the sentries and killing them — but having gotten down to the town, things had all gone awry.

Oh, he'd managed to have one of the men set explosives, and had thought it a jolly thing to see the sheep blown to pieces, and some houses set afire.

But them sneaky sheep fellers had been better organized than he'd reckoned on — like a damn little military unit they'd been, and he hadn't even got to kill the Sheriff. That fact irked him most of all, for Prosper Peterson had nurtured a mighty hatred for lawmen of every color and stripe — and though he had jimmied bulls before, and found satisfaction in it, for this particular badge-toting bull, he wished to do more, so much more. He planned to kill Sheriff Damn Whipple slowly and painfully, whittle away at his hide, make him *beg* for his death to come faster, then make him beg more.

He'd thought about all these things as they'd ridden away to safety.

The two men Peterson had lost in the raid did not matter to him a damn — he hadn't liked either Knoll or Greene anyway. All that mattered now was killing that damn Sheriff — then going back to wipe out the Sheep Town.

Bat Jenkins was an old friend, and a clever man as well. He had saved Peterson's life more than once in the war, and had his back ever since. Bat's only weakness was that he preferred to do things without violence, whenever he could.

Musta been weak to start with, though the war weakened some men that way as well.

Anyway, soon as they failed, he knew he should have listened to Bat, done what he'd suggested.

Won't make that mistake twice. Bat's got the brains, best I make use of him now.

Peterson spurred his horse on, drew level with Jenkins, and signed for him to stop. They all came to a halt and he said, "What to do now, Bat, my old friend?"

"The Sheriff'll try to bring in a U.S. Marshal, I reckon," said Bat Jenkins. "He'll head Cheyenne way for that. Or he might try to get through to Pine Bluffs. Closer in miles, but some of it mighty hard going, and risky as well. If I was him though, that's where I'd go, if I just wanted to save my own skin."

"Don't matter where he *thinks* he's goin', Bat, damn you. Nor where you'd want'a go, you bein' him — which you ain't. Only matters where we can *catch* him."

"Where we can *kill* him, you mean?"

"Naw. *Catch* him." Prosper Peterson's eyes went all wild again, and he laughed as he spoke. "Maybe I'll slow roast him, this one. I'm gonna play with him like he's a mouse, and I'm one'a them tigers they poke a big chair at — rile 'em up for a show."

Bat Jenkins' own eyes did not betray him, nor did his voice. He looked evenly at the man who used to be his friend — used to be halfway decent at one time — and he said, "There's only really two ways the Sheriff can go, that first little bit. He'd be a fool to head north, get himself killed by Indians — and he's *not* a fool. Lucky for us, Prosper, both trails south intersect at one point. Two miles from where we are now."

They had ridden to that place directly, bedded down in a hollow, spent the night. Deputy Vinton Waits had been sent to inform Pinckney Barron they had the Sheriff and Cleve Lawson hemmed in.

Young Vin had wanted to stay in the town when he got there — he'd had enough of the outlaw life already, but he could not very well say so. He was in it now, up to his neck.

And when Pinckney Barron sent him back, the boy lacked the required imagination and forethought to ride away from that place as quick as he could. Like the dang fool he was, the young Deputy done exactly what he was told — and in the morning, he found himself sitting around a small camp-fire with seven other outlaws, and wishing he'd listened up better to old Uncle James.

Should have been nine of them there, not just the eight — but one had crept away during his watch. Must have walked his horse out of there a good ways before mounting up, for not one of them heard him escaping. Young feller that escapee was — kind of a lazy one, but with enough brains to seize the opportunity to hightail it when his chance came.

Bat Jenkins offered to track the kid down right away, bring him back — but Peterson said no. Said they'd find the kid sometime later, and do unto him what he deserved. Of course, if Peterson *had* let Jenkins leave, ol' Bat would not even have searched for the runaway. Would have just gone and kept going, to Montana at least, maybe further.

Truth was, most of them outlaws wanted to leave. Prosper Peterson was a whole heap of trouble — a six-foot pile of dangerous explosives with a fuse that was already lit. The only thing they weren't sure of, was the length of Peterson's wick. Unfortunately, none of them fellers trusted the others enough to say one word about it. But that one feller leaving, it sure put the idea of it firm in all of their heads.

Bat Jenkins was possessed of more sense than all the rest of those men put together — now that the cleverest of them had taken his leave — but not even Bat figured the Sheriff would leave the Sheep Town so soon. He'd considered it possible, but not as likely as him leaving in, say, a day or two, after getting more prepared. And Bat also figured the Sheriff would have a dozen or more of them sheep fellers with him, armed and loaded for bear.

Bat Jenkins planned not to be there when the Sheriff arrived. He didn't yet know *how* he'd escape, but he'd decided on it for certain.

I ain't stickin' around in the hope ol' Prosper grows back some brains. Just don't seem like part of his future — and I'd rather live a long life than find out how this ends. I been on the owl hoot trail too long, might be time to turn honest, else I end up loco like Prosper.

There was a good sized bounty out for Prosper Peterson — problem was, the states it could be collected all had bounties on Jenkins himself. And besides, he wasn't much of a shot — and loco or not, you wouldn't get a second shot at Prosper if your first missed.

So Bat cooked up some breakfast and ate it with the seven other men. Or rather, six other men, and whatever Prosper had become.

Anyways, there was eight of them there.

They were all done eating now, and were seated on logs around a fire, warming their hands on their coffee cups. It was yet a cold morning, no sun having reached their camp through the trees.

There was surprisement all 'round, when pretty soon after daylight, those with sharp ears heard a wagon rumbling along the trail toward them.

"Well, I swan," Bat Jenkins exclaimed as he jumped up from the log and onto his feet. "Wagon coming, two horse team."

Prosper Peterson sniffed at the air like a rabbit, cupped

a hand around his ear and said, "How many troops mounted, Colonel?"

Bat ignored the fact that he'd never been a Colonel, listened a few moments longer as he tried to come up with an escape plan. But when nothing came to mind, he told Peterson the truth. "No troops, Prosper, only the wagon."

"It's a trap!"

"Maybe not," said Bat Jenkins. "We best get in place though, they're moving at a fair steady clip."

"Whoever it is," Peterson growled, "they's mine, all mine, y'hear? Any one'a you kills 'em, I'll shoot your damn privates off, and make you eat your own liver. Mine they are, all mine for some games. I'll show you boys how to play, and you'll rightful thank me for the learnin' of it!"

CHAPTER 37

"IF YOU FIND YOURSELF KNEE-DEEP IN DUNG..."

Sheriff James Whipple half expected them outlaws to be waiting up ahead at that crossroads.

Ten or so minutes before, he had asked Cleve to pull up the wagon, give the horses a breather, and draw up a "just in case" battle plan.

Once they'd stopped, Whipple said, "To track us so easy to Wolf Town, Peterson must have a good tracker with him. If he's been here awhile, he'll have spent some time learning the trails, and know just where to expect us. That be the true of it, Greene?"

By now, Greene knew where his best chance of survival lay — and it sure weren't with Prosper Peterson. "That's just how it is," he agreed. "Tracker's a feller called ... well, I shouldn't say, he's the one treated me best all along, and he ain't done a violence to no one. But it splits fair he'd know where to go, best spot for an ambush. Such a place be close up ahead?"

Whipple shot Cleve a worried look. "It's the only place

they can be sure to intercept us. A smart man'd already be there."

"That's where they are then," said Greene. "Unless the tracker's made a run for safety — I'd not be surprised if he did, he ain't no fool." His voice raised up into a panic then. "If Prosper sees me, works the play out..."

"Peterson will shoot you on sight, yes?"

"Seems high likely, Sheriff. Man's gone completely loco. Best shootist I ever saw too — bad combination."

"We can't go back, and we can't go around," said the Sheriff, as he ran his hand over the stock of that lovely short Yellowboy.

It was Cleve who spoke then. "My old daddy always reckoned, if you find yourself knee-deep in dung, you best keep on goin' 'til you're through it, and *then* clean your boots."

Whipple closed one eye, looked along the barrel of the carbine. "He have any advice for when you're neck-deep?"

"Same thing applies, is my best guess," said Cleve. "But as I remember, my daddy weren't much of a thinker, and that was his downfall." He smiled then, and the smile grew into a laugh."

"Glad you find our peril amusing," said Whipple.

"Well," Cleve said, rubbing some at his chin, "I remember how I used to hide from him when I was little — and a plan occurs to me now. That might amuse you too, Sheriff, if you'd like to hear it."

Cleve explained the plan real quick, and it being a simple one, it seemed about right to the Sheriff. So they moved some of the straw, and shoved Greene over to one side of the buckboard. Then James Whipple climbed in there too, with his Winchester beside him, and his Remington six-gun to hand.

Then Cleve spread the straw over the top of 'em, decided it looked right enough, climbed back on the box and got moving.

Way he figured it, them fellers might not even remember him from the robbery. Only two had got close enough for a *good* look at him — and of those two, Prosper Peterson, by all accounts, was wrong in the head.

And perhaps they would not even be there.

Ain't much of a plan, Cleve thought as he got the horses moving — *but even a bad plan is better than no plan at all.*

That's about how it worked out.

It was slightly downhill to the crossroads, and the trail particular smooth there. He didn't push the horses too hard, but kept plenty in reserve, case he got the chance to make a run for it, get in front of the outlaws.

Sure enough, sound of shots started echoing around, and though none seemed like they came close, men were shooting from both sides.

Cleve hunkered down low, give that span of horses their head, and they sure proved their worth. Just about flew over the top of the ground, barely seeming to touch it. Almost like ghost horses they were, with a wing on each foot.

It was going pretty well to begin with. But when he come 'round a slight bend in the trail, right before the crossroads themselves would have come into view, the whole damn trail was horses, a string of seven all tied there, one side to the other, all the way to the trees. Three men standing there with them too — three men all with their guns out.

Nothing else Cleve could do but to rein in his horses, slow down and pull on the brake, so that's what he did.

And there, in the middle of the trail before him, was a tall well-built man in a brown derby hat, and a blue bandana worn at his throat.

It was all Cleve could do not to go for his gun in that moment. But he knew he was dead if he tried, and with nothing achieved. The three men in front all had six-shooters pointed right at him; he heard men coming out from the bushes both sides now, and there were other noises further back too, where the firing had come from.

At least two more coming, that means.

So Cleve put his hands up instead, left his Winchester right where it was in full view, and his six-gun hidden under his shirt.

We're dead men, he thought. But what he *said* was, "What's this about? All I got's my rifle here, and twelve dollars, but you're welcome to take what I got."

The others hung back a little, and had all surrounded him now, every gun trained right on him. But Prosper Peterson walked on up past the horses, came and stood about four feet away to the right, from where Cleve sat with his hands up.

Then, with the light of recognition in his eyes, Prosper Peterson said to Cleve, "You still don't see so good, do you, Friend?"

Cleve looked at the man, thinking of how he was loco

— but then, the remembrance came to him, of what he had told the damn snake at the robbery. Cleve blinked, craned his neck sideways and forwards some. He peered toward Peterson in the manner of a man almost blind, and said, "You know me, Mister?"

"Know you?" Peterson laughed. "Listen up, boys, this feller wants to know do we know him?"

Cleve's mind could work quick when he needed it to. He remembered now that the Sheriff knew too, about what he'd said at the robbery — how he'd told that Blue Bandana feller his eyes were bad, so he wouldn't be seen as a threat.

Maybe worked in their favor right now. Leastways, Cleve hoped it did.

He made out like he was trying to focus on Peterson again, then said, "Hey, I know your voice now. You're that feller killed that damn sheep man for us, last week when you robbed the stage. Appreciate it kindly, Mister, whoever you are. Fine work you and Pinckney Barron's doin', riddin' the place a'them scab-herders. Why, I wish I had me a bottle here, so's I could share a drink with you."

That sure tickled Peterson's fancy. "Hey, he's a cattleman, boys — but we might as well rob him while he's here." Then he busted out laughing as he holstered his gun, and turned around this way and that, all the better to watch his men laugh it up with him.

Right then would have been the best moment.

Right then, Sheriff James Whipple had his Remington ready to fire in Peterson's direction.

Right then, Cleve was waiting for Whipple to shoot, waiting for the moment where he would jump to his left, shoot whoever he could, take some cover and fight these damn outlaws to the death.

But right then, the Sheriff held out hope that those men were taken in by the trick; held out hope that Peterson would take Cleve's gun and his money, then allow him to drive that wagon on through — and that they would be free, on their way to Cheyenne, where Greene would give evidence to cut off the head of the snake, that damn Pinckney Barron.

But right then, right in that moment they might have been safe, and been on their way — Deputy Vinton Waits came straggling along up the trail; heard what Prosper Peterson said; and in a panicked tone yelled, "That's Lawson, Mister Peterson, kill him!"

CHAPTER 38
LAST TIME I SEEN BAT JENKINS...

By this time, Prosper Peterson was in a wild and robustly advanced state of madness. But years of riding the owl hoot trail prepares a man certain ways; helps him react to certain things without wasting time thinking — makes him jump sideways, for instance, at a certain tone of voice, and go for his guns.

And that was what happened *right then*.

A great many things happened at once then — leastways in the same moment or two — so that whatever happened, it happened so quick, that these next dozen things all happened at once, far as time more-or-less goes.

Prosper Peterson jumped left, hit the deck and rolled, just in time so that James Whipple's shot almost missed him completely — but somehow shot off one of his fingers. The one next to the small one, it was, though no one yet knew it.

That same moment, Cleve Lawson went left, pulled his gun out from under his shirt, fired it at the outlaw that side of him — not much of a shot, with Cleve in such a hurry and scrambling. But that feller squealed in pain, shot in the foot how he was, Cleve having got lucky.

As a reflexive action, that feller lifted his gun up to shoot — but Cleve had his feet proper planted by then, and he put one right through the man's heart. Outlaw fell on the ground, nevermore to do robbing or killing.

Other things happened, too, in that moment — indecisive actions, so-called.

Problem was, every last dang one of them outlaws was dead-afeared of Prosper Peterson's madness — not to mention his guns — and they were under strict orders not to do any killing, no matter what.

Them indecisive actions — so-called — led to some of them pulling their guns but not firing, just pointing the weapons at men who, natural enough, took unkindly to it. That's a damn fool action at any time, and those two fellers deserved to get killed then, on account of their own chuckleheadedness. They got just what they earned — one shot by Cleve, one by Whipple — and both outlaws expired soon after.

One of the other outlaws, though, was *plenty* decisive — the cleverest of them, Bat Jenkins. He'd recognized Cleve right away, and been half *expecting* the Sheriff to come up shooting from under the straw — it was what *he'd* have done, after all. So as soon as Bat saw a movement from the straw; saw Prosper Peterson dive; saw the makings of violence and death — ol' Bat used his knife, not his gun. He turned quick, cut the rope that tied his horse to the others, leaped onto its back, and was galloping away down that trail, 'fore you coulda said 'Save your own skin.'

The two outlaws nearest to him hesitated a moment, then seeing what Bat had done, them fellers followed his lead — jumped onto their horses they did, and flew out of there fast as steam trains on a long downhill run.

Only man hadn't moved was the one who thought slowest of all — seemed like when the Lord handed out brains, Deputy Vinton Waits had neglected to go wait in line. Perhaps he'd gone back for a second dose of good looks, 'stead of lining up where he was meant to.

So when all the shooting and running and riding away was unfolding, young Vin stood there like a fish out of water, his eyes darting this way and that and his mouth flopping open, just watching the whole frolic unfold from back thirty yards away. Hadn't even raised up his gun yet, which maybe saved his life, him not being a threat when Cleve and Whipple was working out who they should shoot next.

Right at the start, when Prosper Peterson hit the ground and rolled, he'd then scrambled for the nearest cover he saw — went right under the wagon, he did. He pressed that big six-gun of his against the underside boards of the wagon, and commenced to fire shots on up through it. Two bullets he fired in one spot, before moving the pistol a foot or so to the left, then firing two up through there.

Them first two shots went right up through the back of the witness — ended Robert Greene's life, without Peterson even having known the man had been in there.

Second pair of shots was less lucky, but still damn

effective — they both hit the Sheriff, but neither one killed him.

Whipple had seen Prosper Peterson head underneath, but he'd been busy to start with, on more immediate business — killing another man. By the time he picked up the rifle to blow some big holes through the boards toward Peterson, he was already hit through the foot, then the next bullet after that smashed into his elbow. Took the stuffing right out of him that did — he lost his grip on the Winchester, and it clattered away to the ground as he scrambled over the backboard to get to the box seat.

While that was all going on, Cleve fired one under the wagon, just missing Peterson's shoulder — but he had to jump for it himself as the outlaw turned his six-gun on Cleve.

Landed right on the Sheriff, Cleve did — his big knee planted itself on the Sheriff's shot elbow as he scrambled toward his Winchester. Must have been mighty painful, for Whipple cried out, and he nearly passed out from the pain.

That was when Vinton Waits finally came to his senses, aimed his rifle at Cleve where he kneeled on the box seat and said, "Don't you move, Mister Damn Lawson." Then he smiled at his cleverness and added, "You can come on out, Mister Peterson — they ain't goin' nowhere but Hell."

CHAPTER 39

HACKLES

The widow Winnifred Roach had been so tired when she got to bed, she had cried herself right to sleep, and not woken "til daylight came pouring in through her window.

I've overslept.

She heard noises in her kitchen, felt a pang of regret about what happened the previous night. The men would all be up, she imagined. Gabe would perhaps be annoyed with her for not being up to make breakfast — but he would be getting on with things, rather than wake her.

The three of them must be out there — and yet, she heard no talking. Then she just about jumped out of bed when something wet touched her hand.

Turned out to be the nose of Cleve's dog, the lovely ol' Jimbo. He had slept under her bed.

"Good boy," she said. "We'd best let you outside."

Her room had no door that led outside the way Gabe's did. She decided to dress first, before letting the dog out.

She could smell the food being cooked, yet still not a word could she hear. Perhaps they were all as exhausted as she, and simply didn't feel like talking.

As Winnie pulled on her boots and tied the laces, she hoped things would not be awkward between her and Cleve.

After what happened with Cleve the previous night, she had headed straight for home; she had not looked back once; she had not seen Gabe stride toward Cleve and deliver that one vicious punch to his belly.

She opened her door and said, "Jimbo, outside now, good boy." The dog squeezed through the doorway in front of her, wagging his tail as he headed for the front door. She crossed behind him, not even looking to her right, where the three men would be.

She opened the door and let the dog out, then, leaving it open, she held her head high and turned to face the men — but only her brother was there.

"I made flapjacks and bacon," he said as he put the two plates on the table. "Won't be as good as yours, but I figured you needed the sleep."

"Alright," she said, as she walked across and took her seat. "Thank you."

"All a bit burned," he said, "but better than starving."

She drank some of the coffee he'd made — at least he was good at that, and she felt better right away. Then she chewed the parts of the bacon and flapjacks that weren't so burnt as the rest, and the pair ate in silence.

Finally, she couldn't stand it any longer. She looked up, caught Gabe's eyes and said, "Where are our guests?"

His countenance changed right away — got that look on him he always did when his hackles were up. "Where do you think?"

"I don't know," she said. "That's why I asked."

Far as hackles went, she could get hers up with the best of 'em.

"They left early."

"Left? Left without you?"

A look of bewilderment crossed Gabe's face and he said, "You could not have believed I'd go with them?"

"Why would you not?" She thumped her hand down on the table, and the cups and plates rattled.

"What sort of a brother do you think I am, Fred?" He shook his head at her, puzzled. "After what that damn snake Lawson done to you, I told them they were on their own; to leave here at dawn; and for Lawson to never come back."

"What have you *done?*"

Winnie Roach's chair clattered across the floor behind her as she jumped to her feet. She ran to the front door, looked this way and that, then turned and strode to the gun rack, took down her Sharps.

"What are you *doing,* Fred? Surely you—"

"You fool," she cried, rushing to the drawer where the spare shells were kept. "Are you coming or not?"

"But what he *did...*"

"That sweet man didn't do a thing. Oh, you fool, Gabe, you fool. I don't know what you saw, but you misunderstood. I kissed him, and he pushed me away, that's all he did. I should not have slapped him, it wasn't his fault, but I was upset when he rejected..."

"Oh, no," said Gabe then, and he strode to the gun rack himself, took down his Winchester. "I'm sorry, Winnie, but I thought ... I assumed he'd ... oh dammit, let's go, I'm sorry."

She took her hat down from the hook, pushed it down on her head as she stepped out the door. "What if those men are out there waiting to ambush them?"

"It'll be alright," Gabe said, keeping his voice calm. "We'd best hurry is all."

But he had a bad feeling about it, and he wasn't the only one.

CHAPTER 40

THE DEVIL'S OWN MAN

Cleve had already emptied his six-shooter and was reaching for his fully loaded Winchester, when young Vinton Waits pointed his rifle at. And Cleve's hand just hung in the air for what seemed a long moment of deciding — he was inches away from the rifle stock, but maybe less inches from death.

"Don't," said Sheriff James Whipple. "Don't, Cleve. The boy can shoot."

Cleve raised his hands in the air instead. Stared back at the crooked damn Deputy in disgust. "We just about done it, Sheriff," he said.

Not much as last words go, he thought, *but nobody cares, so I guess it don't matter none anyway.*

As Prosper Peterson emerged from under the wagon, Cleve closed his eyes. If he had to die anyway, he had seen enough ugliness already — instead of seeing more, he would spend his final moments picturing the face of the beautiful Winnie Roach.

"What the damn hell's the smile for?" It was Prosper Peterson speaking, he knew, but Cleve wasn't falling for that. He kept his eyes closed, kept seeing that lovely face in his mind, went right on smiling.

Next thing he knew, Peterson shoved him a mighty one, and as he flew rump over sconce, Cleve's eyes opened in time to see the blue and white of a cloudy sky above, a flash of the sun in the East — then the whole thing spun all too quick, his face thumped the dirt, and he couldn't see nothing but dust.

Do something, Cleve, don't just lay here!

He jumped to his feet just in time to see Peterson pointing Cleve's own Winchester at him. The man's lips were curled back in a snarl, exposing two blackened teeth, and he said, "We's gon'a have some fun now, Friend. Come tie him up now, young Vin, and this other damn sneak as well."

Prosper Peterson knew what he was doing. Loco or not, he'd had some years of practice already. Such things become second nature after awhile. He stood in perfect position to shoot both Cleve and the Sheriff, them being more or less in a line. Would not have mattered much anyway, as he was the only one of the three with a gun now.

It took a long couple of minutes for Vinton Waits to get the rope, for he had to catch a horse first. The gelding he'd hired from the livery was long gone, as were the others, for the most part. But Prosper Peterson's animal was well trained, and not much scared of gunfire, so he'd stuck around — what took the time was, the horse didn't trust the young Deputy far as he could kick him.

Finally Vin caught him. He tied the horse to the branch of a tree and came back with the coil of rope. "Sorry, Uncle," he said, as he commenced to lash the Sheriff's hands together, and tie him to the seat of the buckboard. Once Vin had trussed Whipple good, he left him right there. Then he walked around behind Cleve and tied his hands tight behind his back, just as Peterson ordered.

"Now walk him over here, and lash him to the tailgate of the wagon." Young Waits did as he was told, while the crazed outlaw grinned like a hungry coyote and said, "I'll practice on this one and we'll see just how much a man can take — then I'll get to the *real* prize." Then he cackled a demented one and added, "That prize is you, Sheriff, case you ain't worked it out yet. Fancy eatin' some bits of your friend?"

"Forget about hurting him," Whipple said, "he ain't nothing at all. I'm the man you have business with."

There was nothing Cleve could do. Even while Prosper Peterson taunted James Whipple, he never took his eyes off of Cleve, never pointed the gun anywhere but his chest. Not until the Deputy had lashed Cleve tight to the back of the wagon, did Peterson step away to go look at the Sheriff.

Prosper Peterson's lip curled back in that grin of his. "You's shot up bad, Sheriff Whipple. That's hurtin' you somethin' fierce, I wouldn't reckon, that elbow bein' all bullet-smashed how it is."

"Ain't but a scratch," the Sheriff answered. "About even to your own wounds, in my estimation."

"Me? I ain't been touched, you fool," Prosper Peterson answered. "Bullets can't touch me no more, I'm Prosper Damn Peterson, the Devil's own man in the West."

"Sad thing," said Whipple, "when a man's gone so loco he don't notice he's missing a finger."

The outlaw's face twitched a little, his gaze shifted quick to his hand, then his eyes opened wide as he studied it. "Now *there's* quite the thing. Ha. Would not never have noticed I reckon — thanks be to you, Friend Whipple, for pointing it out. But we Devil's men don't feel pain, and I'd not be one hooter surprised if the damn thing grew back."

By now Deputy Waits had noticed the partially uncovered body of Robert Greene in the buckboard. He brushed off some of the straw and said, "Hey, Mister Peterson, they got Greene in here dead as a maggot."

Whipple called out to his nephew then, one last try to bring him back to goodness; one last try for a witness; one last try so that he and Cleve might survive. "Greene was alive, Vin, and was going to be our witness to lock up Pinckney Barron."

""Til I killed the skunk like he deserved," crowed Peterson with glee.

"Listen, Vin, it's not too late. Kill Peterson now and turn witness yourself, and I promise, you'll be a free man."

Cleve had craned his neck around and been watching young Vinton's eyes. He saw a flicker of goodness in them eyes when Vin heard his Uncle's words — but then Prosper Peterson laughed it up big, and the young Deputy smiled with him. And right then Cleve knew there was nothing much left, no humanity left in the boy — and he sure enough knew they would die here, out on this trail.

"That's right funny, Uncle," said Vin. "I'm to be Sheriff, you know, and *help* Mister Barron — and help Mister Peterson too. I'm with *them* now, and I'll be a rich man before long. You coulda been too, if you wasn't so stickled on rules."

Prosper Peterson knew he had won. He held his bloodied hand up against the light of the sky now and studied it. More than half of that shot finger was missing — and what was left was a mess. "Looks maybe better than ever, I reckon," he said. Then his lips curled back into a smile at Whipple, and he rubbed at the stubble of his chin as he added, "I'll get back to you soon, Sheriff. But first, I got some right painful business to transact, with your oversize shortsighted friend."

CHAPTER 41
LITTLE JACK

Winnie and Gabe had wasted no time saddling their horses and hightailing it after their new friends. Gabe told the livery feller to send four good men to catch them up soon — but they didn't have time to wait for them.

"Tell them to head for the crossroads," Gabe added. "Just before there's the best place for an ambush. If we've already left when they get there, I'll leave a sign pointing which way we've gone. Then they won't have to waste time studying tracks. And take this dog here inside, and don't let him out."

Ol' Jimbo didn't take kindly to being left behind — *again* — but when the livery feller produced a good bone for him to chew on, he consented to stay.

Gabe and Winnie had a lot of ground to make up — but being on horses, they were able to make use of a shortcut, a path that no wagon in existence could possibly take.

It was less a path than the merest suggestion of one —

indeed, Gabe did not even know of it, for it was a secret known only to Winnie and her horse.

It was surpassingly steep, that little shortcut, and it took a real top-notch horseman — or horse*woman* — to travel it safely. Gabe Roach was a pretty fair rider, and his sister had figured him up to the task. But Winnie, she was a natural-born horsewoman — and not only that, her horse was a match for any in Wyoming Territory.

When they came to the steep-sided shortcut, she was a little in front. Gabe said, "Wait, let me go ahead, you'll try it too fast, come undone." But of course, Winnie Roach didn't listen. She would *not* be held back — not by Gabe; not by fear; not by common good sense. She could not have been held back in that moment, not by the Devil himself.

"Go, Little Jack," she called to her horse, and he threw himself at that slippery slope without showing so much as the slightest grail of fear. He was a mustang of mustangs, that fine little stallion.

Winnie was a girl who had always loved to push limits, and Little Jack was her most willing partner. That horse loved the danger as she did, and the pair of them as a team were an all-fired wonder.

A horse cannot dodge and weave if he holds his head high — but that little mustang always ran with his down. As he darted away up the slope now, zigging and zagging and twisting at her merest suggestion, Gabe could only marvel at the sight, before taking off after them.

Little Jack did his job well. Once, near the top, a pebble rolled underfoot and he staggered — but he took it in his stride, he balanced, corrected and scrambled — and a few moments later the wild pair crested the ridge. Winnie drew his reins in a second, surveyed what lay below them and said, "You know the way, Little Jack!"

Then she patted his neck, urged him on again — and they leaped from the crest, launched at the downslope together, joyous, audacious, dissolute, almost flying like birds.

Halfway down it they were by the time Gabe and his mount had got to the top. Gabe Roach's eyes widened in terror at his sister's savage recklessness then — and yet, in the midst of his sensible fear he was proud, as proud then as he'd ever been in his thirty-four years.

She had given him rein and leaned back, leaned back so far that her head touched the tail of the horse, and the pair were a wonderment to see. Then Little Jack stepped on an old rotted log, it broke and gave way, and Gabe's poor heart skipped a beat. The brave horse went down on his haunches, and yet — *and yet!* — Winnie and the mustang, as one, rode it out, and together they came to the bottom of the slope, safe and sound, and Gabe thought they surely must stop.

But neither rider nor horse yet considered to rest — and Winnifred Roach urged Little Jack on faster still, as she threw her weight forward, more over his withers, to help his power and speed.

"Wait for me, Fred," called Gabe. And more cautious than she — he would hit the ground heavier too, if it came to a fall — he urged his horse forward to tackle the treacherous slope.

By the time Gabe and his gelding had picked out a

path, traversed and slid their way down and were safe at the bottom, she was gone — *gone!* — and he knew he could not catch her up. Not only did she have the best horse, she was the best rider he knew, and she weighed next to nothing.

When he next saw her, it was some long minutes later. She was maybe five-hundred yards shy of the ambush point, that place they had feared the outlaws might have waited for Cleve and Whipple and the witness.

Little Jack was tied to a tree at one side of the trail, and for once he looked some worse for wear — but Winnie herself was an absolute brown study of concentration.

She was lying prone on the trail, looking down the sights of the Sharps at the men in the distance. She did not look up at Gabe, but spoke even and calm as if she was in a church praying. "Get your horse to the side lest they notice us, Gabe. Please hurry, take a look at what's happening, I'd have your opinion."

He wasted no time, did just as she'd told him. He tied the horse over near hers, took out the field glasses he always kept in his saddle bags, and came back to her quickly, staying low. He knelt down next to Winnie and surveyed the scene she was watching.

"Dammit, Fred," he said. "That isn't good."

"You call that advice? Little Jack told me that much, even before I stepped down, and he's got no glasses."

Gabe studied what he saw, tried to think. The wagon was stopped in the middle of the trail, slightly turned to the left. It was five-hundred yards away, he reckoned — but her judgment of distance was better. There were dead men off a short ways at each side of the trail.

A pair of legs stuck out into the air, off the side of the box seat. The feet were not tied together. That would be the Sheriff — almost certainly dead.

Part of a dead man could be seen in the back of the buckboard — that would be the witness, of course.

Of those who still breathed, one man was off a ways to the side. He was cradling a rifle, watching the two who were at the back of the wagon. Clearly, those were the two men Winnie was focused on.

One of those two men was Cleve Lawson. His feet were bound together, and his hands were behind him, and clearly, they would be bound too. He was facing this way, eyes open, still with it, standing on his own two feet, still alive — for the moment — and tied to the tailgate of Gabe's own buckboard wagon. Cleve wore no hat, no bandana, not a thing above his waist. His shirt lay in tatters on the ground a few feet away, and his large muscles shone, slick with sweat — and in places, what looked like blood was running down too in straight lines.

A man in a brown derby hat — a big man too, almost Cleve's size — kept on moving. Agitated, somehow abnormal. Sometimes he obscured Cleve from their view, sometimes he went to the side. But at *all* times, the man made his intent exceedingly clear. He brandished a large Bowie knife, the blade glinting, shimmering under the sunlight, the flash of it testament to its sharpness.

And now, the man — at the side he was — stepped close

to Cleve, put the blade to his throat, and stared at him from inches away.

"You struck dumb or what, Gabe?" Winnie's voice was still *mostly* calm — but not completely.

"You don't have a choice," said Gabe, trying to sound as calm as he could, so as not to panic her worse than she already must be. "We both know *I* can't make the shot from here, it's up to you. I know it's near your limit — but the way that man's playing with that knife, he'll pretty soon tire of the game, and finish him off."

"Furthest he gets away is two feet. If I miss, chances are I'll shoot Cleve. Wind's coming and going — when it blows, it comes from that side."

It was the first time she'd called him *Cleve,* rather than *Mister Lawson* — but she didn't even notice.

"If you miss, Fred, the feller will cut his throat anyway. If you don't take the shot, same result. We can't get any closer to shoot from without being seen. Soon as he moves to the side again, take the shot. It isn't your fault if you miss — the shot *must* be taken."

"But—"

"No buts, Fred. You're the only person I know who could make that shot." He tried to convince himself it was possible, but could not quite believe it. "You can do it. Five-hundred yards. You can do it."

"Four-eighty," she said. "But if a puff of wind comes as I—"

"You'll make the shot."

He went quiet, watched through the field glasses. Slowed down his breathing, just as he knew she was doing.

She breathed in—

—

— and breathed out

—

—

And the man in the brown derby hat—

— jumped away to the side

—— raised the knife to the sky

——— drew it back...

...and Winnie Roach squeezed the trigger of the Sharps, her mind gone so still, and so quiet, quiet as the truth.

CHAPTER 42
THE SHOT

She had never known a gun could make such a noise. The silence of her mind, her inner stillness and truth and belief — all of these things were shattered by the great booming sound.

As the bullet went on its way she cried out, cried out like a bird — a bird who's discovered she's not just a pile of feathers, but there's something inside her as well; something that *matters*.

And Winnie Roach could not look, could not bear to see what she'd done — for the moment she'd fired, a puff of cold wind touched her cheek, like the kiss of a dead man.

Deputy Vinton Waits heard the shot too, saw the result, and somehow it seemed otherworldly, impossibly perfect, and he was afraid. He did not think, but he acted — he put in the licks, ran right to the horse, jumped on it and rode for his life. Did not even hear the words, "Come back you coward, come back," as he rode away.

Cleve Lawson had known it was coming. His eyes,

unbeknown to Peterson, were about as good as eyes get —
in the West, that can be good indeed, for men become
accustomed to looking across greater distance than city men
do. Their eyes can adapt, become stronger — "til they hit
maybe forty or so, when finally, the years take a toll.

Cleve had been faced that way all along; had noticed
Winnie Roach arrive; seen her dismount; seen her set up
her rifle on a log she'd rolled onto the trail; seen her brother
show up almost two minutes later. Cleve had known right
away it was Winnie, he could tell by the way she had
moved, by her womanly stance. He'd figured the distance
between them at five-hundred yards — he also knew she
had a Sharps. And he knew she could shoot, *really* shoot.

But Cleve was a practical man, not given to wild ideas
of perfection — so he knew too, that five-hundred yards was
a little too far, even for Winnie.

If the wind were completely still, maybe.

But he felt the wind on his cheek, the slight gust of it
coming and going. He knew what that wind would do to a
bullet, knew he would probably die from her shot — if
Peterson didn't get on with it and kill him first.

And then, as Prosper Peterson raised up his knife to
pretend once again he would finish things — but rather, to
take another small slice, as he'd already done several times
— the shot came speeding toward them. Cleve smiled one
last time as he closed his eyes, and he pictured her beautiful
face again.

A nice way to go.

As for Prosper Peterson himself, he was no normal man
any more. Perhaps madness, while taking some senses

away, causes others to become more tuned in, become somehow finer than ever. Maybe Prosper *sensed* the big bullet coming — seems unlikely he could have *heard* it in time — he turned to face it, his head jerked around as it came, the great booming sound the Sharps made as its deadly load split the air.

Gabe Roach felt the zing, the bullet's aliveness, felt time almost stop as it flew to its target, saw the man in the derby hat turn. Saw the bullet meet the man's forehead — an inch below the brim of that brown derby hat — and go into him, right between his eyes. Saw a small hole that blossomed, and the blank surprised look as the life faded out of the outlaw. Saw him fall, slow at first, and then fast, thump the dirt to rise nevermore, and cause no more grief.

"You did it, Fred," the almost breathless Gabe gasped. He felt like his strength was gone from him, and the effort to speak was so great it surprised him. But he made the effort again, said, "You did it. You did it."

But Winnifred Roach did not hear him — she slumped down into the dirt, lost her grip on the rifle, and her face fell into her hands.

She howled along with the sound, the resounding echo of the Sharps as it filled all her senses, and tears ran fierce from her eyes — and she hoped a small hope against all the vast dread that she felt.

Then Winnie took a deep breath, opened her eyes, and said, "Does he live? Cleve. Did I...? Have I...?"

Still, she could not bear to look. Instead, she looked at her brother, did not comprehend his look of admiration.

"Look and tell me, Gabe, please."

She watched Gabe smile at her, turn his head, raise the field glasses up and look through them again.

"By the speed his mouth's moving," Gabe said, "my guess is, Cleve is fine. You killed the right man, Fred, shot that filthy killer right between his damned eyes. Cleve is fine, Winnie, just fine. Best we get ourselves there and untie him."

CHAPTER 43

ROLL WITH THE PUNCHES

Winnie Roach crossed the ground to Little Jack in a hurry. She pushed the Sharps into the scabbard and mounted the brave little stallion, in one practiced motion.

And again, Gabe found himself left behind. "Wait, Fred," he called. "Wait up, in case there are others."

Little Jack made it there in a twinkling. He came in so fast Cleve leaned back, for it seemed to him then the horse surely must hit him, and he could not move out of the way, being tied to the buckboard.

The horse came skid-sliding to a halt, not two yards away, and Winnie Roach was dismounting before it had stopped. Without so much as a glance at the man she had shot, she jumped from the horse, let momentum carry her the two steps to Cleve, and her arms were already around him before either one spoke.

"Thank you," he said, as she pressed her whole self against him.

"Oh, Cleve," she said, holding him tight, heedless of the blood from his wounds that were seeping onto her shirt. Then as Gabe arrived and dismounted, she started to kiss Cleve's face, kiss his cheeks and his mouth and his nose and his forehead, hugging him the whole time. "I thought I had killed you," she cried, and she kissed him again, right on the lips, as if Gabe was not even there.

Cleve half did not want her to stop — but Gabe Roach was approaching, watching the whole thing. "Gabe, listen, please," said Cleve then. "How about you untie me 'fore you hit me, treat a man fair? I don't reckon I could survive one more of your punches, not while I'm tied as I am, and can't roll with it some."

"There's no time for that," Gabe told him. "Who was the man who rode away? And where are the others? We need to get after them."

Winnie stood back away from Cleve then, pushed herself back to arm's length. She looked at Cleve's bare chest, the blood on him, the blood on her shirt, as if it was all some new thing she'd not noticed before, and she came to her senses.

"He can't go with us, Gabe," she said. "Can't you see the man's injured."

"Oh no you don't," said Gabe. "You've done your share, Winnie, I can't risk you—"

"Little help over here might be nice," called Sheriff James Whipple from where he was tied to the seat of the buckboard.

Gabe and Winnie both stopped like they'd heard a ghost speak — maybe thought that they had.

Cleve said, "He's shot some, you better attend to him, then come back and untie me."

"Untie Cleve," said Gabe, "and try not to kiss him while you do it, if you can manage." Then he walked the few steps to the Sheriff and said, "Sorry. Thought you were dead. Shot in the foot, huh? I'll untie you first then take a look."

Whipple said, "Just cut these dang ropes off and leave me, get after the my nephew. He'll be riding for town to tell Barron what happened. The others all run off, I reckon. Didn't give the appearance of men who would be coming back."

Cleve and Winnie made a point — mostly — of not looking at each other, while she cut the ropes to untie him. Cleve flexed his wrists where the ropes had cut into them, did the same for his ankles. He picked up his shirt, but it was cut into pieces, well beyond wearing.

"Give me that," Winnie said, and he did. She took the canteen from her horse, used the rest of her water to wet the cleanest part of the shirt, used it to wash out Cleve's wounds. There were many, and some were still dripping — but at least Prosper Peterson hadn't gotten around to actually cutting much off.

Cleve didn't look at Winnie's face while she did it, but he watched Gabe the whole time instead. For some reason Cleve did not understand, Gabe Roach took no interest at all now in what they were doing.

Gabe had taken Whipple's boot off and examined the foot. "I've seen healthier feet on dead horses, but no permanent damage is done," he said, then moved on to looking at the shot elbow. "It's busted up bad, Sheriff. No shooting for you for awhile. I've got four men on their way, one'll take you back to Wolf Town to the Doc."

"Thanks, Gabe," Whipple said. "You best get going right away."

Gabe turned to Cleve and said, "You up to coming?"

"Wouldn't miss it," said Cleve.

"I'm coming too," Winnie announced. She was surrounded by brave men, but the tone of her voice was one which made all of them quake. Cleve was glad it was not up to him to tell her to stay.

So when Gabe Roach offered resistance against her, Cleve thought it the bravest thing he had seen a man do.

"You can't come, Fred, there's—"

"Don't *call* me that!"

Her eyes flashed a warning, but Gabe went on anyway.

"Alright ... *Winnifred!* There's only two horses."

"There's four!"

"They belong with the wagon, and besides, there's only two saddles. Wait here with the Sheriff, Cleve and I will go after the Deputy, time's a'wasting."

"Then one of *you* must stay," she told him, her jaw jutting out in defiance, and Cleve could not imagine a time he'd ever seen something so lovely, yet infuriating too.

"You're wasting time, Winnie," Gabe growled.

"No man rides my horse, you know that, Gabe. *You* can stay if you want, but no man touches my horse — not now, not ever!"

"Please," Cleve said to her. "We have to get moving quick."

"Unharness that horse on the right," she said, pointing to it. "He's the better mount of the two. You can borrow my saddle and bridle — Little Jack and I don't really need them."

She stepped straight to her horse and commenced then to undo her saddle — and Gabe moved just as quickly to unharness one of the span from the buckboard.

"Best take my shirt, Cleve," said Whipple. "Can't ride off all over the countryside half-shucked in that manner — it just isn't seemly — and besides, you'll be needing a shirt to bleed into. Can't go bleeding all over a borrowed saddle."

They readied the horses, reloaded their guns, and the Sheriff wished them good luck as they left him behind.

"Remember, try to take Vinton alive," he called as the three rode away. "He's our best chance for a witness, so Barron doesn't go free."

CHAPTER 44
WORLD'S BIGGEST
CHUCKLEHEAD

When Deputy Vinton Waits rode off in his panic, he had no thoughts at all in his head — that head was just about solid bone, and such room as was in it, was mostly filled up with fear, right at that moment.

So he ran and then rode away, helter-skelter, on Prosper Peterson's horse — weren't like Prosper had further need of it.

First problem for Vin, that horse did not like him — wasn't his fault, not really. Truth was, that horse never liked no one at all, not even his owner.

Second problem — somewhat related — the horse showed his displeasure by bucking, and running toward every low-hanging branch on the trail. And while Vin was no great shakes as a horseman, the fear that he felt from the unnatural, otherworldly thing he thought he just saw — namely, a bullet coming from out of the nowhere, and lodging in Prosper Peterson's skull, right in between his two eyes — was enough to keep Vin in the saddle, him being afraid of ghosts and the like, for fear is a strong motivation.

So the horse bucked and twisted, tried to run up against things, then galloped as fast as he could, attempting to dislodge this new rider he'd took so much dislike to. When all that didn't work, he tried pulling up sharp, then he stopped completely, twisted his neck back, and attempted to bite Vinton's leg.

By this time, young Vin Waits was just about done with. He stopped fighting that horse, and just sat, he felt so defeated — just sat in the saddle and said, "I'm sorry, Horse, but you see, you're the only chance I had. I'm sorry your owner got dead, but it wasn't me done it."

Seemed like the horse done relaxed then, and stopped fighting Vin too.

That was when the young Deputy began to explain to the horse, how otherworldly agents — ghosts maybe — had taken it into their minds to shoot Mister Peterson dead.

And while Vin Waits would have gone close to winning, if ever a contest was organized for *World's Biggest Chucklehead,* he was not quite so stupid as to keep on ignoring the facts.

Not quite.

The facts of it came to him now, as his mind — such as it was — began working again. And thinking not coming so easy to Vinton, he found it some easier to use his voice when he did it. And so, he explained all his thoughts to the horse, more or less, while he nutted it out.

"*It was them sheep folk come after us, maybe, from where Uncle James had been to last night. Must be I just* never seen 'em, and they had one'a them big buffalo guns, and maybe just made a lucky shot from up on a hill back behind."

Now, one of the things about that horse was, it had been with Prosper Peterson awhile. It had gotten used to his madness, and part of that madness was, Prosper talked aloud to himself as they rode along.

To a horse who doesn't like no one at all, one fool man is much the same as another. And the horse, being soothed by Vin's ramblings, now consented to walk along quietly, without trying to dislodge him.

"This is some big improvement," Vin said — more to himself than the horse, but the result was the same — and the horse then consented to trot some, and even to travel at a slow canter before they'd gone too much further.

Vin Waits was a spooney, let's not be untruthful about it — but even *he* was clever enough, before long, to notice he had to keep talking for the horse to behave.

So he talked, and the horse sorta listened, not caring what the words were, but only that they kept coming. And before too long, they were making good progress back toward La Grange, to warn Pinckney Barron about what had happened.

Seemed like no one had followed him so far, though the Deputy realized after a time — and told the horse so — that whoever shot Prosper Peterson might soon be coming after him too.

CHAPTER 45
THE PROBLEM WITH WITNESSES

An hour ago, Pinckney Barron had walked down the street to visit Romulus Hogg. Both men were in mighty fine spirits — for it seemed like more profits were well on their way, and their futures looked rosy indeed.

"Let's ride out to our new property," the tall-booted Barron had said to his over-wide friend.

Pinckney Barron wasn't much of a horseman, but fancied himself one these days. But Hogg wasn't falling for that, the man liked his comforts.

"Let's take my new buggy, shall we, Pinckney? I've a new horse to draw it, quite sleek and fast, you really must have a drive."

As they traveled toward Norris Ricks' place, they discussed the situation.

"I do prefer to test the limits atop a fast horse," Barron boasted, "but this *is* a fine buggy, and comfortable too, as you said. Now listen up, Romulus, and I'll fill you in.

Peterson and all the others have the Sheriff pinned down at the Sheep Town."

"Whipple?"

"He somehow worked out by the tracks that his nephew was involved in Ricks' killing. Damn fool Deputy tried to kill him but missed, and Whipple escaped."

He steered to the right of the trail to dodge a low branch, as Hogg said, "Are you certain they'll take care of the Sheriff? If he gets back—"

"Don't worry," Barron said with a cruel smile. "Prosper Peterson is *the* most dangerous man — besides me — I've ever met. We're going places, Romulus, my friend. And by the way, I have more good news!"

"My favorite sort," said Hogg, before stuffing half of a cream-filled cake into his mouth and commencing to chew as if his very life depended on it.

"After Sheriff Whipple escaped," Barron said, "he went to Cleve Lawson's. The pair are together — and they'll *die* together too. If they haven't already." He screwed his face up in distaste and wagged a finger toward Hogg's cheek to tell him to clean it. "We're getting richer by the day."

"But I don't hold a mortgage over Lawson's property," said Hogg, wiping the cream from his cheek then licking his finger. "Delicious," he added, "are you sure you won't have one?"

Barron ignored the offer, so Hogg took another from the bag for himself — he had a second bag for when this one was empty, and if he had to eat them himself, he would certainly manage.

"Forget the damn food, Hogg, and *listen*. You've missed

something important. The *Sheriff* is going to be dead — and he's the one keeping local records regarding the land."

"I still fail to—"

"You're as slow as Waits sometimes, I swear. Romulus, listen. With Whipple and Lawson both dead, we'll just forge the documents, take Lawson's land as well."

The banker's jaws were about to chomp down on a fresh cake, but he stopped mid-bite, used his mouth for speaking instead. "Oh, I don't know, Pinckney, that's pushing things. The man has family, and—"

"So you *don't* want half of your damn seven-thousand back from the robbery? It was overly generous of me to offer it, but I did so in good faith of our equal partnership. But if you've lost your nerve now—"

"Alright, alright," said the banker, raising his hands in surrender. "But that reminds me, Pinckney, wherever is my *watch*? You promised you'd get it back for me, and it was my father's, and his—"

"Here, stop complaining," Barron said, reaching into his inside coat pocket, and handing the watch to his friend. "Hey, who's that riding toward us? Take the reins, Romulus, quick, and let's stop, I may need to shoot at whoever is coming."

Pinckney Barron, relieved of the reins, picked up the scattergun he'd brought along. He had never been much of a shot — in truth, he had rarely fired a weapon, and did not even know how to properly clean one. But he had other men to clean them for him — and from close enough quarters, a double-barrel scattergun was pretty much foolproof.

They were right out front of Norris Ricks' place now, and there should not be anyone coming — certainly not a lone rider. Neither Barron nor Hogg was prepared enough to have brought along field glasses. But as the buggy came to a halt and the rider came closer, Barron recognized who it was.

"It's our future Sheriff," he said to the banker, and they laughed — more with relief than because it was funny. Though it *did* tickle both of them somewhat, that such a simpleminded young fool would soon be installed to a position of power, where they could pull his strings to their liking.

"Greetings, my clever young friend," said Pinckney Barron, raising his left hand in welcome. "You're the bearer of good tidings, I trust?"

Vinton Waits got a puzzled look on his face and said, "I didn't tied nothin', Mister Barron, I'm not sure what you..."

His voice trailed off as he drew the horse to a halt beside the buggy, but the animal whirled away a half-turn — being an outlaw's horse, it was ever ready to leap into action, did not like to stand facing buggies or anything else.

The two rich men shot a superior look at each other, as much as if to call the boy stupid, then Barron said, "What I meant to ask, my dear Vinton, was, have you brought me good news?"

The Deputy said, "Mister Barron, sir, there's a..."

Then he clamped his mouth shut, looked from Barron to Hogg, his eyes darting back and forth a few times, and it was clear he was panicked.

"It's alright, young Vin," Barron assured him. "We're all

equals here, you can consider my friend Romulus one of us from now on. You may speak on any subject at all, he's with us all the way. The Sheriff is dead, yes?"

"Mister Barron, he ain't, as far as I know, and we got a bad problem."

"What is it? Spit it out, boy, what is it?"

"They shot him, Mister Barron, sir — they done killed Prosper Peterson, shot him right between his two eyes. Shot some of the other boys too, and the rest all run off!" Vin looked back behind him, clearly panicked, as if he was sure they were coming to get him.

"Dammit, Waits, how could that happen? Where are the others? How many still left?"

"None I reckon, Mister Barron, that's what I been sayin'. They's all gone, there's only *us* left, you and me." He looked around at his back-trail, then faced Pinckney Barron again.

"Listen to me, young Vinton, listen." Barron thrust his two hands out in front, as if making a passage for his words to flow along, from his own self to Vin Waits.

"Yessir," the boy answered, a look of concentration on his face now.

"First, is anyone following you?"

Vinton looked behind again a few moments, closed one eye like he was thinking hard on the question. Then he turned and said, "Maybe."

"Maybe?"

"What I mean is, I don't really know. I never *seen* who shot Mister Peterson, and the others was all tied up, so I know it weren't them."

"*Who* was tied up?"

"Uncle James and Cleve Lawson, a'course."

"Were they shot?"

"Uncle James been shot up some, but still alive when I left. Just his foot and a elbow, I reckon. He ain't goin' nowhere, that's for certain."

"So you didn't see who shot Prosper? But you're *sure* he was killed?"

"Yessir, Mister Barron, that's it to rights. Bullet came outta nowhere, shot him right between his eyes, then I run and got on his horse and at first, the horse wouldn't run straight, but then after awhile I worked out—"

"Stop, Vin, forget that. Go back to the start, and be quick now. What happened when you ambushed the Sheriff?"

"Cleve Lawson was driving a buckboard with straw in the back, and we all started shootin', but not to kill no one, 'cause Mister Peterson wanted to kill folks slow now instead. But then when Lawson stopped, Uncle James come up shootin' from under the straw, and shot off Mister Peterson's finger. Three of our men jumped on horses right then and rode right away like damn cowards."

"Damn!"

"Uncle James and Lawson killed the rest, and Mister Peterson went under the wagon and shot Uncle James, then I got there and saved the damn day, that was *me* done the savin', true as I'm here right now."

Barron wore a grave look now, but still he spoke calmly. "Good boy, Vin, well done. Tell me, what happened then?

"We tied 'em up, then Mister Peterson was cuttin'

Cleve Lawson up some, when the bullet come from nowhere. And now Mister Peterson's dead, and I'm here to warn you about it, and that's all up to now, except for the thing about the horse that you said not to tell."

Pinckney Barron rubbed at his clean-shaven chin a long moment. He looked to his friend then for help, but Romulus Hogg only shrugged his round shoulders and said, "Don't look at me, I'm only a banker."

Alright," said Barron, before commencing to count out the facts on his fingers. "Sheriff Whipple and Cleve Lawson are alive; *Someone* is helping them; All our men are dead, or have fled, and are unlikely to ever return; *But* there are no living witnesses that can testify against me." Four fingers he had out by now, and he sat staring at them, like he thought they might tell him exactly how to proceed.

Vinton Waits also stared at the fingers, but finding no answers forthcoming, he said what he *knew*. "But they *know,* Mister Barron, they know it was *us* done the killings. Know it was *you*."

"Know *what,* boy? Spit it out. What *do* they know exactly? And how?"

"Witness, a'course. They had a witness who told 'em, your man Greene it was. He told 'em it was you done the orderin' about who to kill. What we gonna do, Mister Barron?"

"Wait. *Had? Had* a witness, did you say?"

Vinton Waits was still on that horse, and it seemed impatient to be going along on its way. Didn't like the company maybe. It refused to stand still, and spun right around now, full circle — but the Deputy managed to subdue it before giving his answer. "Prosper killed Greene, so he's dead now, but they *know*. What we gonna do, Mister Barron?

"It's alright, Vin, it's alright. There's no witnesses who can implicate me now."

Romulus Hogg's eyes darted toward Waits, then back to Pinckney Barron, then he poked the latter in the ribs. And under his breath he said, "But there's still—"

"It's alright," Barron said firmly, placing a hand on the banker's thick arm, before turning to face the Deputy again. "We *do* have a problem, young Vin. You're a clever boy, so you understand it — you tried to kill the Sheriff, and he'll come for you, or send someone else. We need to take care of *that* little problem first. How would you like to own this fine ranch, my good friend?"

"Me, Mister Barron? Own Norris Ricks' ranch for myself? Why, I'd sure like that fine, but—"

"We need to set up an ambush ourselves, right here and now, before all this goes any further."

"Alright, Mister Barron, but—"

"I believe you know *just* how to do that, right here at Norris Ricks' place, same way you and Prosper did it to Ricks. Can you do that, my clever young friend? If I draw them in here, get them in place? Can you do it?"

"I can, Mister Barron," Vin said, as he looked across at the driveway that led to the house. He smiled a wide one, then looked back to Barron and nodded with certainty. "Can't believe it, my very own ranch — thank you, Mister Barron, thank you. I surely can do it, I can."

"**G**o on ahead, Vin," Pinckney Barron said. "Make certain the undertaker's left, we don't need a witness."

The impatient horse was just happy to get going, and Vinton Waits let him canter up Norris Ricks' driveway. He could see the fresh tracks that the undertaker's wagon had left — one set going in, one set going out — and for the briefest of moments, the Deputy's mind snagged a little on how it could be, that Barron and Hogg had not crossed paths with the undertaker on their way here. There was only this one trail back to La Grange after all, at least for a wagon.

But Vin was so thrilled to go look around his new place, his boyish excitement won the battle for his attention, and he let that small nagging doubt disappear from his mind.

"But the undertaker's back to town by now," said Romulus Hogg once Vin rode away. "Why did you—?"

Barron smiled, released the brake — he was still on the

driver's side of the buggy, though he didn't have the reins — and beckoned for the banker to get them moving up the driveway. "You're right of course, Romulus. There *is* just one witness that could see me convicted of murder — and we can't afford to take any chances."

"You're going to let them kill the young fool?"

The buggy trundled along and they watched the young Deputy dismount up ahead, and tie his horse to the porch rail.

Barron caressed the big scattergun that lay across his lap. "No. We can't be seen to be aiding him in any way. I'll have to kill him myself before they arrive."

"But perhaps the boy *could* kill Whipple and Lawson — and whoever else comes after him now."

"No." Barron shook his head. "Where Prosper Peterson failed, that young gump cannot possibly succeed. Waits failed to kill the Sheriff already, and that was one against one — *and* he had the advantage of surprise on his side."

"I forgot about that. You're right I suppose, Pinckney — we don't know how many will come. So what do we do?"

"I'll splatter his brains, then we'll wait for the Sheriff or whoever else to show up — it shouldn't be long — and we'll tell them Waits did it himself. We'll say he confessed to the murder of Ricks, and he could not live with the thought of it."

The banker looked plenty alarmed then. "But I can't be here when you do it. It was bad enough being nearby when that sheep man was shot — and if I'd have known it was you on that horse, I'm not sure I could have kept myself from looking in your—"

Pinckney Barron slapped his friend's face, hard as his little hand could manage. Wasn't hard at *all* by Western standards — but it got the job done, the banker being more-or-less a Nancy. Barron raised his hand up again and said, "Pull yourself together now, Hogg. Or do I need to do something about *you?*"

The terrified Romulus Hogg rubbed his face with one hand, held the reins with the other as he cowered. "No. No, of course not," he said, his eyes wide with fear. "I'm sorry, Pinckney, I'm just worried they'll know I'm involved. I don't have your ... your *flair* for all this."

"Don't worry," Barron growled, "I got flair enough for us both. You just do your job, and all the rewards will be ours. Peterson was good, but the man was cracked in the head. We'll get some new men to take over, start again soon, once things settle down in a week or two. We'll get rid of the sheep folk, the Sheriff, and anyone else who tries to stand in our way."

"It's all getting so unseemly. I don't know, Pinckney. Could the sheep men not—?"

"No! No they could *not*. You don't know this, Romulus — but I had a man scout their town several weeks back. They've built a fine little township out there. Quality buildings, real prime location. I *want* it. *All* of it." Barron swayed with the buggy's movement as he watched Vinton Waits come out of the house and turn to close the door behind him.

"What about the Sheriff?" said Hogg. "He *knows* you told all those men to do all the things they've been doing. He *knows,* Pinckney."

"Yes, he knows. But he has no *proof.* No judge would convict me on hearsay, and Whipple's a stickler for rules. He's never once stepped outside the law, despite numerous chances to do so. He knows I'm the top man — but without a witness to testify to it, he won't do a thing except wait. Wait for me to slip up. And *that* isn't going to happen. I'm too damn good."

Barron pulled on the brake and they came to a halt near the house, then the pair of rich men climbed down. Hogg stood by the buggy, feigning interest in one of the wheels. But Pinckney Barron — carrying the scattergun pointed at the ground — walked toward the young Deputy.

Vinton Waits was in a world of his own. He had walked halfway across to the outhouse, to the spot where Norris Ricks died, and that's where he'd stopped. He was making lines in the air with his hands, working out how to kill whoever was coming. "Get 'em to stand here, Mister Barron, on the same spot where Ricks died, and I'll be all ready for 'em. I'll shoot from down there," he said, pointing. "You be sure to stand off to the side though, don't get behind 'em."

Such small brains as Vin had was all being used on the planning. He had not yet even looked up, though he'd heard Pinckney Barron approaching.

"You best hide that shotgun you brought, Mister Barron, so they don't get 'emselves an attack a'the nerves, and cut you down 'fore I kill 'em."

"Good idea, my clever young friend," Barron said as he stopped walking. "Here, why don't *you* have it?"

As Deputy Vin Waits looked up, he was smiling.

Pinckney Barron was too.

Last thing young Vin seen was the beastly cavernous barrels of that scattergun, less than two feet away from his handsome young face.

But a half second later, that face was a whole lot less handsome — for it had turned mostly to liquid and got sprayed across the dirt, when Pinckney Barron squeezed both the triggers, and done his own dirty-work for the very first time.

CHAPTER 47
WISH IN ONE HAND

C leve sure marveled at the way Winnie Roach rode that horse. Just a blanket on its back and a short length of rope on his neck, and she and that fine little stallion were leading the way.

As for Cleve, he was none too comfortable. That horse had been a wonder at pulling a wagon, but he weren't no great shakes as a mount. He would have been passable fair, if Cleve had his own saddle.

Wish in one hand, spit in the other, and see which one fills up first.

It was no use wishing, he knew. He had the saddle he had, and was grateful for that.

Problem was, Winnie Roach's saddle had been custom made — made for a girl five-foot-two, not a six-footer like Cleve. Even with the stirrups adjusted as low as they could be, he pretty much rode standing up, and he sure wasn't used to it.

By the time they went past his own ranch, Cleve's

legs were already beginning to tire, and he was considering asking the others to stop and rest up a minute. He had never been short on grit, so he stuck it out and kept going.

Halfway between his place and Norris's, just as they came over the ridge that separated the two, the blast of a shotgun resounded from somewhere ahead.

They pulled up right away, and Cleve briefly considered stepping down off the horse — but instead, he took his feet from the stirrups and stretched out his legs, worked his ankles back and forth too as he spoke. "Don't reckon the Deputy had a scattergun with him. And he could not have got one from my place, I keep it well hid."

"We'd best keep on moving," said Gabe. "He won't catch himself. You want to swap horses awhile, Cleve? I really don't mind."

"No, I'm fine," Cleve answered. "I'll play the cards I got dealt." He put his feet back in the stirrups and got that horse moving again. But by the time they got close to Norris's place, he was just about ready to fold.

When they halted to look at all the tracks outside Norris's place, it came as a relief. Cleve looked about, wary, then stepped on down to the ground. Never felt quite so happy to have dirt underfoot, though he moved like a man who was eighty. He hadn't ever been *much* of a tracker, but he would have been happy to look at them tracks for an hour, if it kept him off of that horse.

"Waits stopped right here several minutes," he announced. "Never dismounted while he spoke to whoever drove the buggy."

"What are these other tracks?" Winnie asked, pointing at some further along.

"Undertaker's wagon, come for Norris's body, earlier than these by the looks. You can see here where the second wagon crossed over the top of 'em."

"Tracks all lead in here," called Gabe from over where the trail met the driveway. "Just a single horse and buggy, plus the horse Waits is riding."

Winnie studied Gabe's face, then Cleve's. "A trap? He'll be waiting for us, won't he?"

They all kept their eyes and ears open, silent a moment.

Gabe rode back toward Cleve, looked down at him. "Is there another way in?"

"There's *always* another way in," Cleve replied. "But here, there's only one way we wouldn't be seen — and Vinton Waits know's it's there. That's the way him and Peterson musta went, to kill my friend Norris."

"Don't forget about that shotgun," said Winnie. "Perhaps it belonged to your friend?"

"No, Norris never owned one. Always said they weren't hardly sporting. He only ever really used rifles, though he did own a six-gun as well."

"If you're right, Mister Lawson," she said, "the shotgun belongs to whoever arrived in that buggy."

"Wheels of it look *almost* evenly weighted," Cleve said. He was down on his haunches, and looked up now from his inspection. "I'm no tracker, but from the almost even weight, I'd reckon there's two men came in it. One's likely to be the damn banker, and he owns a two-seater buggy."

"Why him?" said Gabe.

"Skunk holds a mortgage over Norris's place. He'd be out here quick as he can to inspect his new acquisition. Also, he's fat as a pig, which accounts for the slightly uneven weight on each wheel. Which means the other feller might be small — no prizes for guessing who that is. They's friends, I guess, if snakes can have friends."

Gabe nodded thoughtfully. "Can they shoot?"

Cleve scoffed good at that one. "Barron and Hogg? Wouldn't reckon. Hogg was on the stagecoach when it got robbed — had a full strongbox with him, yet still didn't carry a gun. The teller keeps one under the counter, of course. But Hogg wouldn't know which end bit."

"So, maybe Barron owns the shotgun?"

"If it is him? Might yet turn out to be someone else. Still, Barron seems likely. Who knows, maybe they come out together, had a disagreement. Maybe."

"Maybe a lot of things," Winnie said, sliding the Sharps from its scabbard. "I say we head in there, cautious, and fight it out with them."

Gabe tried to stop her, of course. "You're staying right—"

"Ha," was all she said. Little Jack read her thoughts and took off up the driveway.

Cleve leaped onto his horse, took off behind Gabe, who was already chasing Winnie.

She slowed Little Jack, allowed them to catch her, and Gabe took the lead, before Cleve called, "I know the place best, let me go ahead, just be ready to head to the right, and keep well apart."

But as they came into view of the house, guns out and prepared for a battle, the sight before them was a surprise.

Pinckney Barron and Romulus Hogg both stood still, in the middle of the house yard, their hands raised high above their heads.

And a few yards away, laid out flat on the ground, was the headless corpse of what seemed to be Vinton Waits.

CHAPTER 48
SQUEAL LIKE A BANKER

They slowed their horses, and all three kept their wits about them, expecting more trouble. But it soon enough became obvious, none would be forthcoming.

One at a time the men dismounted, and handed their reins to Winnie. She had put the Sharps back in the scabbard, and waited there now with the horses, half-distance between the house and the buggy. Cleve kept his rifle trained on Barron as he approached, while Gabe followed him, off to one side, ready to shoot at anyone else who popped up too sudden.

"Thank goodness you're here," Barron said. "We had no idea what to do about this poor man."

Cleve thought how easy it would be just to shoot Barron now — murder him, just as the man had caused others to be murdered. But Cleve could not do it, he had a strong moral code, though the skunk sure deserved it. "No idea, huh?" he said. "You got some explainin' to do, Barron."

"Explain I shall, Cleve, my friend," Barron said, a smirk overcoming his features. "It's poor Vinton Waits lying there — killed himself right here in front of us, didn't he, Romulus?"

The hatless banker nodded his head with such vigor, it caused his great jowls to wobble — but he kept his mouth clamped tight shut, did not speak a word.

"Killed *himself* — with *your* gun?" said Gabe Roach. He still had his rifle at the ready, and kept watch all around him.

"Mister Roach, isn't it?" said Pinckney Barron. He put down his hands, reached one out toward Gabe as if to shake his in greeting, even though there was a distance of five yards between them. "I believe we may have met in La Grange once, would that be the case?"

Gabe glanced at the proffered hand in disgust, left it to hang in the air there, untouched, and stayed put right where he was. "How could I forget? It was at your saloon. You insulted my friends and myself, then ran off to hide, while your hired muscle did all your fighting. Weakness doesn't become a man, Barron."

Pinckney Barron's humiliation showed in his expression, but he only drew back the hand, wiped the palm on his britches and said, "I'd *prefer* we all become friends — but have it your own way. Perhaps later, when we've sorted this out." Then he shot a glance to where Winnie waited behind on her horse and called, "I don't believe we've met, Ma'am, I'm—"

"A damn liar," said Cleve. "Forget about her, Barron, we know what you done, admit it or I'll blow your damn head off." And he looked down the sights of the Winchester, as if he might do it.

"Now, now," Barron said, raising his hands once again, "I'm unarmed, my friend, as you quite clearly see. This is all a misunderstanding."

"Is, is it?"

"Yes, Cleve, of course, let me explain. Unfortunately, your friend Norris Ricks met an untimely end yesterday, and he still owed Romulus here a substantial amount. Now, Romulus is no cattle rancher, as I'm sure you're aware. He asked me to accompany him today to inspect the property and advise him on what to do with it."

"You damn snakes," Cleve said, but Barron pretended not to hear and went on with his story.

"We were just about to turn in off the trail when the Deputy here came toward us — riding hard he was too. That's his horse there, you see, at the porch. He was in a strange mood, and making no sense, so Romulus suggested he accompany us up the drive, and explain what was wrong while we all inspected the property together."

"That a fact?"

"Yes, Cleve, true as I stand here before you. Romulus hoped the boy might buy the place from him, you see? Vinton had previously expressed a desire for property, and indeed, he already owned cattle."

"Which *you* now own again."

"Well, no," Barron said. "In fact, *Romulus* would now be the owner, him still holding a mortgage over the cattle.

But none of that matters. What matters is this — once we came up here, young Vin went into the house by himself, then came out wringing his hands, and carrying on like a man who'd quite lost his senses. He went to our buggy and picked up my shotgun — for a moment I thought he would shoot me!"

"What a loss that woulda been," Cleve growled, but he lowered his rifle.

"Then the Deputy informed us he'd *killed* Norris Ricks — shot him from where he was hiding." Pinckney Barron half-turned then to point out the spot. "Said he did it from those trees down there."

Cleve shook his head in disgust. "And right after he said all that, the Deputy's head just exploded all by itself, huh?"

"Well no, of course not," Barron replied. "He then walked to that spot where he is now, turned to face us and said, 'This was where Mister Ricks was when I killed him. I wanted his ranch, and I know I done wrong, and I'm sorry.' That was what he said, wasn't it, Romulus?"

Right then Hogg looked more like a pig than ever before, as his skin was turning pink from the sun. He'd gone back to his vigorous nodding, but he still didn't speak.

"Your tongue been cut off, Hogg?" said Cleve. "I'd hear from you too. You're mixed in this too, by the looks."

The banker's eyes widened, and he looked back to Barron to save him. Hogg seemed almost to shrink from his fear then, as he cowered away from the hateful gaze of Cleve Lawson.

"Poor Romulus has had a terrible shock," Barron said.

"Surely you can understand that, Cleve. You see, right after young Vinton Waits said all that, he raised the shotgun up to his chin and he fired it. As you can see, it was a most terrible thing for the two of us to witness."

"Terrible," squealed Romulus Hogg.

While all this was happening, Winnie Roach had stepped down from her horse, led all three of their mounts to the porch, tied them all next to the one Vinton Waits had rode in on. Then she'd wandered across to the buggy, and was looking it over while she listened. It was a *fine* buggy.

Cleve laughed at Hogg's squeal, then turned back toward Pinckney Barron, and took two steps toward him. Then he leaned forward so he could stare at the much shorter man, eye to eye from just inches away. "I say you're a damn liar, Barron. I say you been payin' Prosper Peterson to do all your killing. And I say you blew Vinton Waits' poor fool head off yourself."

Barron leaned back away, cried, "How dare you!" — but his smirk did not match his outrage.

The anger Cleve felt was rising. He shuffled forward a couple more inches, put his nose almost up against Barron's and said, "Your overtall boots don't nohow make you a big man — and you know what, little feller? You're the smallest and poorest excuse for a man I reckon I ever saw."

As Cleve had been speaking, the smirk drained away from Barron's face, his look turned to outrage, and finally, his dander was up. Pinckney Barron *hated* being called small, and now he lost his composure and lashed out at Cleve. He *slapped* Cleve's cheek with all the force he could muster — which, even with all the wrath that had built up inside him, did not amount to much force at all.

"That the best you can hit, little feller?" Cleve said, and he leaned back and roared then with laughter. "I've eaten cream pie that was harder'n that slap, and I ain't referrin' to the pastry. You want another free one 'fore I hit you back? Seems a shame I should beat on you, without you get even one punch in. Close your fist this time, little Pinck, there's a good tiny feller, come hit me."

Then Cleve blew the seething Barron a kiss, put his hands behind his back, and jutted his chin out in front of him.

"Don't do it," squealed Romulus Hogg, but it was too late.

Pinckney Barron lunged forward and threw a wild haymaker up at Cleve Lawson's chin. Best you could say for that punch was its aim was on target. Hit right on the left side of the chin where he'd aimed it, and it pushed Cleve's face sideways a little, but that's about all.

Well, that wasn't *quite* fair a description of the damage — for Pinckney Barron was a man unaccustomed to punching, and his feeble technique had caused damage to his own hand. He stood now, clutching his right hand in front of him, then he glared up at Cleve, furious with anger at the way he was standing there laughing.

"That there punch would not have knocked the skin off the top of a custard," Cleve announced. Then he spoke as one would to a baby, when he added, "Have you hurt your little baby hand, my fine little man? How about one more for luck?"

Cleve had never picked on a small man in his life; never made fun of one; never took unfair advantage of *any* man, if it came down to brass tacks. But he knew of the terrible things Pinckney Barron had done, the crimes he'd committed, the good men he had killed. A thousand Pinckney Barrons would never be worth one Norris Ricks, and Cleve knew now, could see it, this evil, terrible man, was about to get away with it all — and Cleve could not take it no longer, and lost himself up to his temper.

When Barron rushed at him again, all flailing hands and kicking feet and flashing teeth trying to bite him, finally, Cleve hit him back.

Cleve did not hit the man's face to start with, but punched his body instead. He drove his big meaty fists into Barron's ribs, and at that time, he was still in control of his faculties, mostly. But the evil deeds Pinckney Barron had done kept coming into Cleve's mind, and soon he lost himself to it, as if in some sort of a trance, and it seemed for a moment he'd kill the snake right then and there.

Then Cleve heard Gabe's voice — it seemed at first to be coming from a great distance — and he felt himself being dragged, and he lashed out some more, landing punch after punch on Gabe Roach, as Gabe struggled to contain him.

Then Cleve heard Winnie's voice, heard her panic, and the shrillness of it cut through to wherever his mind was — and the world, all its sounds and its sights, came back into focus. As he and Gabe stopped their struggling — for Gabe Roach had stepped in to stop Cleve beating Barron to death — they looked up and saw Winnie near the buggy, screaming at them to stop.

Pinckney Barron was standing behind her, his face bloodied, his jaw hanging sideways, all broken. But his left arm was wrapped around Winnie's throat from behind, and his right hand held a pistol to the side of her head.

Gabe's rifle was too far away, but Cleve scrambled the two yards to his own; picked it up, jumped to his feet, and aimed it at Barron in one fluid motion. Then he froze as he heard Barron speak.

"No-no, Cleve, I'll kill her." Pinckney Barron sounded strange as he spoke, for the froth and blood from his busted up mouth made his half-hoarse, half-gravel voice sound three-quarters drownded. But his meaning, they all got clear enough. "Either one of you moves, I'll blow her damn pretty head off."

"**L**et the girl go, Barron," Cleve cried, still looking down the sights of the rifle. "You're only making things worse."

No clear shot.

"Worse? Worse than *dead?*" Barron's eyes narrowed, and his busted features formed into a snarl of a smile. "You'd have killed me just now if your maggoty friend there hadn't stepped in to save me."

"Don't harm her, please," called Gabe, with only the slightest hint of anguish in his voice. "There's no evidence against you, as you said. We all know it, Barron. I'll tie Cleve up so he doesn't go loco again, then you and Hogg can leave in the buggy. But if you do something foolish now — it's not worth it, Barron, you know that."

In the moments that followed, it seemed Pinckney Barron had seen the sense in those words. But perhaps he had spent too much time with Prosper Peterson — had enjoyed being part of the killing, and the madness was somehow contagious — for that snarling look settled once again on Barron's features, and he said, "Small man am I, Cleve Lawson? Who's small *now?*" And he tightened his grip at her throat, causing Winnie to make choking sounds.

"Listen to him, Barron," Cleve called then. "There's no evidence against you, that's true. Sure, we all know what you done, and we know you got away with it too. But if I killed you, I'd hang for the murder — it was right of my friend here to stop me. Let her go, we'll call it all square, and me and the Sheriff'll move away to Montana, we already decided on that."

"It's a good deal, Pinckney," squealed Romulus Hogg. "Please, do *not* hurt that woman! There's been too much bloodshed already."

If it wasn't for Pinckney Barron's tall boots, he'd have been the same height as Winnie. But he shaded her by a few inches as he used her for cover. Still, he was clever enough to stay down behind, and only small parts of his head could be seen at any one time.

"You know," Barron said then, "maybe I missed my true calling. I never felt bigger and stronger than I do right now." He sniffed the girl's hair as he held her. "It'd be *fun* to kill her, Cleve ... just to see the look on your face. You care for her, don't you? Yes, you do, I can tell. Why don't you just try to shoot me, Cleve, see where the shot goes?"

"If you don't let her go soon, I will."

"Cleve, no, d—" Winnie cried, but the arm tightened down on her throat again, and she choked on the rest of her words.

"Don't worry, Ma'am," Barron said. "He won't risk

shooting, I promise. Thing is, Cleve Lawson can barely see — from that distance, we two are just a blur, he can't tell which of us is which. Cleve is not shooting anyone, are you, my friend?"

"That true, Cleve?" said Gabe. And no one made a sound, as a long moment passed, then another.

Cleve looked down the sights of that Winchester, and in a tone that sounded defeated, he asked Barron, "How did *you* know I don't see so well?"

"Everyone knows," Barron laughed. "*Someone* must have told me. Yes, I believe it was my good friend, Romulus Hogg."

As Cleve Lawson watched, Pinckney Barron laughed — and his head moved a few inches sideways. *Not far enough.* Cleve continued to wait for a chance, and said, "That true, Romulus Hogg, what your *good friend* here says?"

"I ... I ... you said so, while we were being robbed, I recall, Mister Lawson, don't you remember? Such a thing gets spread around I suppose, by folks who were there."

"Not the question I asked."

"I *must* have told him," said Hogg.

"But you didn't *need* to tell Pinckney Barron that, did you?" Cleve's voice had slowed down, just a little, as he slowed his breathing, getting ready to shoot. "You did not need to tell him, because he already knew. He was there, giving the orders to the man who did the killing. In fact, Mister Romulus Hogg, you're a witness as well — just as poor simple Vin Waits was."

"Shut up," Barron said. "Don't listen to him, Romulus, he's trying to—"

"He'll kill you, Romulus Hogg, same way he murdered Vin Waits."

"Shut *up*," Barron growled.

"He'll have to kill you now, Hogg, you saw him blow Vinton Waits' head off."

"*Shut up, Shut Up, SHUT UP*," Barron cried. "I would *never* do that, Romulus, you know I would nev—"

"Shoot him, Lawson," cried Romulus Hogg then. "He killed Waits, he—"

That's when Pinckney Barron turned the pistol on Hogg, and in doing so loosened his grip on Winnie's throat, exposing the top of his body and all of his head.

Three or four things all happened at once, more-or-less just-about, way they do when push comes to shove and lives go on the line:

Winnie broke away from Barron's grip — Barron fired his six-gun at Hogg — and Cleve squeezed the Winchester's trigger as Winnie dived for safety.

Before Winnie's dive got her all the way to the ground, two bullets crossed paths in the air — one of them lethal, one not — then Romulus Hogg started squealing, his right hand clamped to his left shoulder. His look was two helpings of terror, a cupful of shock, and a biggity spoonful of pain, all rolled into one.

Pinckney Barron stood stock still a moment, just stared at Cleve Lawson, eyes wide. The gun dropped from his hand then the tiny murderer fell — fell for what seemed a long time — for he had some mighty tall boots that he had to fall from, and they held him in place there awhile "til he finally toppled.

He fell face down in the dirt, which busted his already broken-up features some more — but it made no difference, not really.

And though the hole in his forehead was not so perfectly neat in the middle as his man Prosper Peterson's had been, it turned out it *was* hole enough — hole enough on its way in; hole enough where the bullet had tore through his brain; and *more* than a big enough hole where it made its way out — so that Pinckney Barron was dead before he hit the ground.

CHAPTER 50
JUMPING THE BROOM

Cleve stood, holding the Winchester, pointing it still at the dead Pinckney Barron.

As Hogg moaned in the background, Gabe calmly said, "Cleve, it's all over, let me have that weapon." He took two steps forward, reached out and took it. Cleve seemed almost not to have noticed, and Gabe walked away with the rifle.

Then Winnie was on her feet running, running to Cleve, and she crashed into him with such force he almost lost his footing. She smothered him, kissed him, hugged him so tight he barely could breathe — and she hung from his neck the whole time, her feet dangling in the air above his.

"Oh, Cleve," she said, "darling Cleve. I thought he would kill me for certain."

And now, as she kissed him, he came partway back to his senses, and he kissed her right back.

A few moments later — might have been five or fifty, far

as the smitten Cleve Lawson could tell — a harsh sound interrupted the moment.

It was Gabe Roach clearing his throat, plenty loud, a few yards away to the right.

Cleve looked into Winnie's loving eyes one more moment, then he took control, lifted her off him, placed her down on the ground at arms' length.

He nodded at her, a small nod, but slow and deliberate — and that one small nod told her the main thing she needed to know — then Cleve turned to his right to face Gabe.

To Cleve's astonishment, Gabe Roach was smiling — but his head was cocked to one side, and his eyebrows were raised. The expression he wore was *a riddle wrapped in a conundrum* — at least, that's what Norris Ricks would have called it.

These are the queerest folk I ever met.

Maybe he's just happy he has an excuse to punch me again. I don't doubt he's enjoying the practice.

Cleve sighed a deep one, ran his fingers through his hair, and commenced to roll up his sleeves. "Here we go again, Gabe, I guess. I wish you'd go easy on me, I'm gettin' low on teeth."

But Gabe Roach only laughed and said, "If you two are going to keep doing that, I think you should get married first and do it in private — you're scaring the horses."

Cleve's eyes could not have gotten no wider and still been contained in his head. "Married? *Married?* But what about *you?*"

"No, you won't catch me jumping the broom," said

Gabe. "I'll admit, I'm a fool in my own way — but not fool enough ever to marry."

Cleve's head spun toward Winnie, and she looked up at him, her shining eyes so adoring, he could barely stand to look into them. And in an incredulous tone, he said, "You two leaped the book?"

"Pardon?" she answered, with a tiny shake of her head.

And Gabe said, "Are you gone wrong in the head there, Cleve Lawson? Maybe I hit you too hard yesterday — why would you think...?"

Even Romulus Hogg stopped his moaning to watch things unfold.

Then Gabe's eyes narrowed and he said, "Lawson. If this is another crack about us sheep folk wedding our kin—"

"Oh my," said Winnie then. And to the surprise of both men, she commenced then to giggle. The giggle turned into a chuckle, and the chuckle to a chortle, and before long her amusement found voice in great peals of laughter she could not contain.

The men looked at her dumbstruck to start with, and then looked at each other, and in the end both shrugged their shoulders. When she finally slowed down — grew a little bit quieter — Cleve and Gabe cocked their heads to one side like a pair of confused pups, and at the same time, both said, "What?"

Winnie bit her top lip to keep some control of herself then, and she smiled sweetly at Gabe before stepping toward Cleve. She stood in front of him, looked up into his eyes and said, "Cleve, darling Cleve. You've misunderstood the whole time — little wonder you acted so strangely. Did you not notice we had separate bedrooms? It was *Matt* I was married to — Gabe is my *brother,* you fool."

"Well I swow," said Gabe, staring at Cleve. "You thought...? Oh my. I moved into Winnie's house six months ago, after Matt ran off and left her, you chucklehead." He shook his head slowly, then looked at his sister and added, "You sure you want to marry someone with even less brains than a sheep, Fred?"

"Stop *calling* me that!"

Gabe pointed at Cleve and said, "Is he alright? He looks kind of ... busted."

Winnie looked up at Cleve again and she smiled. "Are you busted, Cleve? I hope not."

"Ohhhh," said Cleve, as he thought back on things. Then he said,"Oh. *OH!* So that means ... I mean, you and me can ... I mean, if it's alright with you, then, maybe we *can* get—"

"*Married,*" she cried. "I accept."

Then Winnie leaped into Cleve's arms and kissed him again.

And this time, *nobody* — not Cleve, and not Gabe, and not even Romulus Hogg — raised any objection. They had plenty of time to squawk their displeasure, if they'd at all had a mind to — for that kiss was the first that both parties had felt free to indulge in, and so it went on 'bout as long as a small thirsty horse can drink from a cool mountain stream on a hot summer's day in Wyoming.

CHAPTER 51

COMMUNITY MINDED, THEM BANKERS

Wasn't much left to sort out after that, and it sorted itself, for the most part.

While Gabe and Winnie were attending to Hogg's wounds, Cleve came over, took out his own watch, looked at it a moment then shook it. Then he said, "Thing's broken again. We'll need to know the time for the Sheriff to put in his report. What time you got, Mister Hogg?"

The self-important Romulus Hogg had not yet pinned the watch chain to his coat, but he quickly produced the watch from his pocket, and as the chain dangled, he cleared his throat and he said...

Well, he didn't say nothing at all — because Cleve snatched that watch from his hand, and said, "If I'm right, the inscription on this should read *Romulus Hogg the Second*. Quite a piece of evidence this, if it does — ain't that so, Romulus Hogg the Dang Third? I seen Prosper

Peterson take such a watch with my own two eyes, and I weren't the only one seen it."

"I ... now, now, Lawson, let me explain." The banker was wide-eyed with terror, and if you ever wondered how a pig would look painted bright red, you'd have got a close enough answer right there and then.

The sight of Sheriff Whipple heading up the drive in a wagon, surrounded by armed men on horses, wasn't helping Hogg to feel no more secure.

"Now listen to me, Romulus Hogg the Third," said Cleve then. "Possession of this watch puts you square in the middle of things with your filthy dead friend, by the law."

"But I never knew he was—"

"I know that," said Cleve, and he turned away a moment to wave to James Whipple as the wagon came closer. "So I'll make you an offer, Mister Hogg. I'll say I found this watch on Barron — and you'll sign Norris's ranch and his cattle over to whichever sheep folks' families had members killed during all this. Sure beats being hanged, don't it?"

Then Cleve moved the chain to and fro, so it swung back and forth some.

"Oh, thank you, Mister Lawson, thank you," said the banker, rubbing at his throat, absentminded. Then a look crossed that fat banker's face, like a cat that had got all the cream — and maybe got the cow all that cream had come from as well. "Indeed, I'd be happy to do so. I've come out of this rather well, now I look at it. I hold mortgages over

Pinckney Barron's holdings, you see, and the man had no living relatives."

Cleve smiled a wide one as the wagon pulled up beside them. "Sheriff," he said with a nod. "You missed all the fun, but you got here just in time to hear the good news."

Whipple's arm was tied up in a sling and he looked right discomfited, but he sounded more like himself than ever. "What's that, Cleve?" he said.

Cleve held the pocket watch up to glint in the sunlight, looked at the inscription, then at Hogg. "Romulus Hogg the Third here is the new rightful owner of all Pinckney Barron's possessions."

"And that's good news?" Whipple said.

Cleve smiled at Whipple, then at Winnie and Gabe, then finally at Romulus Hogg. And he said, "Community minded he is, our friend the banker. He's donating all Pinckney Barron's holdings, and Norris's too, to the families who lost men at Barron's hands." Cleve let the watch swing on its chain once again, like the chain was a rope and the watch was a man who was being hanged on the end of it. "Ain't that right, Mister Hogg?"

You never saw a smile fall off a banker's face so fast. "Yes, that's just what I'm doing," Hogg said unhappily. "It won't bring those men back to their loved ones, but it's the least I can do, after all."

"Romulus here was also saying it'll go some way to establishing trust between the sheep men and cattle men," Cleve said. Then he put the watch in his own pocket and added, "I'll borrow this for now, Mister Hogg, I assume you don't mind."

"Quite."

"You'll get the watch when the paperwork's sorted," said Cleve.

Winnie turned to James Whipple and said, "How are *you* feeling, Sheriff?"

"Good as new, more or less."

Cleve leaned in, looked at Whipple's shot elbow, screwed up his face some. The bandage had loosened as he'd driven the wagon, and part of the elbow could be seen. "I wouldn't say new exactly, Sheriff. Seen better lookin' bones after Jimbo's done chewin' on 'em."

"Had worse," said Whipple. "You three sorted out who stands where, by the looks."

It was true. Winnie stood right by Cleve, the two finally together, as it seemed they'd been destined to be. And Gabe stood close by, maybe a yard or two off to the side, watching on. Ready to be on their side when they needed him — or whip Cleve if he ever deserved it.

Hardly seemed likely though, that last thing.

"Turns out these two are brother and sister," Cleve said, "not hitched up like I thought."

Whipple shook his head, lowered his brows and stared at Cleve a few moments from under his hat. "No wonder that dog of yours likes me better than you. Maybe figures you've not yet worked out he's a dog, and may yet try to ride him — plain facts only coming to your mind once someone explains them over and over."

"I tried to warn her against him," said Gabe, "but she's a sheep girl through and through — always did like the mush-headed ones."

"No accounting for love," said Sheriff James Whipple.

And right then, ol' Jimbo — who had never taken too kindly to being locked up, and had made his escape and come a'sniffing all along their trail — came running up Norris Ricks' driveway, flew through the air, landed right beside Sheriff James Whipple, before landing a big sloppy dog-kiss right on his stubbly face.

"Right again, Sheriff," said Cleve, "and ol' Jimbo's the proof of it. No accountin' for love!"

Then he turned to kiss Winnie again, and the others looked away. It was scaring the horses.

CHAPTER 52
CLEVER AS A SHEEP

Cleve Lawson had always believed himself unlucky in love — yet from that day forward, the opposite proved to be true.

He had a few doubts to begin with. Wondered if she might come to her senses, tell him it wasn't working out, and send him off to Montana.

After a month of wedded bliss, he asked her, "Why me?" for about the hundredth time.

This one time, she gave him an answer. "I loved you from the very first day, because you're a real man, Cleve Lawson — a man who can cry a tear for the loss of another he never really knew. A man who stands up for what's right, though it goes against his preference to mind his own business. A man who'll stay true to his woman, no matter what happens. But if you ever ask '*Why me?*' again, you can go to Montana alone, I've heard it enough, and I've answered you now."

"I'm a lucky man," he'd said then. "And I was thinking, maybe we could go to Montana together, start over—"

"No," was all the answer she gave him. "And not another word about it."

That wasn't the first time Cleve didn't get his way, and it surely was not the last either. Some women — the best of them maybe — refuse to be tamed. Men might *think* they've tamed them, but such women, though fiercely loyal and supportive and loving, are just as apt to tell their dear husband to sit on their saddle and rotate, rather than do as they're told.

First time Cleve tried to tell Winnie what to do, it was the very next day after they'd killed Peterson and Barron, and helped the Sheriff bring some peace to the county.

"Soon as we're married this Sunday, I'm taking you to Cheyenne," he had told her. "We're going shopping! We're buying you ten pretty dresses, and a fine little buggy to drive, no more riding for you. You won't need that Sharps any more either, we'll buy you some books about cooking, and a few pretty bonnets, and you'll be a regular lady, the fanciest and prettiest in all of Wyoming."

"How wonderful," she'd said.

He never even noticed the frosty tone of her voice, and thought she had meant what she said. And he replied, "It's all settled then."

"Oh, Cleve," she'd said then. "You really are clever as a sheep aren't you?"

"W-what?"

"Cleve Lawson," she'd said, with her hands on her hips and eyes blazing all sorts of *don't-argues*. "I'll marry you on

Sunday, I will — but it'll be on my *own* terms. *No* pretty dresses, *no* staying at home wearing aprons, and tied to a kitchen. No sewing, no knitting, and no more than a *half* share of cooking and cleaning — yes, in case you're wondering, it's *you* that'll do the other half."

"But—"

"*And,* most important of all, you'll keep your sticky hands off my Sharps, and never — *never* — go near my horse, you'd only teach him bad habits. Buggy indeed! If you got yourself a *real horse,* one like Little Jack, you might one day understand. Hmmph."

One of those peskified newspaper headlines had jumped into Cleve's mind right then:

Bootmaker Lashed by Tongue
- Told to Stop Acting Too Big for His Boots.

And that had been, as they say, most certainly that.

Funny thing happened though, unexpected. Didn't change Winnie completely, but it softened her some.

Oh, she still rode Little Jack at breakneck speed up and down mountains, through rivers and everywhere else she could find that was dangerous — and she still used that Sharps too, saved their lives more than once, became fiercer than ever at such times as she needed to be.

But the softness was to do with her babies. She had always wanted some, but had thought herself unable — turned out it was Matt who'd been firing blanks all along.

Cleve had no such problem, it seemed. In fact, five years later, she had occasion to tell him to stop loading awhile — she was thirty-five years old by then, and Cleve forty-two.

And their children were four, and three, and two, and one — and there was a newborn as well. They named one after Gabe, and one after Norris, and the girls they called Ethel and Irene, after their mothers.

But that first one, they named after Whipple — James Whipple Lawson, they called him.

Sheriff tried to get them to name that babe after ol' Jimbo — caused all sorts of higgle-piggle and hellabaloo, not to mention some quality amusement — but that's another story all its own, and we won't tell it now.

And we won't try to tell you things didn't get hard, won't try to say these fine people did never know heartbreak — for all of us do, when we truly care about others.

But we *can* assure you of this — when they found each other these people found love, and once they did, they never lost it.

And that's as good as things get, I'm sure you'll agree.

THE END

THE DERRINGER

If seven-year-old Roy Stone had done what his Ma told him to, he'd never have known the truth of what happened at all.

He'd never have seen the double-cross, never have witnessed the murders, never seen the killer's blowed-apart finger. But the poor kid saw the whole rotten thing, and watched his mother die on the floor.

"I'm going to kill you," little Roy cried at the killer – but Big Jim only laughed with contempt.

But that little boy meant what he said – and what's more, he believed it.

He would grow up and kill that big man. That was all that now mattered.

Available as an eBook and paperback.

FYRE – A WESTERN

What if you went off to fight for what's right, and someone
told your sweetheart you'd died? What if that same person
told you that she was dead too?
What if that man up and married her? After secretly killing
her family? And what if that man was the brother you
trusted?
And what if, one day, you came home?
A story of trickery and cunning, of brotherhood and truth,
and of war. Of bandits and shootouts and justice, and of
doing what's right. Of a tall man who slithered, and a dwarf
who stood tall as the clouds, and became Billy's friend.

It's the story of how Billy Ray becomes Billy Fyre – and
how, seven long years after being told he'd lost everything,
finally, Billy comes home, to fight for what's his.

Available as an eBook and paperback.